D0772797

CONAN
of Venarium

CONAN
of Venarium

Harry Turtledove

TOR®

A Tom Doherty Associates Book
New York

CONAN OF VENARIUM

This book is printed on acid-free paper.

Edited by Teresa Nielsen Hayden

Map by Ellisa Mitchell

A Tor Book
Published by Tom Doherty Associates, LLC
175 Fifth Avenue
New York, NY 10010

www.tor.com

Tor® is a registered trademark of Tom Doherty Associates, LLC.

Library of Congress Cataloging-in-Publication Data

Turtledove, Harry.
    Conan of Venarium / Harry Turtledove.—1st ed.
        p. cm.
    "A Tom Doherty Associates book."
    ISBN 0-765-30466-X (acid-free paper)
    1. Conan (Fictitious character)—Fiction. I. Title.

PS3570.U76C665   2003
813'.54—dc21
                                        2003040283

First Edition: July 2003

Printed in the United States of America

0 9 8 7 6 5 4 3 2 1

To Robert E. Howard,
L. Sprague de Camp, and Poul Anderson

Contents

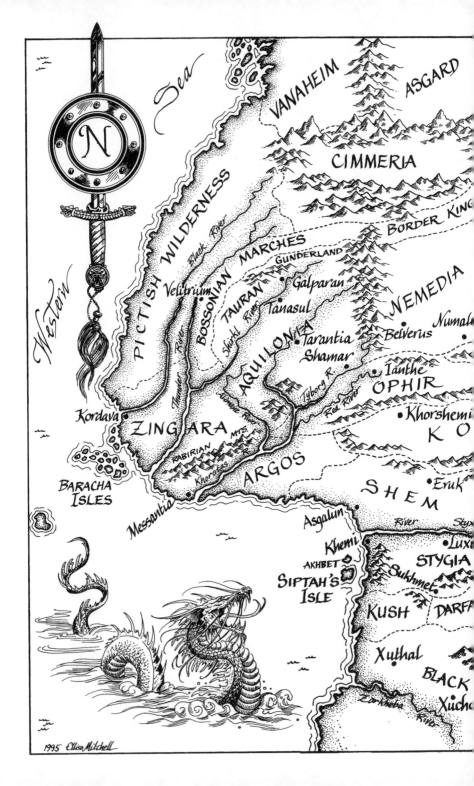

chapter i

The Coming of the Aquilonians

Wagon wheels groaned. Horses' hooves drummed. Above and behind and through all the other sounds came the endless thump of heavy boots in the roadway. Lithe Bossonian archers and the broad-shouldered spearmen of Gunderland made up the bulk of Count Stercus' army. They eyed the small number of heavily caparisoned Aquilonian knights who rode with Stercus with the amused scorn freeborn foot soldiers often accorded their so-called social betters.

"What do they suppose they're going to do with those horses when we get up into Cimmeria?" asked Granth son of Biemur. The Gunderman coughed. He marched near the middle of the long column, and the road dust coated his broad, friendly face and left his teeth gritty.

His cousin Vulth snorted. "Same as they always do," he answered.

"And what's that?" demanded Granth. He and Vulth squabbled all the time, sometimes in a friendly way, sometimes in earnest. Vulth was older—he had to be close to thirty—and taller, but deep-chested, big-boned Granth owned a bull's strength his cousin had trouble matching.

Here, though, Vulth was more interested in sniping at the

Aquilonian aristocrats than in scoring points off Granth. "Why, they'll use 'em to flee, of course," he replied. "They can run from the wild men faster and farther than us poor foot sloggers."

Granth laughed. So did several other soldiers in their company. But their sergeant, a scarred, grizzled veteran named Nopel, growled, "Shut your fool's mouth, Vulth. If the count hears you talking like that, you'll be lucky if he just puts stripes on your back."

"I'm not afraid of him," said Vulth, but his wobbling voice gave the words the lie. Count Stercus hated everyone in his own army with a fierce and rancorous passion. Granth had yet to hear what he had done down in Tarantia, the capital, to be relegated to the gloom of the northern frontier, but it must have been something dreadful.

But, however much Stercus despised his own men, he reserved his most savage loathing for the Cimmerians. How many times had he harangued the army about the barbarous savages they were going to face? More often than Granth could easily remember; that was certain. If Stercus had his way, he would wipe every Cimmerian off the face of the earth.

Peering through the dust as best he could, Granth looked north toward the hills of Cimmeria. Dark forests of pine and fir and spruce robed those hillsides, making them even more somber than if they were of bare rock. Mist clung to the hills; gray clouds scudded low above them.

"Mitra!" muttered Granth. "Why do we want that miserable country, anyway? Why would anybody in his right mind want it?"

Nopel grunted. "Plain you didn't grow up on the border, the way I did. You ever had a pack of those wild wolves come howling down on your farm or village to steal and burn and kill, you wouldn't ask stupid questions like that." The sergeant spat in the roadway.

Abashed, Granth marched along in silence for a while. But

his was not an easy spirit to quell, and before long he said, "You can't even see if anybody lives in those woods."

"Oh, no—you can't see the Cimmerians there," said Nopel. "Don't you worry about it, though. Whether you see them or not, they see you."

More silence followed. More often than not, Gundermen and Bossonians, good-natured men close to the land, would sing as they marched: ferocious songs of what they intended to do to their foes and bawdy ballads about the wenches they'd left behind and the others they expected to find after they beat the enemy. No one in the whole long column seemed to feel like singing today.

Granth looked toward the huge Aquilonian flag a standard-bearer carried at the head of the column. The great gold lion on black heartened him. Aye, the Cimmerians were wolves, but when faced with a lion wolves slunk away. Granth's hand tightened on the shaft of his pike. Let the wolves howl! When the fight came to close quarters, he would make them howl on a different note.

A stream no different from any of the others the army had forded wound down out of the darkly wooded hills and through a verdant meadow. Pioneers ran forward, seeking a ford, and soon found one. The standard-bearer splashed across, the water rising no deeper than his thighs. The Aquilonian knights forded the stream next. Most of them urged their horses forward to form a protective wall to shield the rest of the army against any possible onslaught from the north. Count Stercus and a few of his henchmen, however, reined in just on the far side of the stream.

"You see?" muttered Vulth. "He hasn't the stomach to advance himself."

"No, look," answered Granth. "He's speaking to the foot soldiers as they cross."

"Well, so he is," said Vulth. "Still, actions talk louder than words, or so our grandsire always used to say."

Sergeant Nopel cuffed him, hard enough to stagger him and make him swear. "I don't care what your granddad used to maunder on about," snapped Nopel. "What I say is, you talk too cursed much."

By then, the company had almost reached the stream. Granth drew his sword and held it high so the blade would not get wet and rust. When he crossed, his boots crunched on gravel in the streambed. Cold water poured down over his boot tops and soaked his feet. He cursed resignedly; he had known that would happen. He would have to sit close by the fire tonight—and every other man in the company would have wet feet, too. There would be a lot of pushing and jostling before that got sorted out.

He squelched up onto the north bank of the stream. "Welcome to Cimmeria!" Count Stercus called from horseback, not to Granth in particular but to all the men who were coming up onto dry land just then. "Welcome, I say, for we are going to take this land away from the barbarians and make it ours."

Stercus sounded very sure, though his voice was higher and thinner than Granth would have liked in a commander. He wanted a man who could bellow like a bull and make himself heard across a mile of battlefield. Stercus was young to have a command like this, too, for he could not have had more years than Vulth. His lean, hawk-nosed, pallid face would have been handsome but for dark eyes set too close together and a chin whose weakness the thin fringe of beard he wore could not disguise.

"The savages shall surely flee before us," declared Stercus.

"I hope he's right," said Granth.

"If the Cimmerians ran whenever somebody poked them, Aquilonia would have taken this country hundreds of years ago," said Vulth. "We'll have plenty of fighting to do yet. Don't you worry about that."

Granth looked to see if Sergeant Nopel would tell Vulth

to shut up again. Nopel said not a word, from which Granth concluded the sergeant thought his cousin was right. The Aquilonians trudged north, deeper into Cimmeria.

Iron belled on iron. Sparks flew. Mordec struck again, harder than ever. The blacksmith grunted in satisfaction and, hammer still clenched in his great right hand, lifted the red-hot sword blade from the anvil with the tongs in his left. Nodding, he watched the color slowly fade from the iron. "I'll not need to thrust it back into the fire, Conan," he said. "You can rest easy at the bellows."

"All right, Father." Conan was not sorry to step back from the forge. Sweat ran down his bare chest. Though the day was not warm—few days in Cimmeria were warm—hard work by the forge made a man or a boy forget the weather outside. At twelve, the blacksmith's son stood on the border of manhood. He was already as tall as some of the men in the village of Duthil, and his own labor at Mordec's side had given him thews some of those men might envy.

Yet next to his father, Conan's beardless cheeks were not all that marked him as a stripling. For Mordec was a giant of a man, well over six feet, but so thick through the shoulders and chest that he did not seem so tall. A square-cut mane of thick black hair, now streaked with gray, almost covered the blacksmith's volcanic blue eyes. Mordec's close-trimmed beard was also beginning to go gray, and had one long white streak marking the continuation of a scar that showed on his cheek. His voice was a deep bass rumble, which made Conan's unbroken treble all the shriller by comparison.

From the back of the smithy, from the rooms where the blacksmith and his family lived, a woman called, "Mordec! Come here. I need you."

Mordec's face twisted with a pain he never would have shown if wounded by sword or spear or arrow. "Go tend to your mother, son," he said roughly. "It's really you Verina wants to see, anyhow."

"But she called you," said Conan.

"Go, I said." Mordec set down the blacksmith's hammer and folded his hand into a fist. "Go, or you'll be sorry."

Conan hurried away. A buffet from his father might stretch him senseless on the rammed-earth floor of the smithy, for Mordec did not always know his own strength. And Conan dimly understood that his father did not want to see his mother in her present state; Verina was slowly and lingeringly dying of some ailment of the lungs that neither healers nor wizards had been able to reverse. But Mordec, lost in his own torment, did not grasp how watching Conan's mother fail by inches flayed the boy.

As usual, Verina lay in bed, covered and warmed by the cured hides of panthers and wolves Mordec had slain on hunting trips. "Oh," she said. "Conan." She smiled, though her lips had a faint bluish cast that had been absent even a few weeks before.

"What do you need, Mother?" he asked.

"Some water, please," said Verina. "I didn't want to trouble you." Her voice held the last word an instant longer than it might have.

Conan did not notice, though Mordec surely would have. "I'll get it for you," he said, and hurried to the pitcher on the rough-hewn cedar table near the hearth. He poured an earthenware cup full and brought it back to the bedchamber.

"Thank you. You're a good —" Verina broke off to cough. The racking spasm went on and on. Her thin shoulders shook with it. A little pink-tinged froth appeared at the corner of her mouth. At last, she managed to whisper, "The water."

"Here." Conan wiped her mouth and helped her sit up. He held the cup to her lips.

She took a few swallows — fewer than he would have wanted to see. But when she spoke again, her voice was stronger: "That is better. I wish I could—" She broke off again, this time in surprise. "What's that?"

Running feet pounded along the dirt track that served Duthil for a main street. "The Aquilonians!" a hoarse voice bawled. "The Aquilonians have crossed into Cimmeria!"

"The Aquilonians!" Conan's voice, though still unbroken, crackled with ferocity and raw blood lust. "By Crom, they'll pay for this! We'll make them pay for this!" He eased Verina down to the pillow once more. "I'm sorry, Mother. I have to go." He dashed away to hear the news.

"Conan—" she called after him, her voice fading. He did not hear her. Even if she had screamed, he would not have heard her. The electrifying news drew him as a lodestone draws iron.

Mordec had already hurried out of the smithy. Conan joined his father in the street. Other Cimmerians came spilling from their homes and shops: big men, most of them, dark-haired, with eyes of gray or blue that crackled like blazing ice at the news. As one, they rounded on the newcomer, crying, "Tell us more."

"I will," he said, "and gladly." He was older than Mordec, for his hair and beard were white. He must have run a long way, but was not breathing unduly hard. He carried a staff with a crook on the end, and wore a herder's sheepskin coat that reached halfway down his thighs. "I'm Fidach, of Aedan's clan. With my brother, I tend sheep on one of the valleys below the tree line."

Nods came from the men of Duthil. Aedan's clan dwelt hard by the border with Aquilonia—and, now and again, sneaked across it for sheep or cattle or the red joy of slaughtering men of foreign blood. "Go on," said Mordec. "You were tending your sheep, you say, and then—"

"And then the snout end of the greatest army I've ever seen thrust itself into the valley," said Fidach. "Aquilonian knights, and archers from the Bossonian Marches, and those damned stubborn spearmen out of Gunderland who like retreat hardly better than we do. A whole great swarm of them, I tell you. This is no raid. They're come to stay, unless we drive them forth."

A low growl rose from the men of Duthil: the growl that might have come from a panther's throat when it sighted prey. "We'll drive them forth, all right," said someone, and in a heartbeat every man in the village had taken up the cry.

"Hold," said Mordec, and Conan saw with pride how his father needed only the one word to make every head turn his way. The blacksmith went on, "We will not drive out the invaders by ourselves, not if they have come with an army. We will need to gather men from several clans, from several villages." He looked around at his comrades. "Eogannan! Glemmis! Can you leave your work here for a few days?"

"With Aquilonians loose in Cimmeria, we can," declared Glemmis. Eogannan, a man nearly of Mordec's size, was sparing of speech, but he nodded.

"Stout fellows," said Mordec. "Glemmis, go to Uist. Eogannan, you head for Nairn. Neither one of those places is more than a couple of days from here. Let the folk there know we've been invaded, if they've not already heard. Tell them to spread the word to other villages beyond them. When we strike the foe, we must strike him with all our strength."

Eogannan simply nodded again and strode off down the road toward Nairn, trusting to luck and to his own intimate knowledge of the countryside for food along the way. Glemmis briefly ducked back into his home before setting out. He left Duthil with a leather sack slung over one shoulder: Conan supposed it would hold oat cakes or a loaf of rye bread and smoked meat to sustain him on the journey.

"This is well done," said Fidach. "And if you have sent men to Uist and Nairn, I will go on to Lochnagar, off to the northwest. My wife's father's family springs from those parts. I will have no trouble finding kinsfolk to guest with when I get

there. We shall meet again, and blood our swords in the Aquilonians' throats." With that for a farewell, he trotted away,
his feet pounding in a steady pace that would eat up the miles.

The men of Duthil stayed in the street. Some looked after
Fidach, others toward the south, toward the border with
Aquilonia, the border their southern neighbors had crossed.
A sudden grim purpose informed the Cimmerians. Until the
invaders were expelled from their land, none of them would
rest easy.

"Bring your swords and spears and axes to the smithy," said
Mordec. "I'll sharpen them for you, and I'll ask nothing for
it. What we can do to drive out the Aquilonians, let each man
do, and count not the cost. For whatever it may be, it is less
than the cost of slavery."

"Mordec speaks like a clan chief." That was Balarg the
weaver, whose home stood only a few doors down from Mordec's. The words were respectful; the tone was biting. Mordec
and Balarg were the two leading men of Duthil, with neither
willing to admit the other might be *the* leading man in the
village.

"I speak like a man with a notion of what needs doing,"
rumbled Mordec. "And how I might speak otherwise—" He
broke off and shook his big head. "However that might be,
I will not speak so now, not with the word the shepherd
brought."

"Speak as you please," said Balarg. He was younger than
Mordec, and handsomer, and surely smoother. "I will answer—you may rely on it."

"No." Mordec shook his head again. "The war needs both
of us. Our own feuds can wait."

"Let it be so, then." Again, Balarg sounded agreeable. But
even as he spoke, he turned away from the blacksmith.

Conan burned to avenge the insult to his father. He burned
to, but made himself hold back. For one thing, Mordec only
shrugged—and, if the fight against the invaders meant his

feud with Balarg could wait, it surely meant Conan's newly discovered feud with the weaver could wait as well. And, for another, Balarg's daughter, Tarla, was just about Conan's age—and, the past few months, the blacksmith's son had begun to look at her in a way different from the way he had looked at any girl when he was smaller.

Men began going back into their houses. Women began exclaiming when their husbands and brothers gave them the news Fidach had brought. The exclamations were of rage, not of dismay; Cimmerian women, no strangers to war, loved freedom no less than their menfolk.

Mordec set a large hand on Conan's shoulder, saying, "Come back to the smithy, son. Until the warriors march against the Aquilonians, we will be busier than we ever have."

"Yes, Father." Conan nodded. "Swords and spears and axes, the way you said, and helms, and mailshirts—"

"Helms, aye," said Mordec. "A helm can be forged of two pieces of iron and riveted up the center. But a byrnie is a different business. Making any mail is slow, and making good mail is slower. Each ring must be shaped, and joined to its neighbors, and riveted so it cannot slip its place. In the time I would need to finish one coat of mail, I could do so many other things, making the armor would not be worth my while. Would it were otherwise, but—" The blacksmith shrugged.

When they walked into the smithy, they found Conan's mother standing by the forge. Conan exclaimed in surprise; she seldom left her bed these days. Mordec might have been rooted in the doorway. Conan started toward Verina to help her back to the bedchamber. She held up a bony hand. "Wait," she said. "Tell me more of the Aquilonians. I heard the shouting in the street, but I could not make out the words."

"They have come into our country," said Mordec.

Verina's mouth narrowed. So did her eyes. "You will fight

them." It was no question; she might have been stating a law of nature.

"We will all fight them: everyone from Duthil, everyone from the surrounding villages, everyone who hears the news and can come against them with a weapon to hand," said Mordec. Conan nodded, but his father paid him no heed.

His mother's long illness might have stolen her bodily vigor, but not that of her spirit. Her eyes flamed hotter than the fire inside the forge. "Good," she said. "Slay them all, save for one you let live to flee back over the border to bring his folk word of their kinsmen's ruin."

Conan smacked a fist into the callused palm of his other hand. "By Crom, we will!"

Mordec chuckled grimly. "The rooks and ravens will feast soon enough, Verina. You would have watched them glut themselves on another field twelve years gone by, were you not busy birthing this one here." He pointed to Conan.

"Women fight their battles, too, though men know it not," said Verina. Then she began to cough again; she had been fighting that battle for years, and would not win it. But she mastered the fit, even though, while it went on, she swayed on her feet.

"Here, Mother, go back and rest," said Conan. "The battle ahead is one for men."

He helped Verina to the bedchamber and helped her ease herself down into the bed. "Thank you, my son," she whispered. "You are a good boy."

Conan, just then, was not thinking of being a good boy. Visions of blood and slaughter filled his head, of clashing swords and cloven flesh and spouting blood, of foes in flight before him, of black birds fluttering down to feast on bloated bodies, of battles and of heroes, and of men uncounted crying out his name.

Granth son of Biemur swung an axe—not at some foeman's neck but at the trunk of a spruce. The blade bit. A chunk of pale wood came free when he pulled out the axehead. He paused in the work for a moment, leaning on the long-handled axe and scowling down at his blistered palms. "If I'd wanted to be a carpenter, I could have gone to work for my uncle," he grumbled.

His cousin Vulth was attacking a pine not far away. "You go in for the soldier's trade, you learn a bit of all the others with it," he said. He gave the pine a couple of more strokes. It groaned and tottered and fell—in the open space between Vulth and Granth, just where he had planned it. He walked along the length of the trunk, trimming off the big branches with the axe.

And Granth got to work again, too, for he had spied Sergeant Nopel coming their way. Looking busy when the sergeant was around was something all soldiers learned in a hurry—or, if they did not, they soon learned to be sorry. As Vulth's pine had a moment before, the spruce dropped neatly to the ground. Granth started trimming branches. The spicy scent of spruce sap filled his nostrils.

"Aye, keep at it, you dogs," said Nopel. "We'll be glad of a palisade one of these nights, and of wood for watchfires. Mitra, but I hate this gloomy forest."

"Where are the barbarians?" asked Vulth. "Since those herders by the stream a few days ago, we've hardly seen a stinking Cimmerian."

"Maybe they've run away." Granth always liked to look on the bright side of things.

Nopel laughed in his face; sergeants got to be sergeants not least by forgetting there was or ever had been any such thing as a bright side. "They're around. They're barbarians, but they're not cowards—oh, no, they're not. I wish they were. They're waiting and watching and gathering. They'll strike when they're ready—and when they think we're not."

Granth grunted. "I still say building a little fort every time we camp for the night is more trouble than it's worth." He went back to the base of the trimmed trunk and began to shape it into a point.

"It's a craven's way of fighting," agreed Vulth, who was doing the same thing to the pine. The woods rang with the sound of axes. Vulth went on, "Count Stercus brought us up here to fight the Cimmerians. So why don't we fight them, instead of chopping lumber for them to use once we've moved on?"

"Count Stercus is no craven," said Nopel. "There are some who'd name him this or that or the other thing, sure enough, but no one's ever called him coward. And when we're in the middle of enemy country, with wild men skulking all about, a fortified camp is a handy thing to have, whether you gents care for the notion or not." He gave Granth and Vulth a mincing, mock-aristocratic bow, then growled, "So get on with it!" and stalked off to harry some other soldiers.

After the cousins had shaped the felled trunks into several stakes sharpened at both ends and a little taller than they were, they hauled them back to the encampment. Archers and pikemen guarded the warriors who had set aside their weapons for spades and were digging a ditch around the camp. Inside the ditch, a palisade of stakes was already going up. The ones Granth and Vulth brought were tipped upright and placed in waiting postholes with the rest.

"I wouldn't want to attack a camp like this. I admit it," said Vulth. "You'd have to be crazy to try."

"Maybe you're right." Granth did not want to admit any more than that—or, indeed, even so much. But he could hardly deny that the campsite looked more formidable every minute. He could not deny that it was well placed, either: on a rise, with a spring bubbling out of the ground inside the palisade. The axemen had cleared the dark Cimmerian forest back far enough from the ditch and the wall of stakes that the wild men lurking in the woods could not hope to take the army by surprise.

But then a lanky Bossonian straightening the stakes of the palisade said, "I wouldn't want to attack a camp like this, either, but that doesn't mean the damned Cimmerians will leave us alone. The difference between them and us is, they really are crazy, and they'll do crazy things."

"They're barbarians, and we're coming into their land," said Granth. "They're liable to try to kill without counting the cost."

"That's what I just said, isn't it?" The Bossonian paused in his work long enough to set hands on hips. "If trying to kill without worrying about whether you fall yourself isn't crazy, Mitra smite me if I know what would be."

Another sergeant, also a Bossonian, set hands on hips, too. "If standing around talking without worrying about whether you work isn't lazy, Mitra smite me if I know what would be. So work, you good-for-nothing dog!" The lanky man hastily got back to it. The sergeant rounded on Granth and Vulth. "You lugs were just rattling your teeth, too. If you've got more stakes, bring 'em. If you don't, go cut 'em. Don't let me catch you standing around, though, or I'll make you sorry you were ever born. You hear me?" His voice rose to an irascible roar.

"Yes, Sergeant," chorused the two Gundermen. They hurried off to collect more of the stakes they had already prepared, only to discover that their comrades had already hauled those back to the encampment. Granth swore; cutting trees down was harder work than carrying stakes already cut. "Can't trust anyone," he complained, forgetting that only the day before he and Vulth had cheerfully absconded with three stakes someone else had trimmed.

As darkness began to fall—impossible to say precisely when the sun set, for the clouds and mists of Cimmeria obscured both sunrise and sunset—a long, mournful note blown on the trumpet recalled the Aquilonian soldiers to the camp. Savory steam rose from big iron pots bubbling over cookfires. Rubbing their bellies to show how hungry they were, men lined up to get their suppers.

"Mutton stew?" asked Granth, sniffing.

"Mutton stew," answered a Bossonian who had just had his tin panikin filled. He spoke with resignation. Mutton was what most of the army had eaten ever since crossing into Cimmeria. The forage here was not good enough to support many cattle. Even the sheep were small and scrawny.

A cook spooned stew into Granth's panikin. He stepped aside to let the cook feed the next soldier, then dug in with his horn spoon. The meat was tough and stringy and gamy. The barley that went with it had come up from the Aquilonian side of the border in supply wagons. Cimmeria's scanty fields held mostly rye and oats; the short growing season did not always allow barley, let alone wheat, to ripen.

Had Granth got a supper like this at an inn down in Gunderland, he would have snarled at the innkeeper. On campaign, he was glad he had enough to fill his belly. Anything more than that was better than a bonus; it came near enough to being a miracle.

Someone asked, "What are we calling this camp?" Count Stercus had named each successive encampment after an estate that belonged to him or to one of his friends. Granth supposed it made as good a way as any other to remember which was which.

"Venarium," answered another soldier. "This one's Camp Venarium."

Mordec methodically set his iron cap on his head. He wore a long knife—almost a shortsword—on his belt. A long-handled war axe and a round wooden shield faced with leather and bossed with iron leaned against the brickwork of the forge. A leather wallet carried enough oatcakes and smoked meat to feed him for several days.

Conan was anything but methodical. He sprang into the air in frustration and fury. "Take me with you!" he shouted, not for the first time. "Take me with you, Father!"

"No," growled Mordec.

But the one word, which would usually have silenced his son, had no effect here. "Take me with you!" cried Conan once more. "I can fight. By Crom, I can! I'm bigger than a lot of the men in Duthil, and stronger, too!"

"No," said Mordec once again, deeper and more menacingly than before. Again, though, Conan shook his head, desperate to accompany his father against the invading Aquilonians. Mordec shook his head, too, as if bedeviled by gnats rather than by a boy who truly was bigger and stronger than many of the grown men in the village. Reluctantly, Mordec spoke further: "You were born on a battlefield, son. I don't care to see you die on one."

"I wouldn't die!" The idea did not seem real to Conan. "I'd make the southrons go down like grain before the scythe."

And so he might—for a while. Mordec knew it. But no untried boy would last long against a veteran who had practiced his bloody trade twice as long as his foe had lived. And no one, boy or veteran, was surely safe against flying arrows and javelins. "When I say no, I mean no. You're too young. You'll stay here in Duthil where you belong, and you'll take care of your mother."

That struck home; the blacksmith saw as much. But Conan was too wild to go to war to heed even such a potent command. "I won't!" he said shrilly. "I won't, and you can't make me. After you leave, I'll run off and join the army, too."

The next thing he knew, he was lying on the ground by the forge. His head spun. His ears rang. His father stood over him, breathing hard, ready to hit him again if he had to. "You will do no such thing," declared Mordec. "You will do what I tell you, and nothing else. Do you hear me?"

Instead of answering in words, Conan sprang up and grabbed for his father's axe. For the moment, he was ready to do murder for the sake of going to war. But even as his hand closed on the axe handle, Mordec's larger, stronger hand closed on his wrist. Conan tried to twist free, tried and failed. Then he hit his father. He had told the truth—he did have the strength of an ordinary man. The blacksmith, however, was no ordinary man. He took his son's buffet without changing expression.

"So you want to see what it's really like, do you?" asked Mordec. "All right, by Crom. I'll let you have a taste."

He had hit Conan before; as often as not, nothing but his hand would gain and hold the boy's attention. But he had never given him such a cold-blooded, thorough, methodical beating as he did now. Conan tried to fight back for as long as he could. Mordec kept hitting him until he had no more fight left in him. The blacksmith aimed to make the boy cry out for mercy, but Conan set his jaw and suffered in silence, plainly as intent on dying before he showed weakness as Mordec was on breaking him.

And Conan might have died then, for his father, afraid he would fall to an enemy's weapons, was not at all afraid to kill him for pride's sake. After the beating had gone on for some long and painful time, though, Verina came out of the bedchamber. "Hold!" she croaked. "Would you slay what's most like you?"

Mordec stared at her. Rage suddenly rivered out of him, pouring away like ale from a cracked cup. He knelt by his bruised and bloodied son. "You will stay here," he said, half commanding, half pleading.

Conan did not say no. Conan, then, could not have said anything, for his father had beaten him all but senseless. He saw the smithy through a red haze of anguish.

Taking his silence for acquiescence, Mordec filled a dipper

with cold water and held it to his battered lips. Conan took a mouthful. He wanted to spit it in his father's face, but animal instinct made him swallow instead. Mordec did not take the dipper away. Conan drained it dry.

"You are as hard on your son as you are on everything else," said Verina with a bubbling sigh.

"Life is hard," answered Mordec. "Anyone who will not see that is a fool: no, worse than a fool—a blind man."

"Life is hard, aye," agreed his wife. "I am not blind; I can see that, too. But I can also see that you are blind, blind to the way you make it harder than it need be."

With a grunt, the blacksmith got to his feet. He towered over Verina. Scowling, he replied, "I am not the only one in this home of whom that might be said."

"And if I fight you, will you beat me as you beat the boy?" asked Verina. "What point to that? All you have to do is wait; before long the sickness in my lungs will slay me and set you free."

"You twist everything I say, everything I do," muttered Mordec, at least as much to himself as to her. Fighting the Aquilonians would seem simple when set against the long, quiet (but no less deadly for being quiet) war he had waged with his wife.

"All you want to do is spill blood," said Verina. "You would be as happy slaying Cimmerians as you are going off to battle Aquilonians."

"Not so," said Mordec. "These are thieves who come into our land. You know that yourself. They would take what little we have and send it south to add to their own riches. They would, but they will not. I go to join the muster of the clans." He strode forward, snatched up his axe and shield and wallet, and stormed forth from the smithy, a thunderstorm of fury on his face.

"No good will come of this!" called Verina, but the blacksmith paid no heed.

Conan heard his father and mother quarrel as if from very far away. The pain of the beating made everything else seem small and unimportant. He tried to get to his feet, but found he lacked the strength. He lay in the dirt, even his ardor to go forth to battle quelled for the moment.

Verina stooped beside him. His mother held a bowl full of water and a scrap of cloth. She wet the cloth and gently scrubbed at his face. The rag, which had been the brownish gray of undyed wool, came away crimson. She soaked it in the bowl, wrung it nearly dry, and went back to what she was doing. "There," she said at last. "You're young—you'll heal."

With an effort, Conan managed to sit up. "I still want to go and fight, no matter what Father says," he mumbled through cut and swollen lips.

But his mother shook her head. "Mordec was right." She made a sour face. "Not words I often say, but true. However great you've grown, you are yet too young to go to war." And Conan, who would have and nearly had fought to the death against his father, accepted Verina's words without a murmur.

chapter ii

The Fight by the Fort

Granth son of Biemur looked out toward the woods beyond Fort Venarium. A dirt track led farther north, but the Aquilonian army had not taken it. Instead, Count Stercus seemed content to linger here and let the Cimmerians hurl themselves against his men if they would.

Whatever Granth hoped to see escaped his eyes. One tall, dark-needled tree merged with another until he wished for color, wished for motion, wished for anything but the endless forest stretching out and out to infinity.

Vulth looked out toward the woods, too. Granth's cousin realized that what he was not seeing might be there nonetheless. He said, "Mitra smite 'em, the Cimmerians could be hiding an army amongst those trees, and we'd never be the wiser till they rushed out howling like maniacs."

That made Granth cast another worried glance in the direction of the forest. After a moment, he realized he was foolish to peer ever to the north. Although that was the direction in which the Aquilonians had been going, the barbarians who dwelt in gloomy Cimmeria might as readily come at them from east or west or south.

A harsh chattering came from the woods. Granth's hand

leaped to the hilt of the shortsword on his belt. "What was that?" he said.

"A bird," said Vulth.

"What kind of bird?" asked Granth. "I've never heard a bird that sounded like that before."

"Who knows?" said his cousin. "They have funny birds here, birds that won't live where it's warmer and sunnier. One of those."

"They have other things, too," said Granth. Vulth waved impatiently, as if to say he could not bother to worry about the Cimmerians. That angered Granth, who snapped, "If this was going to be an easy conquest, Count Stercus wouldn't have needed to bring an army into the north. He could have come by himself, and the barbarians would have run away before him."

Vulth looked back toward the camp. Stercus' silk pavilion towered over the other officers' shelters, which in turn dwarfed the canvas tents in which ordinary soldiers slept. "Count Stercus thinks he could have driven the barbarians away all by himself," said Vulth.

Before answering, Granth looked around for Nopel. Not seeing the sergeant, he said, "We all think a lot of things that aren't so. Half the time, for instance, I think you make sense." Vulth stuck his tongue out at him. Before either of them could say anything more, that chattering bird call again resounded from the woods. Granth peered in the direction from which the sound had come. Though he saw nothing untoward, he frowned. "And I don't think that's any natural bird."

"Where are the Cimmerians, then?" asked Vulth.

Granth shrugged. "I don't know, but we're liable to find out before very long."

Mordec slid forward through the forest with the speed and silence that marked the true barbarian. Not a single twig crackled under the soles of his boots; not a single branch swayed to mark his passage. He might have been a ghost in Crom's grim underworld for all he impinged on the world of the living. Nor was he the only Cimmerian gliding toward the invaders' encampment; far from it. The Aquilonians seemed unaware the woods around them swarmed with warriors.

From in back of the trunk of a fat spruce, Mordec loosed a bird call to let his fellow know where he was. Another Cimmerian answered him a moment later. He looked out from behind the trunk. Most of the soldiers who fought under the gold lion on black went about their business, oblivious to the calls. A handful of the enemy—mostly yellow-headed Gundermen who had some small store of woodscraft—looked up at the sounds, but even they seemed more curious than truly alarmed.

A soundless laugh passed Mordec's lips. Soon now, very soon, the Aquilonians would find reason to be alarmed. They had come into Cimmeria before, never yet learning the lesson of how unwelcome they were here. The blacksmith tightened his grip on the axe handle. They would have to find out once more, then.

More bird calls resounded, all around the encampment. Some of them said the Cimmerians were in position, others that the Aquilonian scouts and sentries were silenced. Mordec smiled grimly. The men in the clearing would get no warning before the attack.

Not far from Mordec, a clan chief raised a trumpet to his lips. The discordant blast he blew would have made any arrogant Aquilonian bugler double up with laughter. But the signal did not need to be beautiful. It only needed to be heard from one side of the clearing to the other, and heard it was.

Yelling like demons, the Cimmerians burst from concealment and thundered toward the enemy. Mordec swung up the axe. For most men, it would have been a two-handed weapon. The great-thewed blacksmith swung it effortlessly in one. That let him carry the shield as well.

When the Cimmerians swarmed from the woods at them, the Gundermen and Bossonians yelled, too, in horrified dismay. But they did not break and flee, as Mordec hoped they might. Had they done so, their destruction would have been certain. Other Aquilonian hosts, taken by surprise in the—seemingly—trackless forests of Cimmeria, had come to grief in just that way.

These men, though, however much Mordec despised them both as invaders and as willing subjects—willing slaves—to a king, were warriors, too. The Bossonians might have cried out in alarm, but they began shooting even before their cries had fully faded. And the Gundermen snatched up their pikes and hurried to form lines to protect their archers and companies to protect themselves. True, sweet bugle notes resounded from within the palisade.

Before the Bossonians and Gundermen outside the encampment were fully formed to face the Cimmerian tidal wave, it swept onto them. A blond Gunderman thrust at Mordec. He knocked the spearhead aside with his shield as his axe came down on the shaft and cut it in two. Cursing, the Gunderman grabbed for his shortsword. Too late, for Mordec's next stroke clove his skull to the teeth. Blood sprayed and spurted; several hot drops splashed Mordec in the face. Roaring in triumph, the blacksmith pressed on.

He might have been hewing firewood in the forest rather than men on the battlefield. One after another, Aquilonians fell before him. They wore chainmail, aye, but it did them little good; his axe, propelled by the power of his mighty arm, hewed through the links as if they were made of linen.

When Mordec paused for a moment to snatch a breath and look down at himself, he was surprised to discover a cut on his forearm and another on his left leg. He had no memory of receiving the wounds, nor had he felt them until he knew he had them. He shrugged. They would not impede him. Even if they had impeded him, he would have gone on anyway. Resistless momentum was the Cimmerians' friend; if ever they should falter, if ever the Aquilonians should rally, the superior discipline the men from the south knew could swing the fight their way.

Forward, then—ever forward. Mordec plunged back into the press. An arrow thudded into his shield and stood thrilling; had he not carried the target of wood and leather, the shaft might have found his heart.

He hewed a Bossonian's sword from his hand. "Mercy!" gasped the man, turning pale and falling to his knees. "Mercy, friend!"

"Mercy?" Mordec laughed. He knew some of the Aquilonian tongue, having learned it from traders who now and again dared venture north after amber or wax or furs. But that word had scant meaning in Cimmeria, regardless of the language in which it was spoken. The axe fell. With a groan, the Bossonian crumpled. Mordec kicked the corpse aside, saying, "I am no friend of yours, southern dog."

He hewed through the chaos toward one of the gateways in the palisade. If the Cimmerians could break in with their foes still in disorder, the day and the campaign were both theirs for the taking. They had no general, no single mind moving them hither and yon in accordance with his will, yet most of them sensed that same need. On they came, smiting and shouting.

The foemen in front of them gave ground. A few archers and pikemen ran for their lives, forgetting in their fear they would find no safety in flight. Most, though, put up the best fight they could. And, to take the place of the fled and fallen, more and more soldiers came forth from the camp.

In the red rage of battle, Mordec cared nothing for that. More enemies before him meant more men he could murder. He chopped down another Bossonian. Only a handful of stubborn blond pikemen from Gunderland stood between him and the gate. Countrymen at his side, he stormed against them.

Like any man who grew up among rough neighbors, Granth had done his share of brawling. He had also helped clear out a nest of bandits from hill country near his farmhouse. This mad encounter in southern Cimmeria, though, was his first taste of true battle. If he lived, he knew he would have its measure forevermore. Whether he lived, though, seemed very much up in the air.

One moment, the encampment and its surroundings were as quiet and calm as if they were back in Gunderland and not in the midst of enemy country. The next, after a horrible blast from a horn, a horde of bellowing barbarians burst from the trees and rushed toward the Aquilonians, brandishing every sort of weapon under the sun: swords, axes, spears, sickles, scythes, maces, morningstars, simple bludgeons, eating knives, even a pitchfork. Cimmerian archers sent shafts arcing over the heads of their onrushing comrades.

"Mitra!" exclaimed Granth, and snatched up his pike from where he had laid it on the ground.

"Mitra, watch over us," echoed Vulth, grabbing his own weapon. "And the god had better, for we're in trouble if he doesn't."

"Form a line!" shouted Sergeant Nopel from somewhere not far away. "Form a line, protect your comrades, and fight hard. If they break us, we're ruined. If we stand fast, though, we've got a chance." He strode up to take his place among the men he led, using his example to buoy their courage.

A captain was shouting, too: "You pikemen, ward the archers as you can. They aren't worth so much at handstrokes."

Bossonians were already pouring shafts into the onrushing mob of barbarians. Here and there, a dark-haired Cimmerian would clap his hands to his chest or his neck or his face and fall. Taking a handful of drops from the ocean, however, left plenty more than enough to drown a man. And now the barbarian storm crashed into—crashed over—the Aquilonians outside the palisade.

Any sensible man, Granth realized, would have been terrified. Maybe he was something less than sensible. More likely, he was so desperate, so busy fighting for his life, that he had no time for fear or any other distraction. Anything that took his attention away from simple survival would have meant him lying on the field, a hacked and gory corpse.

As things were, he might have died a dozen times in the first minute of collision. A barbarian swinging a two-handed sword almost as tall as he was thundered toward him, shouting something in Cimmerian that Granth could not understand. But even a two-handed sword had less reach than a Gunderman's pike. Granth spitted the foe before the Cimmerian could slash him.

To his horror, the barbarian, though bellowing in anguish, tried to run up the spear so he could strike with the sword, but slumped over dead before he could. Granth had to clear the pike in a hurry; had he not, some other Cimmerian would have cut him down. At his right hand, Vulth speared an axe-wielding barbarian. With the enemy still on the pike, Granth's cousin could not defend himself against another Cimmerian, this one swinging a wickedly spiked morningstar. Granth had no time to thrust, but used his pikestaff as if it were a cudgel, clouting the Cimmerian in the side of the head.

The enemy warrior wore a leather cap strengthened with iron strips. That kept the shaft from smashing his skull like a melon. But, though the blow did not slay, it stunned, leaving the barbarian dazed and staggering and easy meat for Vulth's newly freed pike.

As the Cimmerian fell, Vulth bowed to Granth as if to an Aquilonian noble. "My thanks, cousin," he said.

"My pleasure, cousin," replied Granth, as if he were such a noble. He looked over the field: a mad, irregular excuse for a battle if ever there was one. Everywhere he saw Cimmerians surging forward, Bossonians and Gundermen giving ground. Raising his voice above the din of the fight, he said, "Looks to me as if we're in trouble, cousin."

"Looks to me as if you're right," agreed Vulth. Granth and he had to fall back several paces or be left behind by their retreating countrymen, which would have left them cut off, assailed from all directions at once, and doomed to quick destruction. Vulth risked a glance back over his shoulder. "Having a fortified camp behind us doesn't seem so bad any more, does it?"

"As a matter of fact, no," said Granth, doing his best to preserve the grand manner. "All those men inside the camp look pretty good, too—or the rogues would, if they'd only come out and fight."

There he was not being fair to his fellow soldiers. As fast as they could arm themselves, they were rushing forward into the fray. But to Granth, as to the other men who bore the brunt of the savage Cimmerian onslaught, their friends entered the fight at what seemed a glacial pace.

The barbarian who hurled himself at Granth had eyes that put the Gunderman in mind of flaming blue ice. He roared out a wordless bellow of hate and rage, his face contorted into a mask of fury that might have made any foe quail. His only weapon was a rusty scythe, but he swung it as if he had been reaping men for years. Granth jabbed with the pike to keep the warrior off him. The Cimmerian, who wore a wolfskin jacket over baggy woolen breeks, howled incomprehensible, oddly musical curses at him.

That the Gunderman did not mind. When the barbarian reached out with his left hand to seize the pikestaff and shove it aside so he could close, however, Granth quickly jerked it back and then thrust forward again. He felt the soft, heavy resistance of flesh as the pike's point pierced the man who sought to slay him. The Cimmerian howled. Granth twisted the pike to make sure the stroke was a killing one, then jerked it free. The barbarian fell, blood and bowels bursting from his belly.

Again, though, he and Vulth had to retreat to keep from being surrounded and cut off. "How many damned Cimmerians are there?" he shouted.

"By Mitra, they're all damned," answered his cousin. "But there are too many of them on the field here."

That there were. They forced the Gundermen and Bossonians back and back, until the men from the south were fighting desperately to hold the barbarians out of the fortified encampment. If the Cimmerians forced themselves into the camp, Count Stercus' army was probably doomed. That seemed all too plain to Granth — and to the howling savages who forced their way ever forward despite the reinforcements issuing from the camp.

A Gunderman to Granth's left slumped to his knees, bleeding from a dozen wounds that would long since have slain a less vital man. "What are we going to do?" cried Granth. "What can we do?"

"Fight," said Vulth. "This is where we'll win or lose, so we'd better win."

Granth fought, and fought hard. If the battle were to have a turning point, he and his comrades would have to make it here. If not— He shook his head. He would not think about that. It might befall him, but he would not think of it before it did.

"Fight hard!" bellowed Mordec. "By Crom, we can break them here. We can, and we must! Fight hard!"

Although he and his fellows had battled to the very gates of the Aquilonians' camp, they could not force their way in-

side. For one thing, the pikemen and archers at the gates battled back with the careless fervor of men staring disaster in
the face. For another, more men kept coming forth from the
encampment to add their weight to the fray. And, for a third,
archers galled the Cimmerians from behind the ditch and palisade surrounding the camp.

Mordec smashed at the tip of a pike seeking to drink his
blood. The iron head flew off. He roared in triumph. But the
Gunderman he faced defended himself so fiercely, first with
the pikestaff and then with his shortsword, that Mordec could
not slay him. At last, balked of his intended prey, the blacksmith sought and soon found an easier victim.

Inside the encampment, a bugler blew a long, complex call.
The Aquilonians outside the gate that Mordec faced fell back
into the camp. The foot soldiers who had been hurrying out
to help defend the place parted to the left and to the right. A
great shout of victory rose from the Cimmerians, who loped
forward, ready to taste at last the sweet fruit for which they
had struggled so long and hard.

But they rejoiced too soon. The archers and pikemen had
not given way from despair, but because they were clearing
the path for their comrades. That sweet-voiced Aquilonian
bugle cried out once more—and the armored knights who up
until then had not joined the battle thundered forth against
the Cimmerians.

The horsemen had used the whole width of the encampment to go from walk to trot to gallop, and when they struck,
they struck like an avalanche. Here in the hilly, heavily for-
ested north, cavalry was not much used. Not only was there
little room for horsemen to deploy, but most of the few horses
in Cimmeria were mere ponies, ill-suited to carrying heavy
men and their armor of iron.

Shouting out the name of King Numedides as if it were a
thing to conjure with and not that of a slavemaster, the Aqui-

lonian knights slammed into the oncoming Cimmerians. Lances and slashing swords and cleverly aimed iron-shod hooves and the surging power of armored men and horses took their toll. The Cimmerians fought back as best they could, but their swords and spears would not bite on the knights' thick plate, or on the iron scales the horses wore to protect their heads and breasts.

Mordec's axe was a different story. When he brought it down between a horse's eyes, the beast foundered as if it had run headlong into a stone wall. Agile even in his well-articulated armor, the rider tried to scramble free. The blacksmith's countrymen swarmed over him. Their blades probed for every chink and joint in his suit of iron. He screamed, but not for long.

Yet even as he died, his comrades spurred ahead, spearing and hacking, their great mounts whinnying fiercely and rising on command to their hind legs so they could lash out with their front hooves. Along with Numedides' name, the knights cried out that of Count Stercus, and, whenever they did, one of the foremost riders gaily waved. His visor was down, so Mordec could not see his face, but he fought like a man who had no regard for his own life. Again and again, he urged his charger into the thickest part of the press. Again and again, the other Aquilonians followed to save him from his own folly—if folly it was, for even as he risked himself he routed the Cimmerians.

Had they been used to facing armored horsemen, they surely would have acquitted themselves better. But the Aquilonian knights had, along with the advantages of armor and momentum, that of striking from above and, greatest of all, that of surprise. Never had any of their foes here, no matter how ferocious, tried to stand against such an onslaught.

With the mercurial nature that marked the barbarian, the horde of Cimmerians who had been rampaging forward now suddenly turned to panic-stricken flight. Turning their backs to the knights who pressed them, they dashed for the safety of the woods.

"Stand! Hold fast, you fools!" shouted Mordec. "You but give yourselves into the enemy's hands if you run from him!" His was not the only voice raised trying to stem the rout, but all resounded in vain. Faster by far than they had advanced on the Aquilonians' camp, the Cimmerians fled from it.

And they paid the inevitable price for their folly. Laughing at the sport, the Aquilonian knights speared them down from behind, as if they were so many plump partridges. Bossonian archers sped the Cimmerians on their way with cleverly aimed shafts. More than a few bold warriors from those gloomy woodlands suffered the humiliation of taking their death wounds in the back.

Mordec had to run away with the rest. Had he stood at bay, alone, he would only have thrown his own life away— and for what? For nothing, not when his countrymen thought only of escape. And so, cursing fate and his fellow Cimmerians in equal measure, he ran. He was among the last to leave the field: a small sop for his spirit, but the only one he could take from the sudden rout and disaster.

He had almost reached the safety of the trees when an arrow pierced his left calf. He snarled one last curse at the Cimmerians who had given up the fight too soon, and limped on. Once hidden from the now rampaging foe, he paused and tried to pull out the arrow. The barbs on the point would not let him free it from his flesh. Setting his teeth, Mordec pushed it forward instead. Out came the point. He broke off the fletching and pulled the shaft through the track it had made. Then he bandaged the bleeding wounds with cloth cut from his breeks. That done, he limped on toward Duthil.

When Mordec came upon a dead man who had fallen still holding on to his spear, he pried the other Cimmerian's hand, now pale from loss of blood, off the spearshaft and used the weapon as a makeshift stick to keep some of his weight off the injured leg. He would have gone on without the stick; he was determined enough to have gone on with only one leg. But having it made his progress easier.

"Home," he said, as if someone had claimed he might not go there. And so the Aquilonians had. They had done their best to stretch him out stiff and stark like the warrior from whom he had taken the spear. They had done their best, and they had failed: he still lived, while more than a few of them lay dead at his hands.

In the larger sense, his countrymen had lost their battle. Mordec, though, stubbornly reckoned his own fight a triumph of sorts.

A wounded Cimmerian, too proud and fierce to beg for his own life, glared up at Granth. The Gunderman hesitated before thrusting home with his pike. "Seems a shame to slaughter all these barbarians," he remarked. "The healers could keep a lot of them alive, and they'd fetch us a good price in the slave markets, eh?"

Vulth and Sergeant Nopel both guffawed. His cousin said, "You try to sell a slave dealer Cimmerians, and he'll laugh in your face and spit in your eye. But he won't give you a counterfeit copper for 'em, let alone the silver lunas you're dreaming about."

"Why not?" Granth still did not slay the barbarian at his feet. "They're big and bold and strong. Mitra! We found out everything we wanted to know about how strong they are."

"And you should have noticed none of them surrendered," said Vulth. "They aren't known for yielding to another man's will"—he rolled his eyes at the understatement—"and what good is a slave who won't?"

Before Granth could answer, the Cimmerian on the ground hooked an arm around his ankle and tried to drag him off his feet. Only a hasty backward leap saved him from a grapple. His cousin speared the Cimmerian, who groaned, spat blood, and at last, long after a civilized man would have, died.

"You see?" said Vulth.

"Well, maybe I do at that," admitted Granth. "They're like serpents, aren't they? You're never sure they're dead until the sun goes down."

"When the sun goes down, more of them come out," said Nopel. "Now get on about your business."

Granth obeyed, sending the Cimmerians he found still breathing on the field out of this world with such speed and mercy as he could give them: had they won the fight, as they had come so close to doing, he would have wanted a last gift of that sort from them. Vulth and Nopel and most of the Gundermen and Bossonians acted the same way. No one who had stood up against the barbarians rushing out of the woods could have reckoned them anything but worthy foes.

Count Stercus rode up as the foot soldiers continued their grisly work. Excitement reddened the commander's usually pale cheeks and made his eyes sparkle. "Well done, you men," he said. "Every barbarian you slay now is a barbarian who will not try to slay you later."

Granth and Vulth and Sergeant Nopel all nodded. "Aye, my lord," murmured Nopel. The sight of Stercus cheerful startled them all. The nobleman had despised his soldiers. Victory, though, seemed to have changed his mind.

He said, "We shall seize this country, such as it is, and hold it for our own. Farmers will come north from Aquilonia and take their places here, to prosper for generation upon generation. Fort Venarium will be their center, and one day will grow into a city that can stand beside Tarantia and the other great centers of the realm."

That sounded good to Granth. Only one question still troubled his mind. He was bold, or rash, enough to ask it: "What about the Cimmerians, my lord?"

Nopel hissed in alarm between his teeth, while Vulth made a horrible face and then tried to pretend he had done no such thing. But Count Stercus' good cheer was proof even against impertinent questions. "What about the Cimmerians, my good fellow?" he echoed. "We have smashed their barbarous horde." His wave encompassed the corpse-strewn field; that many of the corpses were those of his countrymen seemed not to have come to his notice. Grandly, he continued, "Now we subdue their haunts in these parts, and compel them to obedience. Surely every Cimmerian man and woman, every boy and every little girl"—his voice lingered lovingly over the last few words—"shall bend the knee before the might of King Numedides."

From all that Granth had heard and seen, the fierce folk of the north bent the knee to no man. He started to say what he thought; he was as forthright as any other Gunderman. But the thought of what Vulth and Nopel had done a moment before gave him pause, and Count Stercus rode off before he could speak. He did not care enough about the argument to call the commander back.

"By Mitra, slaughter goes to his head like strong wine from Poitain," said Vulth in a low voice. "You'd hardly know he was the sour son of a whore who led us here."

"He didn't bite this fool's head off," agreed the sergeant, jerking a thumb toward Granth son of Biemur. "If that doesn't prove he's a happy man, curse me if I know what would."

"Do you suppose holding the Cimmerians down will be as easy as he says?" asked Granth.

Before answering, Nopel spat on the blood-soaked soil. "That for the Cimmerians," he said. "I'll tell you this much: we have a better chance now that we've smashed the manhood of three or four clans. What can they do but submit?"

Vulth stopped to search a dead man. He rose, muttering to himself and shaking his head. "I've not found any plunder worth keeping. The poorest, most hardscrabble Bossonian carries more in the way of loot than these dogs."

"What do we want with them, then?" wondered Granth. He had also searched corpses. He had found nothing worth holding on to but a curiously wrought copper amulet on a leather thong around the neck of a fallen enemy swordsman, and even that could not have been worth more than a couple of lunas at the outside. He had taken it more as a souvenir of the battle than in the hope of selling it later.

"They're here. They're on our doorstep. If we don't beat them, they'll come down into the Bossonian Marches, into Gunderland, maybe even into Aquilonia proper," said Nopel. "Better we should fight them, better we should whip them, in their own miserable country."

"Well, so it is," said Granth. The sergeant's words made good sense to him. He strode across the field, looking for more Cimmerians to finish. Carrion birds had already begun to settle on bodies indisputably dead.

Conan's bruises healed quickly, thanks to his youth and the iron constitution of the barbarian. He was not only up and about but busy in the smithy only a couple of days after his father beat him. But, though he might have been strong enough to go after Mordec, he chose to remain in Duthil instead. Belatedly, he had come to realize his father was right. If he went to fight the Aquilonians with his father and they both fell, who would tend to his mother? She had no other kin left alive in the village; she would have to rely on the kindness of those not tied to her by blood, and such kindness was always in short supply in Cimmeria.

As well as he could, Conan tended to the forge and the rest of the smithy. No large jobs came his way while his father was gone, for most of the other men of Duthil had gone with Mordec into battle. But Reuda, who was married to Dolfnal the tanner, came to Conan asking for a cooking fork. "Must I wait until Mordec comes home?" she said.

He shook his head, pausing for a moment to brush his thick mane of black hair back from his forehead with a swipe of the hand. "Nay, no need," he told her. "Come back tomorrow, just before the sun goes down. I'll have it for you then."

"And if I am not satisfied with your work?" asked Reuda. "If I see I would sooner have your father's?"

"Then save the fork and show it to him," replied Conan. "If you are sorry with what I give you, he will make me sorrier that I did not suit you."

Reuda rubbed her chin. After a moment's thought, she nodded. "Aye, let it be as you say. If you'll not work your best for fear of Mordec's heavy hand, nothing less will squeeze that best from you."

"I am not afraid of him," said Conan fiercely, but an ingrained regard for the truth compelled him to add, "Still, I would not feel his fist without good cause." Reuda laughed and nodded and went back to her husband's tannery, taking the stink of hides and sour tanbark with her.

Conan went to work straightaway, choosing an iron bar about as thick as his finger. He heated one end of it white-hot, then brought it back to the anvil and, with quick, cunning strokes of the hammer, shaped that end into a loop about two inches long. That done, he used a cold chisel to cut through the extremity of the loop, giving him the two tines he would need for the work. Some forks had three tines, but that was as yet beyond his skill. He did not think Reuda would complain if hers proved to be of the ordinary sort.

Heating the iron again, he bent the tines on the heel of the anvil until something close to a right angle separated them. That way, he could work on each of them in turn more conveniently. Careful hammerstrokes flattened the tines. Conan heated the metal once more and brought the tines back to their proper position. He set the fork aside and let it cool.

When he could safely handle it without tongs, he used brass rivets to bind a wood handle to the iron shank. He looked the work over to see if Reuda could find any way to fault it. Seeing none, he took the fork to the tanner's wife fully a day earlier than he had promised.

She examined it, too, plainly with the same thing in mind. Seeing nothing about which she could complain, she gave the young smith a grudging nod, saying, "I think it may serve. When your father comes home, we'll settle on a price."

"All right." Conan nodded. Almost all business in Duthil was done that way. The Cimmerians minted no coins; the few that circulated here came up from the south. Barter and haggling took the place of money and set costs.

When Conan left Reuda's kitchen, he saw Glemmis, who had taken word of the Aquilonian invasion from Duthil to the nearby village of Uist and then, no doubt, gone on to fight the men from the south. Glemmis limped up the street toward him; a filthy, blood-soaked rag covered most of a wound on the man's left arm.

Conan's heart leaped into his mouth. "The battle—!" he blurted.

Glemmis spoke a word Conan had never imagined he would hear: "Lost." He went on, "We hit the Aquilonians a hard blow, but they held us, and then—Crom!—their cursed horsemen cut us down like ripe rye at harvest time." He shuddered at the memory.

"What of my father?" asked Conan. "What of the other warriors who left our village?"

"Of Mordec I know nought. He may well be hale," answered Glemmis with a certain rough kindness. "But I can tell you truly that many fell. Eoganan, for instance, I saw go down, a Bossonian's arrow through his throat. We've not known such a black day for many long years."

Had he got away safe by running first and fastest? Even so

young, Conan saw the possibility and scorned him for it. But before long other men started coming home to Duthil, many of them wounded, all hollow-eyed and shocked with defeat. Even Balarg the weaver, who prided himself on never seeming at a loss, looked as if he had grappled with demons and come off second best. Women began to wail as some men did not come home again, and as survivors began bringing word of those who never would.

Several returning warriors had seen Conan's father where the fighting was hottest, but none could say whether Mordec lived or had fallen. "I will wait, then, and learn," said Conan, "and if need be avenge myself on the Aquilonians." When he told Verina what he had learned, his mother started keening, as for one dead.

But Mordec did come back to Duthil, limping in with a spearshaft clamped in his left fist to help bear his weight. His right arm briefly slipped around Conan in a rough embrace. "We'll fight them again," said Conan. "We'll fight them again, and we'll beat them."

"Not soon." Mordec wearily shook his head. "Not tomorrow, or next week, or next month. Not next year, all too likely. We lost too much in this round."

"What then?" asked Conan, aghast.

"What then?" echoed his father. "Why, the bitter beer of the beaten, for beaten we are."

chapter iii

The Temple Out of Time

Conan saw his first Aquilonians a few days after his father came home to Duthil. By then, the villagers had a good idea of who would never come home again. Women's keening went on night and day. New mourning had broken out only the night before, when a Cimmerian died after taking a fever from his wound.

The invaders marched up the same track the village men had used in retreating from the lost battle. The archers advanced with arrows nocked and bows ready to draw. The pikemen with them were broad-shouldered fellows with hair the color of straw. They too were alert against any ambush that might burst upon them from the woods. Not least because they were alert, no ambush came.

All told, pikemen and archers numbered perhaps a hundred: more than three times the number of warriors Duthil had sent into the fight. Eyeing them as they approached, Conan said, "They don't look so tough."

Mordec stood beside him, still leaning on the spearshaft that did duty for a cane. The blacksmith said, "One of us would likely beat one of them, despite the armor they wear. But they do not fight by ones, as we do. The pikemen fight

together, in lines that support each other. The archers shoot
volleys at an officer's command, aiming where he points. It
makes them more dangerous foes than they would be otherwise."

"A coward's way of doing things," sneered Conan.

His father shrugged. "They fought well enough to win a
battle. We in Duthil cannot stand against that whole company. We have not the men for it. They would slaughter us."
That would have been true before the villagers went off to
war. It was doubly true now that so many of them had not
returned. Conan bit his lip at the humiliation of submitting
to the men from the south, but even he could see Mordec
was right: resistance would only lead to massacre.

As the Aquilonians drew ever nearer, more and more villagers came out into the main street—the continuation of the
track the invaders used—to eye them. None of the men held
a weapon in his hand. None had anything more dangerous
than an eating knife on his belt. Could looks have killed,
though, their eyes—and especially the eyes of the women who
stood shoulder to shoulder with them—would have mown
down the archers and pikemen by the score.

At a shouted command, the pikemen shook themselves out
into two lines in front of the archers. They made no fuss about
the order. They did not argue about it or hash it over, as
Cimmerians would have done. They simply obeyed, as if it
was something they heard every day—and so it plainly was.
"Slaves," muttered Conan, mocking the first military discipline he had ever seen.

The man who had given the command strode out in front
of his soldiers. A scarlet crest affixed to the top of his helm
singled him out as an officer. Hand on the hilt of his sword—
the pommel was wrapped with gold wire, a sure sign of
wealth—he strutted into Duthil. He bawled out something in
his own language.

"He says his name is Treviranus, and asks if any here can

put his words into Cimmerian for him," said Mordec. He took a hitching step forward and spoke in Aquilonian. The officer answered him, then talked at some length. Mordec interrupted him once or twice. "I'm telling him to slow down," he whispered to Conan.

Although Treviranus scowled, he did speak more slowly after that. Despite Mordec's wound, his grim appearance and even grimmer manner would have given any man pause. The blacksmith translated for the folk of Duthil: "This Aquilonian says we are now the subjects of King Numedides. He says this part of Cimmeria belongs to the Aquilonians by right of conquest."

He was careful not to take credit for Treviranus' words himself, but to attribute them to the officer who uttered them. Conan thought his father wise for that. Anyone who declared Cimmerians subjects and a conquered people proved only that he knew nothing of the freedom-loving folk among whom he moved.

Through Mordec, Treviranus went on, "There will be a garrison in the village or near it, as this officer chooses. We will have to feed the garrison and provide for it. If we ambush any of the soldiers, the Aquilonians will take hostages—ten for one—and kill them." The officer added something else. So did Conan's father: "Kill them slowly."

A low mutter ran through the crowd. In Cimmeria, only the most abandoned, most desperate robbers used such tactics. "Now I speak for myself," said Mordec. "I say we must do as the Aquilonians tell us for now, for they have shown themselves stronger than we are. And I say we must watch what words pass our lips, for they will surely have some man or other among them who understands Cimmerian."

Conan had not thought of that. He watched the soldiers. Sure enough, one of the pikemen walked up to Treviranus and casually spoke to him in their language. The officer glanced at Mordec through narrowed eyes. He raised his hand as if about to give some order. Conan tensed, ready to hurl himself against the invaders. But, whatever Treviranus had been about to do, he seemed to think better of it. He spoke a single sentence, aimed at Mordec like an archer's arrow.

"He asks, do we understand?" said the blacksmith in Cimmerian.

Slowly, reluctantly, the men of Duthil nodded. They had fought these fair-haired men from the south, fought them and been defeated. Remembering the loss helped the men submit without too much more shame. Their womenfolk were even slower and more reluctant to acknowledge that the Aquilonians had the upper hand for the time being. One by one, however, most of them did nod at last.

Conan did not, would not. He could be beaten; the bruises he still had from his father's hard hands proved as much. But submission was not in him, nor would it ever be. He glared daggers at the Aquilonian officer.

Treviranus noticed that volcanic blue stare. He spoke to Mordec again: a question. The blacksmith set his free hand, the one not clenched on the spearshaft, on Conan's shoulder. That was as much to hold him back as to identify him. Mordec answered in Aquilonian, then said, "He asked if you were my son. I told him aye," in Cimmerian.

"Tell him I hate him, too, and I'll kill him if I can," said Conan.

"No," said his father, and the hand on Conan's shoulder suddenly gripped like a vise. Despite the pain shooting through Conan's arm, not a sound came from him. Quietly, Mordec went on, "Remember what I said about watching your tongue. And remember what he said—if he dies, so do ten of ours. There is no striking them." He added one more word, too low for the Cimmerian-speaking enemy soldier to catch: "Yet." That Conan understood. Now his head did move up and down.

Another stream of words meaningless to Conan came from

the Aquilonian officer. "He says their commander is called Count Stercus," said Mordec, pitching his words to carry not just to his son but to all the folk of Duthil. "He says this Stercus is a hard man and a harsh man, and warns us against angering him." Treviranus hesitated, then said something else. Mordec frowned and translated that last sentence, too: "He says we would do better not to let Stercus' gaze fall on any of our women, especially the younger ones."

That made the Cimmerians standing in the street mutter more among themselves. Several men put protective arms around the shoulders of wives or daughters. Their sense of chivalry was rude, as befit their material setting, but no less real for that.

Conan's eyes went to Tarla, the daughter of Balarg the weaver. She was still a girl, no more a woman than Conan was a man, but it was on her, after his mother, that his protective instinct centered. Just for a moment, his gaze and hers met. Then she looked modestly down to the ground.

The Aquilonian officer spoke once more. "He says his people have come here to stay, and we had better get used to it," said Mordec.

Liar! Conan did not shout the word, but he wanted to. Looking at the faces of his fellow villagers, he knew he was not the only one in whose heart rebellion flamed. Oh, no—far from it.

Granth and Vulth and a pair of Bossonian archers stood sentry outside the encampment the new garrison had made by the Cimmerian village. It was a little past noon, but Captain Treviranus had ordered sentries on alert at all hours of the day and night. Granth wasn't the least bit sorry Treviranus had given that order, either.

One of the Bossonians, a tall, rangy bowman named Benno, peered into the shadowed woods. "The captain said panthers lurk among those trees," he said. "By Mitra, I should like to make a cape from the skin of a panther of my own killing."

Vulth pointed toward the village just above a bowshot away. "You want panthers, Benno, look that way first. Every house there holds 'em."

"That's the truth!" exclaimed Granth. "Did you fellows spy that one brat, the son of the wounded fellow who was doing the translating for Treviranus? By the look in his eye, he wanted to murder the lot of us."

"Oh, that one," said Benno. "Aye, I noted him—a face like a clenched fist. He'll make a bigger man than his father, and his father's far from small. Did you see his hands and feet? Too big for the rest of him, like a wolfhound pup's before it gets its full growth."

"I saw the lad, too, and I tell you he is no wolfhound." Vulth spoke with great conviction. "He is a wolf."

"All these Cimmerians are wild wolves, and they bite hard." Granth thought back to the fight by Fort Venarium. Those roaring, bellowing barbarians who kept coming, kept killing, despite wounds that would have slain a civilized man on the instant were enough to chill the blood. And, absent the Aquilonian cavalry, they might have—probably would have—won.

And then, as if speaking of the boy were enough to conjure him up, he emerged from the woods only fifty yards or so from the sentries. A quiver of arrows was slung on his back. He had a bow in his right hand. In his left, he carried three long-beaked woodcocks by the feet. After a wary glance to make sure the Aquilonians were holding their place and not pursuing him, the young Cimmerian went on toward his village.

Benno stared after him, jaw dropping in astonishment. "Did you see his bag?" whispered the Bossonian. "Did you see it?"

"Woodcock make mighty fine eating," said Granth. "Fry

the breast in butter, do the legs the same way. If you feel like it, you can cook up the guts, too—fry 'em along with everything else."

"Oh, yes. Every word true," said Benno nodding. "But they are easier to frighten into nets than to take with the bow. To bring home three like that—Mitra! I am glad the boy was not shooting at us in the battle."

"For all you know, he was," said Vulth.

Benno looked surprised in a different way. "It could be," he admitted, "though I saw no children amongst our foes—or amongst the slain afterwards."

The other Bossonian bowman was a scarfaced veteran named Daverio. "Anyone who shoots like that is no child in my book—especially not if the dog is shooting at me," he said.

"True enough," said Vulth. "He'd put a worshiper of Asura on a pilgrim boat for his last journey, sure as sure."

"A fat lot you know about that," jeered Granth.

"I don't care to know anything about the people who worship Asura, and nobody who worships Mitra should," answered his cousin. "People say it's the same black slave who takes every one of those pilgrim boats down the river to the sea, or wherever they end up when all's said and done. That's not natural, you ask me."

Benno and Daverio both nodded. So did Granth. Benno turned to what was uppermost in his mind: "Mowing down woodcock like that isn't natural, either. It's closer to supernatural than a good many things I've seen sorcerers do."

"If he shoots one of us, we burn him and nine of his neighbors," said Vulth. "Even barbarians understand that kind of arithmetic."

"I hope so," said Granth. "Sometimes barbarians will kill without counting the cost. That's what makes them barbarians."

Daverio shrugged cynically. "That will probably happen

once or twice. Then we'll kill ten or twenty Cimmerians, or however many it takes. Before long, the ones we leave alive will say, 'Don't do anything to King Numedides' men. It hurts us worse than it hurts them.' "

"And so it will—except for the poor Gunderman or Bossonian who gets it in the neck," said Vulth.

The four sentries looked at one another. The same thought filled all their minds—as long as it is not me.

Conan got used to the presence of the invaders with a boy's speed and ease. He soon came to take light-haired men walking through the village for granted, and learned to tell Bossonians from Gundermen by looks rather than by weapons of choice.

And he began learning Aquilonian. Before long, he had picked up almost as much of it as his father knew. That amused Mordec, in a grim way. "You've got a good ear, son," he said. "I don't suppose it will matter much, but it's there."

"Why do so many people here have trouble with the other language?" asked Conan in puzzled tones. "It's only more words."

"People seem to," said Mordec. "You don't notice the Gundermen learning Cimmerian, either, do you?"

"I've seen one man trying," answered Conan. "He was doing his best to talk with Derelei, the miller's wife."

"Aye, and I know what he was doing his best to ask for, too," said Mordec. "Derelei is a very pretty woman, and she knows it a little too well. But aside from that, the invaders don't bother. Why should they? They beat us. We're the ones who have to fit ourselves to them, not the other way around."

Why should they? They beat us. The words tolled in Conan's mind like the mournful clangor of a brazen bell. "What can we do, Father?" he asked. "We have to do something. If we don't, we might as well be so many sheep."

"One day, the time will be ripe," said Mordec. "One day, but not yet. Patience, lad—patience. For now, we mourn and we heal. The time will come, though. Sooner or later, it will. And when it does, we will know it, and we will seize it."

Patience came hard for the boy, even harder than it would have for a man. Days came when Conan dared not look at an Aquilonian, for fear he would hurl himself against the foeman to his folk and bring disaster down on Duthil. When such fits took him, he would flee the village as if it lay in the grip of a deadly pestilence, and would go alone to hunt in the forests and on the hillsides nearby.

Mordec said never a word to him about those jaunts. The blacksmith could have used his son's help in the day-to-day work of the smithy, but seemed to sense how Conan needed to escape that which had become intolerable for him. While the boy stalked woodcock and grouse, squirrel and rabbit, he imagined he went after bigger game: Gundermen and Bossonians and the fearsome armored Aquilonian knights he had heard of but not yet seen. And hunting for the pot, though he did not fully realize it, helped him gain some of the arts he would use in war.

Spring slowly moved into summer. In that northern land, days grew long and almost warm. The sun rose in the far northeast and set many hours later in the far northwest. Some of Cimmeria's perpetual mist burned away. The sky was a watery, grayish blue, but blue it was nonetheless. Even the conifer-filled forests seemed—less dour, at any rate. Ferns growing by the bases of the tree trunks added splashes of brighter green to the scenery.

Silent as the beasts he stalked, Conan slipped through the woods. When he came to the edge of a small clearing, he froze into immobility. His eyes scanned the open space ahead to make sure he disturbed nothing before he ventured out from the concealment a pair of pines gave him. Not even a savage Pict from the rugged country west of Cimmeria could have walked more lightly on the land.

Once out in the clearing, Conan froze again, watching, listening, waiting. Something seemed to call him, but not in a way to which he could set words. He frowned, then went on. Whatever it was, he would find it.

He frowned again on the far side of the clearing. He had been through these woods many times, yet he did not recall this particular track. Shrugging, he silently strode along it. It took him in the direction he wanted to go. That it might also take him in the direction it wanted him to go never entered his mind.

Some little distance down the trail, he stopped, his head turning this way and that. The frown that harshened and aged his features grew deeper. Birdsongs were scarcer now than they had been in springtime, when returning migrants vied for mates. Still, he had been able to hear the calls of doves and finches and the occasional distant, strident shriek of a hunting hawk.

Not here, not now. Silence had settled over him, soft as snowfall. His eyes flicked now to the left, now to the right, now up, now down. The forest looked no different from the way it had before he set foot on this treacherous track. It looked no different, but somehow it was. That muffling drift of silence lay thick upon the land. Even the buzz of flies and the hum of gnats were softly swallowed up and gone.

"Crom!" muttered Conan, as much to hear his own voice — to hear anything at all — as for any other reason. The grim god's name seemed to reverberate through the trees, carrying farther than it had any business doing. But Crom would not help him if he came to grief. He knew that only too well. The god might have helped breathe life into him, but, now that he had it, keeping it was his own lookout.

He nocked an arrow before pressing on down the trail. He

could not have said why, save that the unnatural silence oppressed him. Against silence, what could an arrow do? Nothing Conan could think of, yet having a weapon instantly ready to use heartened him.

On he went, his perplexity mounting at every stride. These woods felt more ancient than the ones with which he was so intimately familiar, as if the trees had been brooding here since the dawn of time. He scratched his head, wondering why and how such certainty filled him. Again, he could not have said, but fill him it did, more so with each step he took.

That feeling of age immemorial soon began to oppress him worse than the silence, to raise in his breast a dread nothing natural could have caused. He needed a distinct effort of will to halt, and another, greater, one to turn around and seek to go back. When he did, ice walked along his spine. The track that had led him forward vanished behind him. It might never have been there at all. When he turned again, though, it still ran straight ahead of him.

"I'll go on, then," he said. This time, the tree trunks and branches might have drunk up his words; he barely heard them himself. Crom might have held some power in this primordial wilderness, but Conan himself had none, or so it seemed.

That might have been the judgment of the wilderness, but it was not Conan's. Defiantly, he pressed ahead. The path went past an enormous fir—easily the largest Conan had ever seen, and one he would surely have known well had it grown anywhere near Duthil—before turning sharply to the left. The blacksmith's son followed it, but then stopped in his tracks in astonishment at the sight of what lay ahead.

The gray stone ruin might have sprung from the dawn of time. It was, without a doubt, a temple dedicated to some god, but which? Not Crom, surely; he had neither shrine nor priesthood. Perhaps some mystic convulsion has sent it spinning down the centuries from its own proper era to that in which Conan lived. It might have been a temple from the great vanished island of Atlantis, from whose few scattered survivors the Cimmerians drew their descent. Of that, however, Conan knew next to nothing.

He warily approached the fane. The immense stones from which it was made, albeit only crudely carven, were fitted together with consummate skill; not even the blade of a knife could have slipped between one and another. What had been an entryway still offered ingress of sorts, though the lintel stone had fallen and partially blocked the way in.

With a boy's agility, Conan twisted past the fallen stone. No sooner had he done so than a strange, weird piping filled the air. He could not have said whether it came from a musical instrument or the throat of some curious bird. All he could have said was that it made the hair on his arms and at the nape of his neck rise with horror and dread at its intimations of ancient wickedness.

The entryway twisted left and then right before opening out on an immense courtyard paved with stones of the same dusky gray as the rest of the temple. They were joined as cunningly as all the other masonry, with the result that only a few bushes and saplings had managed to take root between them. In the center of the courtyard stood an altar of white marble made all the more dazzling and brilliant by contrast to its surroundings.

Strange figures and glyphs had been carved onto the altar; the pedestal of a statue rose from it. Only the feet and legs of that image now survived. One quick glance at them was enough to make Conan look away, dizzy and sick. If those remains did that to him, he shuddered to imagine what he would have felt had the statue survived in its entirety. Some things were well lost in the mists of time.

Behind the altar, one of the paving stones suddenly swung down on a clever pivot whose workings had defied the eons. Conan, intent on trying to make sense of the antediluvian carvings on the altar stone, did not notice the silent operation until a curious, hungry hiss forcibly brought it to his attention.

That sound sent him springing back. Even more than the roar of a hungry lion or panther, a serpent's hiss screamed danger! to all around. And, as the great snake issued forth from the den where it had slept since some forgotten age of the world, Conan's eyes went wide with dread. Serpents in Cimmeria were most of them small, slinking creatures that fed on frogs or mice. Even a viper that might steal a man's life would be no longer than his forearm.

This snake, though, could have devoured the blacksmith's son and scarcely shown the bulge he made. It had to be forty feet long, and broad in proportion. When it opened its mouth to taste the air, poison dripped from fangs longer than an index finger. Its lidless golden eyes held old, old knowledge and even older evil.

Those terrible eyes fixed on Conan. The snake hissed again, this time as if glad the opportunity to break its age-long fast was so thoughtfully provided. A tongue a foot and a half long flicked out—in the direction of the young Cimmerian. The fearsome serpent glided straight toward him.

With a cry of horror and abhorrence, a cry springing from the instinctive revulsion of warm-blooded life for the scaly, slimy primeval reptile, Conan let fly. His shaft struck the snake just to one side of a nostril, and bounced away after scraping an all but harmless scratch in the creature's armored hide. The serpent hissed furiously and reared on high, as if to crush the life from the man-thing that had presumed to resent being devoured. Yet it was not primarily a constrictor. Faster than a springing panther, it struck.

Conan, with the tigerish instincts of the barbarian, leaped back out of harm's way in the very nick of time. He was already fitting another arrow to his bow, and loosed again. This arrow stuck behind the snake's head: a wound, yes, but one more likely to enrage than to cripple. The snake's mouth gaped wider than ever. The sound that burst from it might have come from a bucket of water cast onto red-hot iron. It struck again, seeking to avenge itself with envenomed fangs.

Again, though, the stroke fell short. Conan had another arrow ready, too. This one pinned the serpent's tongue to its lower jaw, piercing the soft flesh that wide-spread maw had exposed. Now the snake's hiss came muffled, but its rage, if anything, redoubled. It slithered after the Cimmerian. If it could not strike him, it would smash him to jelly in its monstrous coils.

He drew back the bowstring to the ear and let fly once more—and at last found a vital spot, for the shaft pierced the serpent's left eye and penetrated deep into its tiny, savage brain.

The serpent's death throes went on for the next quarter of an hour, and came closer to killing Conan than anything it had done while alive. In its tormented thrashing, it overturned and smashed the ancient altar and everything that remained of the dreadful statue atop it. Whatever the creature depicted might have been, it was only shards of marble now.

At long last, the serpent lay still. Conan approached the great corpse with a hunter's caution, for he knew that even a seemingly dead snake often had one final bite left to give. He tapped the snake's snout with the end of his bow, held out at arm's length before him. And sure enough, the serpent snapped convulsively, but only on empty air.

When he was sure it would in fact move no more, Conan drew his knife from his belt and used it to pry the snake's mouth open. Then, stoically ignoring the fetid reptilian musk that rose from the creature, he dipped the heads and upper shafts of the arrows remaining in his quiver in the greenish venom still dribbling from its fangs. That done, he cut out one of the fangs and, handling it with the greatest of care lest he be poisoned himself, dropped it into the quiver.

He peered down into the chamber whence the serpent had crawled, wondering whether another of its fearsome breed still lingered there. But of that there was no sign; only the one, it appeared, had come through the ages with this ancient shrine. Shaking his head in wonder, Conan left by the twisting pathway he had used to enter.

Once outside the temple, he followed the track past the enormous fir. Then he stopped, suddenly wishing he had taken both fangs instead of the one. He turned around.

The fir was not there.

Conan took several steps back toward where it had stood. He still saw no sign of it, and rubbed his eyes in disbelief. A tree like that could not simply have vanished off the face of the earth—except that it had. He rubbed his eyes again, which did nothing to make it reappear. Instead of leading back toward the temple from forgotten days, the track took him to a part of the woods he knew well.

He rubbed his eyes again and scratched his head, wondering whether he had somehow imagined the entire episode. But when he unslung his quiver and examined the arrows it held, he saw that their heads and the upper inches of their shafts were discolored by the venom of the titanic serpent's needlelike fang. Whatever his experience had been, a dream it was not.

He decided to set those arrows aside, not to take them on ordinary hunting trips but to save them for panthers, wolves, bears, Aquilonians, and other dangerous game. Now he had no trouble retracing his steps to Duthil. His return journey took him past the encampment Count Stercus' Gundermen and Bossonians had set up near the village. As always, the invaders—the occupiers, now—were alert, with sentries posted all around the palisade. Conan snarled a soft curse he had heard from his father. No one could hope to surprise them.

He had nearly reached his home village when he suddenly

stopped in his tracks. "No one could hope to surprise them by day!" he exclaimed, as if someone had claimed otherwise. "But by night—"

From then on, he ran as if his heels had sprouted wings. "What is it, Conan?" called Tarla as he dashed past Balarg's house. He did not stop—did not so much as slow—even for her, which proved if anything could how important he thought his idea was.

"Father!" he panted, skidding to a stop in the smithy's doorway.

Mordec was giving a new axehead an edge with a foot-powered grinding wheel. As he took his foot off the pedal, the shower of sparks from the axehead died away. "What is it?" he asked, unconsciously echoing Balarg's daughter. "Whatever it is, it must be a thought of weight, to have you running through Duthil as if demons dogged your tracks."

That took Conan's mind back to the fane from out of time, but only for a moment. The present and what might lie ahead were more important to him. "If we were to strike the Aquilonian camp at night, we could take the foe by surprise," he burst out, his voice cracking with excitement.

"We could, aye, but what would happen if we did?" asked Mordec.

"Why, we'd be free of them," answered Conan. How could his father not see that?

As he soon discovered, though, Mordec saw further than than he did. "Duthil would be free of them—for a little while," said the blacksmith. "Cimmeria would not. And when the rest of the Aquilonians learned what we had done, they would come back in force and work a fearful vengeance on us."

"Then we need to strike all their camps on the same night," declared Conan. "If we do, they would be gone forever."

"If we could, they would be gone forever," said Mordec. "How do you propose to bring it off?"

"Send men to all the villages," answered Conan. "Tell them to attack on such and such a night. When that night comes, the Aquilonians go." He made a fist to show exactly what he meant.

But Mordec shook his head, which made his square-cut mane of graying hair flip back and forth in front of his eyes. "The Aquilonians might go," he said. "But some of the villagers would say they lost too many men in the first fight, and they will stay home. And some would promise the sun and moon and stars—and then stay home, too. And some would attack, but in a halfhearted way, and be defeated. And King Numedides would send more soldiers, to punish us for our rebellion. And what's an uprising worth when all that's likely to lie at the other end of it?"

Such bitter cynicism took Conan's breath away. "Why did you fight the invaders in the first place, if you felt like that?" he asked. "Why not bend the knee straightaway?"

"If we could have beaten them at once, they likely would have given up the campaign as a bad job and gone home," said Mordec. "They've done that before. Now they've won, though. Now they're settled on the land."

"All the more reason to drive them away," said Conan.

"All the more reason for them to stay," returned Mordec.

They eyed each other in perfect mutual incomprehension. "I never thought you'd turn coward," said Conan.

His father cuffed him, not as prelude to a beating like the one he'd had when he tried to go off to fight with the defeated Cimmerian host but simply as a warning to watch his tongue. "You have no call to use that word for me," said Mordec. "After you have fought in war, you may say what you please, and I will bear it. Until then, you are only bleating out things you do not understand."

"You would not let me fight in war," said Conan sulkily. "Now you blame me because I have not." He did not speak of his exploit with the serpent. He was not sure his father would believe him. He was not altogether sure he believed it himself, and that despite the sinister stains on the shafts in his quiver.

"I do not blame you," answered Mordec. "I say that you are a boy, and I say that war is not a sport for boys."

That dismissal felt like a slight to the younger Cimmerian. Conan decided he would speak of what he had done after all, if only to show his father he was someone to be reckoned with. He asked, "Do you know of an ancient temple lost in the woods not far from Duthil?"

Mordec, though, only shook his head. "No. There is none," he said positively. "If there were, someone would have found it." His eyes narrowed. "Why do you ask? Do the Aquilonians search for such a place?"

"Not that I know of," answered Conan.

"Well, what nonsense are you spouting, then?" demanded his father.

"Nothing. Never mind," said Conan. No, the blacksmith would not believe him. Since that was so, no point to going on. Mordec would but thrash him for telling fables, and he had had enough of his father's hard hands on him.

When Conan kept silence, Mordec nodded in dour approval. "All right," he rumbled. "If you're going to settle down and be sensible, you can finish grinding this axehead. I have a great plenty of other work to do. Get busy!"

From the bedchamber came Verina's weak voice: "Are you nagging the boy again, Mordec? Can't you leave him in peace?"

Muttering under his breath, Mordec answered, "There is no peace in this land, nor will there be until the invaders are gone."

"That's not what you told me just now," exclaimed Conan.

"By Crom, it is," said his father. "I tell you it is useless to strike too soon, and it is. But we shall have a day of reckoning with the foe. Oh, yes—we shall have a day of reckoning indeed." None of the Gundermen or Bossonians in the camp near Duthil would have cared to hear Mordec's voice when the blacksmith made that vow. Conan's father went on, "Meanwhile, though, there's work to be done. Get on with it."

"Don't carp endlessly at Conan," said Verina. "He's a good boy."

Such praise Conan could have done without. More than anything else, he wanted to be reckoned a man, a warrior, a hero. After his battle with the serpent in the temple from out of time, he thought he had earned the right to be so reckoned. But his father would not even hear of the fight. And hearing his mother call him a good boy made him feel as if he peeked out from behind her skirts. He knew she loved him, but it was a love that simultaneously satisfied and suffocated.

He began pumping the foot pedal on the grinding wheel for all he was worth. A coruscating shower of sparks flew from the axehead as he held it to the rapidly spinning wheel. Mordec chuckled grimly as he fed the fire in the forge. Soon the axehead boasted an edge sharp enough for shaving. Conan tested it with his thumb, nodded, and thrust it at his father. "Here."

Not even Mordec could find anything to criticize.

chapter iv

Enemies

When Granth went back to Fort Venarium with a message from Captain Treviranus, he was amazed to see how much the place had changed. A lot more of the forest around the encampment had gone down under the axes of the soldiers still stationed there. The tents had been replaced by barracks halls. A real keep, even if made of wood, was going up in the center of the encampment. A bridge of boats and boards linked Fort Venarium with the way south, the way down to Aquilonia.

Cimmeria was not so safe as to let Aquilonians travel alone with any confidence they would get where they were going. Along with Granth tramped Vulth and the two Bossonian archers, Daverio and Benno. Pointing to a string of wagons coming toward Venarium from the south, Vulth said, "Look. Some of the first settlers."

"Good to see 'em," said Granth. "They may not be soldiers, but the men will know how to fight. Anybody who can draw a bow or swing a sword against these damned barbarians is welcome."

"Pot hunters," said Benno scornfully. "Half of those poor fools can't hit the side of a barn."

"Well, at least they'll be aiming at the Cimmerians," said Vulth. "I'm with my cousin on this." He clapped Granth on the back.

"And they'll be building houses and barns," added Granth. "If we're going to settle this land, we'll have to make it our own."

The horses and oxen that drew the settlers' wagons would soon plow fields in what had been forest. More cattle, along with sheep and goats, traveled behind the wains. They would graze in meadows and crop tender shoots. If the new arrivals also had dogs and cats and swine and hens and ducks, they carried them inside the wagons.

Daverio did not seem very happy to see the settlers coming up toward Fort Venarium. When Granth asked the Bossonian why, he answered, "Because the Cimmerians will want to murder them even more than they want to murder us. We don't take the land itself away from them. These fellows do."

"Too bad," said Vulth. "This is why we came up into Cimmeria, after all: to make it a place where Aquilonians can live and to drive back the barbarians."

"Yes, that's why we came, all right," agreed Daverio. "Now we get to find out whether we've done it."

Sentries at the gate of the encampment gave Granth and his comrades a careful once-over before standing aside and letting them go in. That only irritated the Gundermen and Bossonians. Granth wondered if the gate guards feared they were Cimmerians in disguise. He laughed at the idea. Even with their hair dyed blond, the northern barbarians would have a hard time passing for men of Aquilonian blood.

He had to ask several times before finding out that Captain Nario, the officer to whom Captain Treviranus had written his letter, stayed in a barracks hall not far from what would soon be the keep. The hall had its own guards, which struck Granth as excessive. His disgust must have shown on his face, for one of the guardsmen said, "You'd better wipe off that frown, soldier. We're here on account of this is where Count Stercus makes his headquarters."

Another guard snickered. "That's not all he makes here."

"You shut your fool mouth, Torm," hissed the first guard. "The count heard you make a crack like that, there'd be hell to pay, and you know it."

"He wouldn't hear if you didn't have a big mouth," said Torm angrily. While the guards bickered. Granth and his comrades went inside.

After the daylight from which he had come, Granth blinked a few times to help his eyes adjust to the gloom within. This was plainly a hall for officers. They had more room than ordinary soldiers, and real beds rather than just blankets in which to roll themselves. Some of the officers had body servants, whose bedrolls rested beside their beds. Granth asked for Captain Nario.

"I am Nario," called a man sitting on a bed not far from a guarded door at the far end of the barracks hall. Granth would have bet Count Stercus lived in the chamber beyond that door. He had no time to dwell on that, though, for Nario asked, "What do you wish of me?"

"Sir, I have a letter for you from my commander, Captain Treviranus, up at the place called Duthil," answered Granth.

"Do you indeed?" Nario's smile showed even, very white teeth. "Give it to me, then. I shall be pleased to read it, and I shall write an answer on the spot."

"Yes, sir." Granth handed the officer the rolled-up parchment, meanwhile concealing his own annoyance. He had hoped to deliver the message and be on his way. Now he would have to wait around until Captain Nario not only read what his own commander had to say but came up with a reply.

And then, quite suddenly, he did not mind waiting any more. A very pretty Cimmerian girl carrying a pitcher of wine and two goblets on a tray came into the barracks. She could not have been above sixteen, and wore little enough that she would have had a hard time sneaking anything lethal into the room at the end of the hall. The guards there did not try to search her, but let her in unchallenged.

Granth had stared and stared. So had a good many of the soldiers in the barracks, though they seemed more used to her presence than he was. In a hoarse voice, he asked, "Who is she?"

"She's Count Stercus' plaything," answered Captain Nario, looking up from his writing. He noticed that Granth's eyes had not left the doorway through which the Cimmerian girl had passed: noticed and started to laugh. "Don't hope you'll see her again coming out, my good fellow. She won't come out of there for quite a while."

"Oh." Granth felt foolish. His ears got hot.

Nario laughed again, so Granth supposed his flush was only too visible. He felt more foolish yet. He had been ready to face roaring Cimmerian warriors. How could a nearly naked Cimmerian serving girl unman him so? He mumbled, "She's too young," and looked down at the ground between his boots.

"Our distinguished commander would disagree with you, and his is the only opinion that matters," said Nario in a silky voice. "And now I am going to do you a considerable favor: I am not going to ask you what your name is."

For a moment, Granth did not see what sort of favor that was. He was a young man, and inclined to be naïve. But then he realized what Captain Nario was driving at, and flushed again. This time, he knew precisely the mistake he had made. "Thank you, sir," he said.

"You are welcome." The officer finished writing, melted some sealing wax at a brazier, and used it and a ribbon to close his letter. The seal on his signet ring was of a fire-breathing dragon, which showed in reverse when he pressed it into the wax. He said, "Now you should make yourself

unwelcome, if you follow my meaning, for others more zeal-
ous than I may have heard you and may be curious about
your choice of words."

This time, Granth had no trouble taking the hint. He left
the barracks in a hurry, with Vulth and Benno and Daverio
trailing after him. For a wonder, none of his companions
chaffed him until they were out of the encampment altogether. Then, leering, Benno asked, "Did you want to rescue
the wench or just to keep her for yourself?"

"Mitra!" ejaculated Granth in an agony of embarrassment:
was he as obvious as that? Evidently he was. Gathering himself, he said, "She was too young for such sport. She should
be finding her first sweetheart, not—what Stercus is giving
her."

All that won him was more teasing from the two Bossonians and his cousin. They kept it up just about the whole way
back to Duthil. By the time he handed Nario's letter to Treviranus, he had decided he was never going to say another
word to anyone else as long as he lived.

Men gathered in a little knot in the main—and almost
only—street in Duthil. They spoke in low voices, too low for
Conan to make out most of what they were saying. He got
only snatches: "Her name is Ugaine." ". . . from Rosinish, to
the east of . . ." ". . . a foul lecher, if ever there . . ."

When one of the men noticed Conan, they all fell silent.
He walked up to them, asking, "What is it?"

No one answered right away. No one looked as if he
wanted to answer at all. At last, a farmer called Nucator said,
"Well, maybe you'd best hear it from your father, lad, and not
from us."

Conan glowered, not least because he already stood taller
than Nucator, who was a weedy little fellow. "Hear what?"
he demanded.

"Nucator is right," said Balarg, his voice smooth as butter. "This is a business for men." The rest of the Cimmerians in the knot nodded, plainly agreeing with the tailor.

That they agreed only made Conan angrier. He wanted to fight them all. That would show them who was a man. But the beating his father had given him before going off to war remained too painfully fresh in his memory for him to snarl out the challenge right away. None of these villagers was a match for Mordec—but Conan had proved to be no match for the blacksmith, either.

When he hesitated, nerving himself, a heavy hand fell on his shoulder from behind. "Here, what's toward?" asked Mordec, who like his son had been drawn by the sight of that group of men with their heads together.

Nucator beckoned the blacksmith forward. "We'll gladly tell you," he said, "though we were not sure if you would want your boy to hear of this."

"Stay here," said Mordec to Conan. Fuming, Conan had to obey. His father joined the rest of the village men, towering over most of them by half a head or more. Again, they spoke in low voices. Again, Conan heard bits of what they said, but not enough to tell him what he wanted to know. Along with trying to listen, he kept an eye on his father. Mordec's hard countenance soon darkened with anger. "This is known to be true?" he asked ominously.

"It is," said Nucator. The others nodded.

"A foul business. A most foul business, without a doubt. And yes, my son may know. Better he should have some notion of what manner of men the occupiers are." Mordec's eyes speared Conan. "You remember the Aquilonian captain here warned us to ward our young women when his commander, Count Stercus, came to Duthil?"

"I do, Father, yes," said Conan.

"Well, it would seem he spoke no less than the truth." Mordec spat in disgust. "This Stercus, if the reports be true—"

"As they are," interrupted Balarg.

"If these reports be true," repeated Mordec, slightly stressing the first word, "this Stercus has taken for his own a Cimmerian girl of good family, using her for his pleasure and threatening to turn his Aquilonian dogs loose against the countryside if she does not yield to his desires."

Rage ripped through Conan. "Do you not see? We must slay him! We must slay all the invaders!" He took a step forward, then another, and more than one of the grown men in Duthil gave back a pace before the blood lust blazing in his blue eyes, so like his father's.

"The day will come," said Mordec, stern certainty in his voice. "The day will come indeed. But it is not yet here."

Balarg nodded, as if in agreement. But he said, "If you had not been as hot as your forge to go to war when the Aquilonians first crossed our border, many men from this village now dead would yet walk under the light of the sun."

"By Crom, we had to have a go at driving the invaders out," said Mordec. "We came close to winning, too. If not for their damned knights, I think we would have. Will you say the fighting did not cost us dear? Will you say we have the strength for another battle so soon after we lost the first?"

"I have the stomach for it!" cried Conan, wishing a man's sword swung at his hip.

Neither Mordec nor Balarg paid any attention to him. Each seemed more interested in scoring points off the other than in anything else. Some of the men of Duthil ranged themselves behind the blacksmith, others behind the weaver. To them, the usual squabbles of village life seemed more immediate, more urgent, more important, than driving the men from the south out of Cimmeria.

"What if it were a girl from Duthil?" cried Conan. "What if she came from here, not from some other place? Would you do more than stand and mumble then?"

For all his fury, his voice remained a boy's treble, and the men from Duthil would not heed him. The small arguments, the familiar arguments, were meat and drink to them. Those went on and on. Meanwhile, the camp full of Bossonians and Gundermen just out of bowshot of the village was becoming ever more familiar, too.

Conan stormed off. No one else cared, not even his father, who was wagging a callused, burn-scarred finger under Balarg's nose. Conan stomped back into the smithy. He snatched up his quiver and bow. Only one arrow in the quiver was poisoned; he had set the rest aside for need more desperate than game. For now, if he could not slaughter Aquilonians, he wanted to kill something—indeed, almost anything—else.

Before he could make for the forest, his mother called, "Where are you going?"

"Out to the woods," he replied.

"Would you bring me some water first?" asked Verina. "And would you tell me what the men are arguing about this time?"

He took a mug of water into the bedchamber, helped support his mother with a strong arm, and held the mug to her lips. Then, in guarded terms, he told her of Count Stercus and the girl from Rosinish.

Verina drank again, then sighed. "She probably brought it on herself with forward ways," she said.

"That's not what the men say. They blame it on the Aquilonian count." Conan spoke hesitantly, for disagreeing with his mother made him uneasy.

In any case, she paid no more attention to him than had the men of Duthil. "Mark my words. It will turn out to be the way I said," she told him, and then began to cough. He eased her back down to the pillow. Slowly, the spasm ebbed. She sighed again, this time wearily. "You can go now. Just leave me be. I'll manage somehow," she said.

"Mother, I—"

"Go!" said Verina. Conan stood, irresolute: a posture into

which no one but his mother could put him. Her gesture of dismissal might have come from a queen, not a sick woman lying in a bed behind a smithy. Biting his lip, Conan went.

He ran to the woods as if demons prowled his trail. He might have been glad to see demons, for they would have given him something he could oppose, something he could hope to defeat with arrows and knife and simple strength. But what chased him out of Duthil dwelt within him, and he could not bring it forth to slay it.

Melcer hacked at a pine with his axe as if the tree were a Cimmerian warrior. The farmer, newly come from Gunderland, struck again and again, with almost demoniac energy. The pine tottered, crackled, and began to fall. "Coming down!" Melcer shouted, though no one but him stood anywhere close to the tree that crashed to earth. He grunted in satisfaction and spat on his hands. One more tree down, one more tree towards a cabin in the woods, one more bit of open space in what would become a farm.

"It'll be a farm if I make it one," said Melcer, and methodically trimmed branches from the pine and tossed them onto a sledge. He dragged it back to the small clearing in which his wagon sat. The oxen were cropping grass not far from the wagon. They looked up with incurious brown eyes as he returned.

His wife, Evlea, had cleared a square of grass with a hoe and was planting seeds for what would be a vegetable garden. Tarnus, his son, was only six, but big enough to shoo away the chickens and keep them from eating the seeds as fast as Evlea planted them. Unlike his father and mother, Tarnus enjoyed his job. "Get away!" he yelled, and waved his arms. When the chickens did not move fast enough to suit him, he ran at them making horrible noises. They fled in clucking confusion.

"Don't drive them into the woods," warned Melcer. "If you do, the foxes and weasels will thank you for their supper—and I'll warm your backside."

"Can I tame the foxes?" asked Tarnus eagerly.

"Not with chickens," answered his father. "Where will we get more if they eat these? It's a long way back to Gunderland."

"A very long way," said Evlea, pausing in her labor to wipe her sweaty forehead with a sleeve. The endless work of setting up the farm left her and Melcer weary all the time. After a moment, she went on, "If I had known it was so very far, I don't know whether I would have wanted to come."

That made Melcer angry. "Here we have as much land as we can clear and hold," he said. "Down there, my father had six sons, so I was stuck on one sixth of the land he'd farmed. That made a miserable little plot, and you know it."

"It wasn't very big," admitted Evlea, "but it was safe. We're off the edge of nowhere here. If the barbarians rise up—"

"They won't," said Melcer. "And even if they do, we have soldiers—and we have our own strong right arms." He took the axe off the sledge and flourished it. "And once we get the cabin built, we'll have a place we can defend, too."

In his mind's eye, he saw the farm he wanted to have, with plenty of room for grain and for grazing, with a barn full of cattle and sheep and horses near the cabin, with an apple orchard not too far away, and with the forest pushed back toward the horizon—but not too far, for he would still need firewood. He saw plenty of neighbors, to help defend the place against the wild Cimmerians—but none too near, for he wanted a big parcel of land for himself. He saw Evlea raising up not just Tarnus but three or four more sons, and all of them going on to take land for themselves, carving out homesteads from this gloomy wilderness. He smiled, liking those visions better than any he might have got from an opium pipe.

In between what he saw and where he was now lay an endless ocean of labor. Stolid as most Gundermen, he shrugged broad shoulders. Work had never fazed him. He said, "I'm going back to cut notches in that tree. It'll go into the cabin—the trunk's good and straight."

"All right. I have plenty to do here," said Evlea. "Keep your eyes open."

"And you," said Melcer. His wife nodded. He sharpened the blade of her hoe against a whetstone every few nights. It would make a wicked weapon in a pinch. So far, the barbarians had stayed away from the settlements around Fort Venarium. Melcer hoped the beating they had had at the hands of Count Stercus' Aquilonians would teach them to respect the power of King Numedides and those who followed him. If it did not—if it did not, he would fight as hard as he had to, and so would the rest of the settlers, men, women, and children.

Shouldering his axe as a soldier would shoulder a pike while on the march, Melcer followed the trail of the sledge back to the pine he had cut down. Once he had cut the notches in it, he would have the oxen drag it to the place where he intended to raise the cabin: not far from where the wagon stood now.

He set to work with skillful strokes. He was good with the axe. He could have been a lumberjack if he had not taken a love for the land and for growing things from his father. He had cut one notch and was walking down to the far end of the tree to do the other when a Cimmerian with a bow came out of the woods.

Like most Gundermen and Bossonians, Melcer made a good woodsman. Here, though, he knew he had met his match and more. He was a civilized man who had learned woodscraft as he had learned axework. The barbarian who eyed him from under a mop of hair black as midnight might have sprung from nowhere, so silently did he appear. He had not needed to learn woodscraft; he might have imbibed its lessons with his mother's milk.

Only little by little did Melcer realize the barbarian had drunk of his mother's milk not so very long before. He was man-tall, and handled his bow with the unconscious ease of an experienced archer, but his features, though promising harshness, were not yet fully molded into the form they would one day possess, and no beard darkened his cheeks.

Melcer did not raise his axe in any threatening way, but he did not take his hands off it, either. The young Cimmerian had an arrow nocked, but it pointed at the ground, not at Melcer. Three plump grouse hung by their feet from the barbarian's belt: he was out hunting game, not hunting men. With luck, this would not have end in blood.

Taking his right hand from the handle of the axe, Melcer held it up, palm out, in a sign. "Do you speak my language?" he asked.

Somewhat to his surprise, the youngster nodded. "Little bit," he said, his accent foul but comprehensible. He jabbed a thumb at his own chest. "Conan."

"I am Melcer," said the farmer. Now he held out his right hand. The Cimmerian hesitated, then strode forward and took it. When he did, Melcer got another surprise, for, though Conan was unquestionably a boy, his grip had a man's strength. When Melcer told him, "I have no quarrel with you," he sounded more sincere than he might have expected.

Conan said something in Cimmerian, then stopped and kicked at the dirt, realizing Melcer could not follow him. He dropped back into his fragmentary Aquilonian: "Why you here? What you do?"

"I have come here to make a farm and to raise my family," answered Melcer.

Another spate of Cimmerian. Again, Conan checked himself. Again, he spoke in what bits of Melcer's language he had: "Not your land. You go home."

"No." The Gunderman shook his head. "I will stay here. We have won this land with the sword. We will keep it."

He did not know how much the barbarian boy understood of that, though his shaken head left little room for doubt. Scowling, Conan repeated, "Not your land."

"I say it is." Melcer remembered that when he had said he had no quarrel with Conan, the Cimmerian had not told him anything of the sort. Yet Conan had taken his hand, and showed no sign of going to war on the instant. Melcer pointed straight at him. "Peace between us?"

Now Conan did not hesitate. "No," he said at once. "No peace. You go, then peace."

Melcer might have lacked money and high birth, but he did not lack for pride. "I will not go," he said. "I have come here to make my home. That is what I aim to do."

"You pay." The barbarian nodded emphatically. "Oh, yes. You pay."

"Anyone who tries to drive me off this land will pay," said Melcer.

He had to say it again before the barbarian followed. When Conan finally did, he studied Melcer, showing surprise of his own. Maybe he had not realized the Aquilonians had pride of their own. He undid the rawhide thong that held one of the grouse on his belt, then tossed the bird at Melcer's feet. He pointed first to himself, then to the Gunderman. "Enemies," he said, and loped off into the woods.

Slowly, Melcer stooped to pick up the grouse. He wondered whether the barbarian had meant to say he wanted them to be friends but had been undone by his imperfect knowledge of Aquilonian. A moment later, an arrow hissed through the air and buried itself in the soil less than a yard from Melcer's boot. He hopped back in alarm. If Conan wanted to kill him from ambush, he probably could.

But no more arrows flew from the forest. "Enemies," the Cimmerian called once more, and then everything was still.

After a couple of minutes of wary, watchful waiting, Melcer decided Conan had gone away. The Gunderman thoughtfully hefted the grouse. He would not have given an enemy a gift. Did Conan reckon it an insult, or was it a token of respect? Melcer shrugged. However the Cimmerian had meant it, it would make a tasty supper.

Up went the axe. Melcer brought it down with all his strength. Regardless of whether the Cimmerian fancied the notion, he had a cabin to build, a farm to make, and he aimed to do just that.

Loarn was a wandering peddler and tinker who came to Duthil every year or two. When he did, he guested with Mordec. The blacksmith did tinker's work now and again, soldering patches onto saucepans and the like, but Loarn was a master at it. He also repaired broken or cracked crockery, which Mordec did not attempt. Loarn had a tiny drill and a set of lead rivets so fine, they were almost sutures. By the time he was done fixing a pot and had daubed his repairs with pitch, it would hold water or ale as well as it ever had. He also paid his way with gossip and news and songs and jokes.

Some of the news of southern Cimmeria had not reached him until just before he came into Duthil. When he led his donkey up the lane toward Mordec's smithy, he was fuming. "Aquilonian soldiers, by Crom!" he cried as he came in. "Aquilonian soldiers! What are they doing here? Why didn't you cast them out?" He sounded as if he blamed the blacksmith personally.

Mordec looked up from the nail—almost a spike—whose point he was sharpening. "What are they doing here?" he echoed, his voice half an octave deeper than Loarn's. "Whatever they please, worse luck. Why didn't we cast them forth? We tried. They beat us, which is why they can do as they please for now."

"Disgraceful business," said Loarn, a small, skinny man with a drooping gray mustache. "Disgraceful, I tell you. They stopped me and searched my goods as if I were a thief. They could have robbed me and murdered me, too, and who would have been the wiser? News of the invasion still hasn't spread up to the north, where my clan dwells."

"You can take it with you, then, when you travel that way again," said Mordec, and Loarn nodded his agreement. "Conan!" called the blacksmith, and then again, louder: "Conan! Where has the boy got to, anyhow? Oh, there you are. About time. Here's Loarn, just in off the road. Fetch him a mug of ale and something to eat."

"Aye, Father," said Conan. "Welcome, Loarn." He hurried into the back of the house.

Loarn's eyes followed him. "He's as tall as I am already, and he has how many years behind him? Fifteen?"

"Twelve," answered Mordec.

"Crom!" said the peddler. "He'll have your inches before he's done, then, and maybe two or three more besides."

"I know." Mordec lowered his voice: "I had a demon of a time keeping him from joining the army that fought the invaders. He thinks he's a man now."

"I can understand why," said Loarn. "How did it fall out that they beat you? Such a thing hasn't happened in all the years of my life."

Mordec shrugged massive shoulders. "We didn't put enough men in the field to swamp them, and their knights hit us at just the right time—right for them, wrong for us. Not enough clans joined the fight on our side."

"And now all Cimmeria will suffer because they didn't," said Loarn.

"Take the news north," said Mordec, shrugging again. "If all the clans in the countryside joined against the invaders—" He broke off and laughed. "If that happened, it would be a miracle, and when was the last time Crom worked a miracle in these parts? He's not that sort of god. He wants his folk to work the miracles."

Loarn grunted. He did not quarrel with Mordec; no Cimmerian could have, not where their god was concerned. The blacksmith had spoken only the truth about the dour deity who watched over this tree-draped land and expected the people dwelling in it to solve their own problems without bothering him.

Conan came in just then, carrying a wooden tray with two mugs of ale, and with oatcakes and a slab of roasted pork ribs for the guest in the house. "Thank you, lad," said Loarn, and then, in surprise, "Mistress Verina! I know you're not well. You did not need to trouble yourself for me."

From behind Conan, his mother said, "It is no trouble, Loarn." A moment later, she gave herself the lie, coughing till her face went a dusky purple and blood-flecked foam clung to her lower lip.

"Get into bed, Verina," growled Mordec. He snatched one of the mugs of ale from the tray in Conan's hands and drained it at a single long pull. "Loarn is right—you do yourself no good by being up and about when you shouldn't."

"I do the honor of the household good," said Verina with quiet pride.

The blacksmith ground his teeth in a curious mix of frustration and fury. Verina was willing—was perhaps even eager—to give up, to throw away, her own life to prove a point. Mordec had seen that years before, when her illness first came upon her. He often thought she used it as a weapon, turning her weakness against him where strength would not have sufficed. That he kept to himself. Had he spoken of it, it would only have ignited more strife between them. But he spent as much time away from the smithy as he could.

His absences, of course, only tightened the bond between Verina and Conan. When she began to cough again, the boy anxiously asked, "Are you all right, Mother?" and started to go to her.

She waved him away, saying, "Tend to the guest in the house, if you please. I will do well enough."

Conan grimaced but obeyed. He heeded her better than he had ever obeyed Mordec, against whose iron will his own, equally hard, clashed at every opportunity. The smith grimaced, too, but for different reasons. He did not care for Verina's use of their son to show off her illness, but she had been doing it for years, and he had never found a way to stop her. He wished the mug he had drained had held twice as much ale.

Loarn, tactfully, said only, "Tell me more of the coming of the cursed Aquilonians. When I do go into the north country again, I will need to answer many questions, and I will want to have the answers right."

Before Mordec could reply, Conan did: "Not only soldiers have come to Cimmeria, but also farmers, and their women and children with them. The men from the south aim to take this land away from us forever."

"He speaks the truth," said Mordec. He scowled at Verina, then got off the stool on which he had been sitting. "If you will not go back to bed, at least come over here and sit down. Conan, bring your mother a mug of ale. Maybe it will lend her some strength."

The prospect of helping his mother was enough to make Conan listen to his father. He dashed back to the kitchen to pour the ale. Verina reluctantly perched on the stool Mordec had vacated. Had she and her husband and son been alone in the house, the blacksmith doubted she would have. Instead, she would have stubbornly stayed on her feet until she fell in a faint, which might not have taken long. But with Loarn watching what went on, she did not care to quarrel too openly with her husband.

"Here you are, Mother." Conan hurried up with another mug of ale.

"Thank you, Conan." Verina was polite with him, where she had wasted no courteous words on Mordec.

Loarn tore into his food, as a man will when for a long time he has not eaten so much as he would have liked. After only bones and crumbs were left, he licked his fingers clean and wiped them dry on the checked wool of his breeks. That done, he bobbed his head to Mordec. "I thank you kindly," he said. "You've always made a prime host, that you have, but you've outdone yourself now, times being so hard for you. To the ravens with me if I know how I can pay you back."

"Your company is enough," said Verina, determined to make everything seem as smooth as it could.

But Mordec shook his head. "If you want to repay me, Loarn, spread the word of what's happened here in the south far and wide, so the rest of Cimmeria does learn of it."

"I'd do that anyhow, for my own honor's sake," said the tinker. "I'll gladly do it for yours as well."

At Mordec's direction, Conan brought Loarn blankets and a pillow, so the guest could stretch out on the floor by the forge, whose banked fire and hot brickwork would help keep him warm through the night. Giving Loarn a pillow meant Conan himself would go without one, but he did not grudge the peddler the best the house had to offer. Hospitality toward friends was as important a duty as vengeance against enemies.

Thirst for that vengeance made Conan's blood boil as he waited for sleep in his narrow bed. He imagined Count Stercus abusing Tarla rather than the girl from Rosinish. He imagined himself slaughtering Stercus and all the Gundermen and Bossonians who followed him. Such gore-soaked images helped soothe the boy, as softer toys might have soothed children in softer lands.

For his part, Mordec was also a long time finding slumber.

What would the Cimmerians still free do when they learned some of their cousins had passed into Aquilonian dominion? The blacksmith hoped such news would inflame them to come to their countrymen's rescue. That was what he hoped, but how much truth mingled with hope? The rest of the Cimmerians might easily decide the men of the south had proved themselves weaklings who deserved whatever happened to them. Like its god, this country's people had scant forgiveness in them, scant tolerance for weakness.

But they did have the barbarian's innate love of freedom. Mordec pinned his hopes there. Surely the other Cimmerians would see that, if one part of their land fell under King Numedides' iron first, the rest could easily follow. Surely they would want to make sure such a disaster did not befall them. Surely they would—would they not?

Grunting worriedly as sleep overtook him, Mordec at last began to snore.

chapter

v

Wolves and Demon

Winter came early to Cimmeria, as it did more winters than not. Winds howled down from the north, from the ever-frozen lands of Vanaheim and Asgard. When times got hard, red-haired and blond wolves who ran on two legs might swoop down on Cimmeria to carry off what they could. In a usual year, men from southern Cimmeria could fare north to help drive back the marauders, who even to them seemed savage. Now, though, with Count Stercus and the colonists carving out a toehold for King Numedides of Aquilonia here in the south, the clans near the northern borders would have to shift for themselves if danger came their way.

No word of rampaging Æsir or Vanir came down to Duthil: only one blizzard after another, blizzards that piled the snow in thick drifts and left trees so covered in white, their greenery all but disappeared. Hunting was hard. Even moving was often hard. Winter was the bleak time of the year, the time when folk lived on what they had brought in during the harvest and hoped they would not have to eat next year's seed grain to keep from starving.

For those who did not make their living directly from the fields, those like Conan and his family, winter was an even

chancier season than for most others. If people had not the
rye and oats to give Mordec for his labor, what were he and
Conan and Verina to do? They had had hungry winters before. This looked like another one.

Despite the drifted snow, Conan went hunting whenever
he could. Against the cold, he wore sheepskin trousers and a
jacket made from the hides of wolves Mordec had slain. A
wolfskin cap with earflaps warded his head against winter. Felt
boots worn too large and stuffed with wool kept his feet
warm.

Even with all that cold-weather gear, he still shivered as he
left the smithy. The icy weather outside seemed to bite all the
harder after the heat that poured from Mordec's forge. Now,
instead of the fire in that forge. Conan's breath smoked.

"Out hunting, Conan?" That was Tarla, the daughter of
Balarg the weaver, scooping clean, fresh snow into buckets to
bring it indoors to melt for drinking and cooking water.

He nodded. "Aye," he said, and even the one word seemed
a great speech to him.

The girl's smile was like a moment of sunshine from some
warmer country. "Good fortune go with you, then," she said.

Awkwardly, Conan dipped his head. "Thanks," he said, and
hurried away toward the woods.

Not far from Duthil stood the encampment full of Bossonians and Gundermen. By now, it seemed as much a fixture on
the landscape as the village itself. Sentries stood guard beyond
the palisade around the cabins that had replaced the soldiers'
tents. One of them waved to Conan as he went off toward
the forest. He pretended not to see. Waving back would have
been confessing friendship for the invaders.

He had not been in the woods for long before he heard
Aquilonian voices cursing. He slipped silently through the
trees toward the sound. A supply wagon on the way up from
Fort Venarium to the smaller camp outside of Duthil had
bogged down in deep snow.

"Don't do that!" said a guard as the driver raised his whip to try to lash the horses forward. "Can't you see we need to clear a path for them?"

"Mitra! Let them work. Why should I?" said the driver. "This weather's not fit for beasts and barbarians, let alone for honest men to be out and about in."

Conan did not follow all of that—his grasp of the invaders' tongue was far from what it might have been, though nonetheless surprising for one with but a few months of informal and sketchily acquired knowledge behind him. The gist, though, seemed plain enough. Snarling deep in his throat, he reached over his shoulder for an arrow. He could not have said whether he wished to shoot the driver more on account of his scorn for Cimmerians or his callousness toward the team.

In the end, he did not loose the shaft that would have drunk the soldier's life. Driver and guard never knew their lives stood for a long moment on the razor's edge. They never knew one of the barbarians they despised had stood close enough to kill them, but had mastered his murderous rage and moved on. Silent as snowfall, Conan glided deeper into the forest. He had come forth to hunt game, not men.

Snow buntings chirped in the trees. They were some of the few birds that did not flee to warmer climes when winter came. Conan was fond of them because of that. Even as woodswise as he was, he had a hard time spying them. They were white and buff, almost invisible in the snow. Only when they flew did their black wingtips give them away. Those wingtips reminded him of an ermine's nose and tail tip, which stayed dark even after the rest of the creature went white to match the winter background.

If he got hungry enough, he supposed a stew of snow buntings would keep him from starving. But he would have wanted to frighten them into nets, not try to shoot them on the wing. They were swift and agile flyers, and no one bird

had much in the way of meat. The arrows he lost were unlikely to repay the catch he made.

He did keep his eyes open not for ermine but for other
creatures that went white when winter came: plump hares and
the ptarmigan that feasted on pine and spruce needles through
the cold weather. The hares' black eyes and noses and the
black outer tail feathers of the ptarmigan sometimes betrayed
them to the alert hunter. Because of what they ate at this
season, ptarmigan were less tasty in winter than in summer,
but they were meat, tasty or not, and a hungry man could
not be choosy.

No one and nothing hungry could be choosy in wintertime.
Only little by little did Conan realize he had gone from hunter
to hunted. He had heard wolves howl several times that day,
but not so near as to be alarming. Hearing those howls in the
distance lulled him for longer than it should have when he
heard them closer. Thus it was with a start of horror that he
realized a pack had found his trail.

His first impulse, like that of any hunted wild creature, was
to run like the wind in a desperate search for escape. He mastered it, as he had mastered the urge to murder. Both would
have given momentary satisfaction, and both would have
brought disaster in their wake. Wolves could outrun men.
Any man who reckoned otherwise but doomed himself.

Instead of running wild and exhausting himself, Conan
moved with grim purpose, seeking a spot where he might
make a stand against the beasts to which he was but so much
meat. And, before long, he found one. Had he fled blindly,
he might well have dashed past without realizing it was there.

Two boulders, each of them them taller than a man, came
together to leave a space between them shaped like a sword
point, protecting him from either side. At the very tip, where
there would have been an opening, stood the trunk of a tall
spruce, against which he set his back. He had his bow, his
arrows, and on his belt a long knife his father had forged. The

wolves had their teeth and claws. They also had the innate ferocity of the wild. They had it, and so did he.

Their voices rose to high, excited howls when they realized they had brought him to bay. The first wolf loped toward him, snow flying up from under its feet, red tongue lolling out of its red mouth, slaver dripping from yellowish fangs, amber eyes gleaming with hate and hunger.

The pack leader leaped. Conan let fly. He shot it full in the chest with the one envenomed arrow he carried. He had to be sure, certain sure, of this kill. So potent was the poison that the wolf had time for but the bare beginning of a startled yip before it slammed down dead on the snow. Its blood steamed scarlet beneath it.

Conan's next shaft, driven by all the power in his smithy-trained arms, was in the air less than half a heartbeat later. It sank almost to the fletching in the eye of the wolf closest behind the leader. That beast, too, died in the instant of its wounding. The third arrow, also quickly shot, sank deep into the flank of the next nearest wolf. That was not a mortal shot, but the wolf belled in pain and ran from the man-thing who had inflicted such torment on it.

Three more shafts saw another wolf dead, one wounded, and one arrow flying far but futilely. Some of the yet unhurt wolves began tearing at the carcasses of a fallen comrade. In this desperate time of year, meat was meat, come whence it might. Gore stained the snow. Conan shot another wolf, and yet another, even as they fed.

But more of them kept him in their bestial minds. One sprang over the corpse of the first wolf he had shot while he reached for a fresh arrow. A civilized man would have gone on with the motion, knowing he would complete it too late, or else would have hesitated before throwing down the bow and snatching knife from scabbard—and, hesitating, would have been undone.

No hesitation lived in Conan. With the quicksilver instincts of the barbarian, he abandoned bow for knife, stabbing deep into the wolf's side even as it overbore him. Its rank breath stank in his nostrils as it snapped, trying to tear out his throat. He held its horrible head away from him as he drove the knife home again and again, until his right arm was red with blood to the elbow.

All at once, the wolf decided it wanted no part of him, and tried to break away rather than to slay. Too late, for its legs no longer cared to bear its weight. It sank down lifeless on top of Conan.

The blacksmith's son flung its weight aside and sprang to his feet ere others could assail him. He seized his bow again and nocked an arrow, ready—as he had been ready in the fight with Mordec—to go on even to the death. He might die, but if he did he would die striving.

But the wolves had had enough. Those that still lived and were yet unwounded trotted off in search of easier prey. Conan's shout of triumph filled the silent forest with fierce joy. He killed two wolves that were still writhing in the snow, then went about the grisly business of skinning the brutes— all but the one its packmates had partially devoured. That done, he also cut slabs of meat from the carcasses. At this season of the year, in this harsh country, he would have eaten worse meat than wolf, and would have been glad to have it.

Burdened as he was, he found going back to Duthil harder than coming out from the village had been. He floundered deeper into snowdrifts, and broke through crust upon which he had been able to walk. Despite the cold, he was sweating under his furs and wool by the time he finally reached his home. The heat of his father's forge, which had been so welcome in wintertime, struck him like a blow.

Mordec was striking blows of his own, on an andiron he held against the anvil with a pair of black iron tongs. The smith looked up from his labor when Conan came through the door. "Are you hale, boy?" he demanded, startled anxiety suddenly filling his voice.

Conan looked down at himself. He had not realized he was so thoroughly drenched in gore. "It's not my blood, Father," he said proudly, and set the wolf hames and the butchered meat on the ground in front of him.

Mordec eyed the hides for some little while before he spoke. When at last he did, he asked, "You slew all of these yourself?"

"No one else, by Crom!" answered Conan, and he told the story with nearly as much savage vigor as he had expended in the fight against the pack.

After Conan stopped, his father was again some time silent. This time, Mordec spoke more to himself than to Conan: "I may have been wrong." Conan's eyes opened very wide, for he did not think he had ever heard his father say such a thing before. Mordec turned to him and continued, "When next we go to war, son, I shall not try to hold you back. By the look of things, you are a host in yourself."

That made Conan want to cry out in triumph again, even louder and more joyfully than he had when the wolves ran off into the woods. He said, "I will slaughter the Aquilonians, and plunder them, too."

His father still stared at the rolled-up, uncured hides and at the gobbets of meat on the floor beside them. "Maybe you will," muttered Mordec. "I am not the one to say you won't." He shook his head in slow wonder, then bestirred himself. "For now, though, go put all that in the snow behind the house. It will keep the meat and the skins from going bad."

"All right, Father." Conan moved to obey. "Wolf's flesh is not of the best, I know—"

"But better than nothing," interrupted Mordec. "And if it stays in the stew pot long enough, it loses some of that rank and gamy taste. Oh, and Conan—when you come back in, wash. Your clothes aren't all that's bloody."

Though no more enamored of washing than any other boy his age, Conan only nodded: a telling measure of how exhilarated, and how blood-soaked, he was. As he carried the hides and the meat out to the snow, he heard a clank as Mordec thrust the andiron into the forge to heat it again. Soon the smith's hammer rang once more on red-hot iron. The work always went on.

Melcer's hastily cleared farm had not brought in enough to feed him and his family through their first winter in Cimmeria. He had expected nothing different. When he came north, he had brought with him all the silver lunas he had. Those that remained now rested in a stout iron box buried under the dirt floor of the snug, securely chinked cabin he had run up.

Some of those lunas jingled in his belt pouch as he led one of his oxen toward the rapidly growing town around Fort Venarium. He went armed, of course, with a pike that doubled as a staff in his hand and with a long knife that would do duty as a shortsword on his hip. The barbarians hereabouts seemed cowed, but a man would be a fool to trust them too far, and Melcer prided himself on being no one's fool. Some of the settlers might also try to take advantage of anything they saw as weakness; he intended to show them none.

It had not snowed for several days. Enough people had traveled the road since to have cleared it of drifts. With the ground frozen hard under the snow, the going was, if anything, easier than it had been during the fall, when the roadway turned into a bottomless morass of muck and ooze. Melcer slogged along, alert for wild beasts and wilder men.

A couple of riders trotted north toward him, their mail-shirts jingling every time their horses' hooves came down. He held the pike a little tighter, in case they had trouble in mind. But one of them waved, while the other touched a hand to the edge of his conical helm and called, "Mitra keep you safe on the road, stranger."

"May the god guard you as well," replied Melcer. Both horsemen waved this time as they rode on. Hoofbeats and clinking chainmail faded behind the farmer. He plodded on. So did his ox, with slow, patient, uncomplaining strides.

Seeing Venarium—the town seemed to have taken on the name of the fort—always made Melcer want to rub his eyes. Every time he came here, it was bigger and had a more finished look. By now, it was at least as large as the market town to which he had gone in Gunderland. New buildings, new businesses, sprang up like mushrooms after a rain.

As the farmer walked into town, he saw an Aquilonian knight carrying new horse tackle out of a saddlery that had not existed the last time he came into Venarium. Next door, a farrier in an equally new establishment was shoeing the knight's charger. The horse snorted indignantly as the man drove nails into its hoof. "Hush, my beauty—you know it doesn't hurt a bit," said the farrier, and went right on with what he was doing. After that one protest, the big chestnut let him do it. In the same way that some men had a gift with women, others had a gift with horses.

A woman who looked too prosperous to be a farmer's wife was haggling with a cloth merchant over a length of brocade. Perhaps she was married to one of the other tradesmen in Venarium, perhaps to an officer who had brought her up from the south. A Cimmerian in a pantherskin coat that came down to his knees, a barbaric garment if ever there was one, came out of the cloth merchant's shop carrying a shirt of lustrous green silk, a shirt he might have worn if presented at the court of King Numedides. Civilization spread in strange ways.

When Melcer saw the Cimmerian, his grip on the pike tightened again. But the man of the north was in anything but a warlike mood. Pleased with his purchase, he beamed at Melcer as he walked by. The farmer, caught off guard, smiled back. Out in the woods, he would not have trusted the barbarian for an instant—though the youngster called Conan had caused him no trouble in several visits to his farm. Here in Venarium, even a full-grown Cimmerian seemed safe enough.

So Melcer thought, at any rate, until he rounded a corner and espied a drunken Cimmerian sprawled, oblivious to the world around him, outside the door to one of the many taverns in the new town. A blond Gunderman, at least as sodden, lay beside him in the gutter. Venarium might bring barbarians to civilization, but it also dragged civilized men down to barbarism.

Melcer made his way to a miller's a few doors beyond the tavern. There he bought flour poured into sacks of coarse canvas. He lashed them onto the ox's back, then led it in the direction of the fort. It followed. What choice did it have? It was but a slave. Melcer prided himself on his freedom.

He had to pause at a corner while soldiers led manacled Cimmerian captives toward Fort Venarium. They too would be slaves, either here or down in the mines of Aquilonia. A short life, that, but not a merry one. The difference between the ox and the barbarians was that they had known freedom's sweetness, and knew it was taken from them.

Melcer stopped at a shop that sold what it called notions: little things of the sort a farmer was ill-equipped to make for himself. Melcer bought some fine iron needles for Evlea; she was down to the last one fetched from Gunderland, and had talked about making more from bone. He also bought her a sachet of dried rose petals. Drying flowers in the cool damp of Cimmeria was a losing proposition. And, to give their food a little extra savor, he bought some spices that had made the long journey from Iranistan to Aquilonia and then to the frontier.

How much the spices cost jolted him. The man who ran the shop only shrugged his shoulders. "What I have to sell is what bandits did not steal and what kings did not confiscate," he said. "You pay for all the hardships and robberies on the road."

"What did you pay for your goods?" asked Melcer.

"Less than I'm charging you," answered the merchant. "If you think I will tell you otherwise, you are wrong. I have not seen it written anywhere in the stars that I am not allowed to make a living."

He sent Melcer a challenging stare. Since he was so frank about what he was doing, Melcer saw no real way to quarrel with him. The farmer did ask, "How much would I have to give for pepper and cinnamon in some other shop here?"

"Go ahead and try, friend, and good luck to you," said the other man. "Good luck finding them at all, first. And if you find them for less, bring back what you bought from me and I will give back your money."

That convinced Melcer not to waste his time trying. He led the ox down the street to a tavern that had no drunks from any nation lying sozzled outside it. He tied the beast to a pillar supporting the entrance, then strode inside and ordered a mug of ale. He sat down where he could keep an eye on the ox. It had only the flour on its back; the smaller things he had bought he kept with him. But even an ox with nothing on its back might tempt a thief.

When the Gunderman finished that first mug of ale, he bought himself a second. When he finished the second, the pretty barmaid who had brought it came back with a broad, inviting, expectant smile. Instead of ordering a third, he got up and walked out of the tavern. The smiling barmaid cursed him behind his back. Pretending not to hear, Melcer kept walking. He untied the ox and started back to his farm.

He was inside the forest again and within a mile of his own land when an arrow hissed past his face and thudded into the bole of a fir to his right. He clutched his pike and stared in the direction from which the shaft had come. He saw nothing. He heard nothing. A ghost might have drawn the bow. He

pounded that way anyhow. If a brigand wanted him, he
would go down fighting.

After a few strides through ever thicker snow, he did hear
something: laughter. Snowshoes on his feet, Conan emerged
from behind a pine. "You jump!" he shouted in his bad Aquilonian. "You jump high!" He imitated Melcer's reaction, then
laughed harder than ever.

"Of course I jumped, you cursed son of a dog!" shouted
Melcer. "You could have killed me!"

Conan only nodded at that. "Could have killed, yes. Did
not kill. Too easy. No—" He said something in his own language, then frowned, looking for a way to put it into Melcer's.
When he brightened, the farmer knew he had found it. "No
sport. Is a word, sport?"

"Yes, sport's a word," growled Melcer. "Come down here
and I'll warm your behind for you, you damned murderous
savage. I'll teach you words, by Mitra!"

Only after he had spoken did he wonder how wise he was
to revile a fiery young barbarian with a bow in his hands,
especially when the boy had already shown a regrettable talent
for archery. Conan studied him watchfully. "You not afraid?"
he asked at last.

"Afraid? Hell, no!" said Melcer. "What I am is furious. You
come down here and I *will* wallop you. You deserve it, too."

To his surprise, Conan nodded to him, a nod that was
almost a bow. "You brave man," said the Cimmerian. "I not
play games with you no more." His voice remained a boy's
treble, but it held a man's conviction. Melcer believed him
without reservation. Then the barbarian added. "Not shoot at
you till war time."

Before Melcer could find an answer to that, Conan ducked
behind the pine once more. He did not come out. He said
nothing further. The farmer did not see him move deeper into
the woods, but at last decided that was what he must have
done. Melcer wished he could match the boy in woodcraft.

Shaking his head, the Gunderman went back to the placidly waiting ox. He broke off the arrow's shaft close to the tree trunk. Then he had another thought, and used his knife to dig out the iron arrowhead. How far it had penetrated surprised him anew; Conan might be a beardless boy, but he boasted a man's strength. Melcer put the arrowhead in his belt pouch. It was one, at least, that Conan would not shoot at him in war.

Melcer picked up the lead rope he had dropped. "Come on!" he told the ox. They walked on toward his farm.

Duthil had never boasted a tavern. No one could make a living selling ale there, not when so many families did their own brewing. When the villagers wanted to hash out the way things wagged in the world over a few mugs of amber ale, they gathered at the home of one man or another.

Mordec put down his hammer after finishing work on a stout iron hinge. He left the shop at the front of his own house, slogged through the snow between the door and the street, and walked along until he came to Balarg's home. No Aquilonian soldiers were anywhere in the village. Since the blizzards started rolling in every week or so, the men from the south had been content, even eager, to stay in their own encampment. To them, this was dreadful weather. Mordec chuckled grimly. To him, it was only another winter, worse than some but milder than a good many others.

He knocked at Balarg's door. The weaver opened it. "Come in, come in," he said. "Don't let the heat from the hearth leak out."

"I thank you," answered Mordec. Balarg made haste to shut the door behind him. The two men were careful around each other. Mordec, the stronger of the two, was clever enough to realize Balarg was more clever. And Balarg, for his part, was clever enough to understand not everything in Duthil yielded to cleverness; sometimes—often—straightforward smashing best solved a problem.

"Ale?" asked the weaver.

"Don't mind if I do," said Mordec. Balarg waved to the pitcher and mugs set up on a table by his loom. Mordec filled a mug, took a strip of smoked meat from a tray by the pitcher, and perched on a stool not far from the fireplace. Along with Balarg, four other men sat in the chamber: three villagers and a stranger, a rugged man whose checked breeks were woven in a pattern worn by a northern clan. After a sip from the mug, the blacksmith asked. "Anyone else coming?"

"I invited Nectan," answered Balarg. "Whether he'll come—" He shrugged. So did Mordec. Nectan was a a shepherd, and stayed out with his sheep in all weather unless he could find someone to watch them while he left the flock.

Mordec's gaze slipped to the man who did not come from the village. "And our friend is—?"

Before Balarg could answer, the stranger spoke for himself: "My name is Herth." His voice was almost as deep as Mordec's. "I come from Garvard, up near the border with the Æsir."

Slowly, deliberately, Mordec took his measure. "You are a chieftain there, or I miss my guess," he said, and Herth did not deny it. After another pull at his ale, Mordec said, "It's a long way from Garvard to Duthil. What are you doing here?"

"Now, Mordec," said Balarg.

"It's all right," said Herth, but, before he could say anything more, another knock resounded.

Balarg opened the door. "Nectan!" he exclaimed. "I thought we'd have to do without you. Who's minding the flock?"

"Why, the blacksmith's son." Nectan pointed toward Mordec.

"Is he?" said Mordec. "Just as well, by Crom. Otherwise, Conan would insist on being here."

"Yes, so he would." Balarg's voice had an edge to it, though one so slight that Mordec thought he was the only man in the room who caught it. The weaver must have noticed the way Conan looked at his daughter. One of these days, he and Mordec would have to sit down and decide what would spring from that—if Conan didn't take matters into his own hands by running off with the girl.

Nectan poured himself some ale and started gnawing on a strip of mutton. When he pulled a stool close to the fire, Mordec slid aside to make room for him. He had been out in the cold and the wind for a long time, and had earned the warmth now.

Herth said, "A tinker named Loarn told me what had passed here. I decided to come down and see for myself, and I find it is so. Yellow-haired soldiers who spoke in grunts and trills put their hands on me not far north of here, and I had to bear the insult, for they were many and I but one. Yet though I had to bear it then, I shall not forget it."

"As you say, they are many," answered Mordec. "For now, we also have to bear it, though we shall not forget, either."

"But the longer we bear it, the stronger the Aquilonians become," said Balarg.

"Aye, that's so, curse them," said Nectan, and the other men of Duthil nodded. The shepherd went on, "The fortress they build, the place they call Venarium"—he pronounced the foreign name with an odd kind of contemptuous care—"has already grown harder to take than any hill fort of our folk." He sipped from his ale, then inclined his head to Herth. "Have you seen it?"

"Not yet," replied the northern chieftain. "No, not yet, though I intend to before I go back to my own country."

"Now that you have seen this much, what will you do up in the north?" asked Mordec.

"What needs doing," said Herth. "Loarn spoke somewhat of rousing the clans. By Crom, he roused me, but not everyone cares to hearken to a landless wanderer who makes his living, such as it is, by patching pans and fixing broken jugs."

"What he does, he does well," observed Mordec. "When you speak of a man, you could say worse."

Herth's gaze might have been a swordblade. The blacksmith's might have been another. When they clashed, sparks flew. From off to one side, Balarg said, "Here, friends, it is of no great importance."

Mordec did not reply. He kept his eyes on Herth. After a few heartbeats, the chieftain was the one who looked away, saying, "Well, perhaps it is not. But I say this, and say it true: when I travel through Cimmeria, men will hearken to me." He had a clan chief's pride, sure enough.

"Hearkening is one thing," said Nectan. "Moving is another. Once they have hearkened, will they move?"

"Oh, yes." Herth spoke softly, but with great certainty. "You may rely on that, friend shepherd. Once they have hearkened, they will move."

Conan stood on a hilltop, watching the sheep on the hillside pawing their way down through the snow to get at the grass beneath it. He also watched the woods not far away. If wolves came trotting forth, he had his bow and he had Nectan's stout staff with which to fight them. The staff was of some hard, dark wood with which Conan was unfamiliar. It was shod with silver. "Keep it safe, lad," the shepherd had said when he handed it to Conan. "You'd leave me a poorer man if you should lose it."

A small fire burned close by, sheltered from the north wind by several tall stones. Conan stooped and tossed a few more branches onto the flames. The fire did not give a great deal of warmth, but Nectan had kept it going, and Conan wanted to maintain everything as the shepherd had had it. Nectan doubtless cooked over it and slept beside it. Having to start it afresh in this raw weather would be a nuisance for him.

For that matter, if Nectan did not come back from Duthil until the morrow, the blacksmith's son would have to cook on the fire and sleep by it himself. Nectan had said he would return before sundown, but Conan had seen that promises, however well meant when made, were not always to be relied upon.

Something flew past overhead. Conan did not pay much heed. The greatest eagle might perhaps carry off a newborn lamb, but lambing season was still months away, and no bird ever hatched could hope to seize a full-grown sheep and fly away with it. So Conan thought, at any rate, but the flying thing stooped like a falcon. A stout ewe let out a sudden bleat of agony.

Whatever the creature struggling to lift the sheep into the air was, it was no bird. Its huge wings were black and membranous, while a pair of pointed ears pricked up above its fiercely glowing red eyes. When it snarled, it showed a mouth full of teeth like needles and razors and knives.

Bat? Demon? Conan could not have said, nor did he much care. All he knew was that the thing was harming one of Nectan's sheep. Stringing his bow was the matter of a moment. Letting fly took even less time. His arrow flew straight and true, and sank to the fletching in the flying thing's flank.

It sank to the fletching—but the creature, apparently unharmed, kept right on flapping, trying to take off with the ewe it had chosen. Conan shot again. The second shaft struck within a palm's breadth of the first, but had no more effect. No normal living thing could have withstood such wounds without woe.

"Demon! Filthy, cursed demon from the darkest pits of hell!" cried Conan. He threw down his bow, snatched up a blazing brand from the fire, and ran not away from the thing but towards it, shouting his defiance of anything from this plane or any other that tried to steal what he had vowed to protect. It screamed, let go of the ewe, and flapped toward him.

The foul stench of it almost knocked him off his feet. Reeling, he lashed out with Nectan's staff. The silver at the base of that length of wood thudded against the creature's ribs. Iron-tipped arrows had done Conan no good, but the demon shrieked in anguish at the touch of silver.

"Ha!" cried Conan. He swung again, and again struck home. Suddenly, the demon wanted no more of this manthing who dealt it such cruel blows. However hungry it might have been, no meal was worth the torment it took from silver. Screaming now in fright, it turned to flee.

But Conan struck again, this time with the burning branch he bore in his left hand. He let out a great bull roar of triumph, for the demon caught fire and burned like a torch. It flew off, still screaming and still burning. Somewhere up above the woods, it could fly no more, and plunged to earth. Conan thought he heard a hiss arise when it slammed into the snow, a hiss like that when his father plunged hot iron into a tempering bath. He might have been wrong, but he believed as much until the end of his days.

Having driven off the demon, he hurried to the sheep it had tried to steal. He tended the cuts and bites as best he could, pouring ale from his drinking flask over them to try to keep the wounds from going bad. The ewe repaid his kindness by kicking him just below the knee. The sheep's thick coat of winter wool had likely gone a long way toward saving its life by shielding it from some of the damage the flying demon's teeth and talons might otherwise have worked.

When Nectan returned not long before sunset, he saw at once the blood on the ewe's flanks. "By Crom, Conan, did you fall asleep here?" he demanded angrily. "I'll thump you with my staff if you did."

"By Babd, Morrigan, Macha, and Nemain, I did not!" exclaimed Conan, and told the tale of the fight with the demon.

Nectan listened without a word. Then he went to the ewe and stooped to examine its injuries. When he straightened, his face was troubled. "Those are not the marks of wolf or panther, nor yet of any eagle," he said slowly. "Perhaps you speak truth, where I thought you lied."

"I do," said Conan. "It most misliked the silver at the end of your staff."

"Silver and fire are sovereign against demons, or so I've heard." Nectan shook his head in wonder. "I own I never thought to put it to the test."

chapter vi

The Hunters

Spring came late to Cimmeria, especially to one used to the warmer clime of Aquilonia. Indeed, to Count Stercus what the calendar called spring hardly seemed worthy of the name. True, the sky was gray longer than it was black, where the opposite had held true through the seemingly unending winter. True also, the snow at last stopped falling and then, with even more reluctance, began to melt.

But there was no great burgeoning of life, as there would have been farther south. The trees did not burst into bright green leaf. They were evergreens, and had kept such gloomy color as they originally owned all through the winter, though snow had hidden much of it. Little by little, fresh grass did begin to poke up through the dead and yellow growth of the previous year, but the process was so gradual that days went by without much perceptible change. And birdsongs other than owls' hoots, hunting hawks' harsh cries, and the croaking and chirring calls of grouse and ptarmigan started to sweeten the air.

Birdsongs, however, left Stercus cold. Almost everything that had to do with Cimmeria left Stercus cold. He had written at least a score of letters to King Numedides and to everyone else in Tarantia who might have had influence with the King of Aquilonia, all of them requesting, pleading—begging—that he be recalled to a civilized country once more. Every one of those letters had fallen on deaf ears. Oh, through one of his secretaries Numedides had replied, but only to say that, as Stercus had done such a fine job in the north up to this time, who better to continue to oversee the growth of the Aquilonian settlements there? Count Stercus would not soon see civilization again.

For a little while longer, his sport with Ugaine sufficed to amuse him, to distract him. But the Cimmerian girl was not exactly what he wanted, and for Stercus anything that was not exactly what he wanted soon became something he wanted not at all. When he tired of Ugaine, he sent her back to her home village, though she protested he did her no favors by returning her.

In that, she was mistaken. Fortunately for her, she did not know and never learned how mistaken she was. There were reasons, good reasons, why Stercus had been sent beyond the Aquilonian frontier, why he was unlikely ever to be welcome in Tarantia or even some provincial town of Aquilonia ever again. It was not least because he still so vividly recalled the reasons for his exile that the nobleman had sent Ugaine to Rosinish instead of adding further to his remarkable reputation. Then, too, the girl was already too old to be altogether satisfying or satisfactory.

After he banished her from Venarium, he spent some little while brooding: even if she was not exactly what he had had in mind, had she not come close enough? By the time he began to wonder, it was too late for such worries anyhow, since he had already sent her away. And, in any case, he decided he had been right all along. He wanted what he wanted, no less. Some imperfect substitute simply was not good enough.

Having sent Ugaine back to barbarism, Stercus tried throwing himself into the administration of the lands his soldiers had seized from the Cimmerians. For a few weeks, a stream of directives flew from his pen to the garrison commanders in the conquered territory and to the leaders of the colonists. Then that burst of activity also slackened. The colonists were busy turning their new farms and settlements into going concerns. The officers knew enough to keep their men alert and well fed and healthy without Stercus' telling them to do so. Some of them sent back letters saying as much in very blunt terms.

Count Stercus was no trained, professional soldier, though like any Aquilonian noble he was expected to know enough of the military art to help defend the kingdom in case of invasion. Trained or not, however, he was King Numedides' chosen commander in this gods-forsaken part of the world, however little that delighted him. If he chose to ride forth on an inspection tour to investigate whether the garrison commanders were doing all they said they were to keep the countryside safe, who could gainsay him? No one.

And if, on that tour, he chose to inspect and investigate certain other matters, certain more personal matters—again, who could gainsay him? Again, no one. No one at all.

Granth son of Biemur was taking his turn at sentry-go at the Aquilonian encampment outside of Duthil. Everything there was quiet, which suited him down to the ground. If the barbarians got used to the idea that they had been beaten, they were less likely to shoot a man from ambush or sneak up behind him and slit his throat.

Also, the weather was such that Granth found standing sentry no hardship, as he had during the long, hard winter. The sunshine that poured down on him was watery, but it was sunshine nonetheless: here in Cimmeria, something to be cherished. He tilted his helm back on his head to bask in it as best he could.

"You think you'll be handsome when you're tan?" said Vulth. "I'm here to tell you, forget about that. You'll just be ugly and tan."

Granth glowered at his cousin. "You mean, like you?"

After that, it was Vulth's turn to scowl. The two Bossonian bowmen with whom they shared the watch snickered. Benno said, "We haven't fought the Cimmerians for a while, so you two want to have a go at each other."

Before Granth could come up with something suitably crushing—with luck, something that insulted both Benno and Vulth, and maybe Daverio as well—the sound of hoofbeats distracted him. A horseman emerged from the woods to the south and trotted toward the encampment. The horse was a big Aquilonian destrier, not one of the shaggy local ponies that often seemed too small for their big-boned Cimmerian riders.

Eyeing the charger made him slow to give heed to the man aboard it. When he did, he frantically stiffened to attention. "Heads up, you dogs!" he hissed to his cousin and the Bossonians. "That's Count Stercus, or I'm a black Kushite!"

Vulth and the bowmen almost did themselves an injury by straightening up while at the same time pretending they had never slouched. Count Stercus' pale, nearly handsome face was unreadable as he reined in. But he did not call the pikemen and archers to account. Instead, pointing toward the Cimmerian village ahead, he asked, "That is the place called Duthil, is it not so?"

Vulth was the senior sentry. "Yes, your Grace, it is," he replied, looking as if he wished someone else could speak for him.

That Stercus' eyes were set too close together only made his stare the more piercing. Granth felt glad all the way down to his boots that that stare was not aimed at him. Vulth had done nothing wrong, and had spoken with all respect due Stercus' rank. Even so, Stercus seemed to be sharpening knives for Granth's cousin in his mind.

Yet the Aquilonian nobleman's words were mild enough: "Be so good as to let your commander know I am riding into that village. I aim to know in full the lands we have taken for King Numedides, and everyone in them." The way he said "everyone" made Granth want to hide. Stercus continued, "If by some mischance I do not ride out of Duthil, avenge me in full upon the barbarians." He urged his horse forward. Saddle trappings clinking and clattering, it trotted on toward the Cimmerian village.

"Mitra!" exploded Vulth once Stercus had ridden out of earshot. "He chills the marrow in your bones."

"As long as he chills the Cimmerians worse," said Granth.

"Ah, no." Daverio slyly shook his head. "He wants to warm the Cimmerians up. Or do you forget the native wench he had for himself down at Fort Venarium?"

"I remember her," said Granth. "She was no wench, only a chit of a girl. And he did not let her wear enough in the way of clothes to stay warm."

The Bossonian shook his head again and laughed. "Are you really so young and innocent? There is warm, and then there is warm." He stuck his elbow in Granth's ribs and leered. "You know what I mean, eh?"

"I know what you mean," growled Granth. "And I know if you poke me again, I'll wrap your damned bowstring around your neck."

"I'm not afraid," said Daverio, bristling.

"Enough, both of you," said Vulth. "You don't want to quarrel while Stercus is around. If he catches you at it, he'll string you up by the thumbs and roast you over a slow fire— and that's if he doesn't decide to do something really juicy instead."

Granth watched the Aquilonian commander ride into Duthil. He breathed a sigh of relief when the first Cimmerian huts hid Count Stercus from view. If he could not see Stercus, Stercus could not see him, either. He wished the commander were back in Fort Venarium, but simply having him out of sight would do for now.

Conan ran like the wind after the ball, his mane of coal-black hair streaming out behind him. The ball was stuffed with rags and covered with scraps of old leather begged or stolen from here and there and then erratically stitched together by the boys of Duthil. If they wanted to play games, they had to make their own arrangements. They had to—and they did.

Another lad kicked the ball up the street just before Conan got to it. Conan lowered his shoulder and knocked the other boy sprawling in the mud. The boy was on his feet and running again a heartbeat later. If he could pay Conan back, he would. Conan's clothes were already muddy, but not so muddy as those of the other boys in the game. With his size and strength and speed, it usually took at least two of them to knock him down.

He effortlessly outsped the boy he had flattened. Girls and women and a few men stood in doorways, watching the sport. Sometimes the men would rush into the game, too. Then it would get very rough. Conan waved to Tarla as he sprinted past Balarg's house. He thought she waved back—oh, how he hoped she waved back—but she blurred past before he could be sure.

Two boys between him and the ball. Instead of going after it himself, the closer boy tried to block Conan. Conan might have feinted one way and dodged the other. He might simply have slipped past. Instead, without breaking stride, he smashed into the other boy chest to chest. With a startled yelp of dismay, his foe went flying. Conan ran on.

"Oh, nicely done!" called someone from behind him. Was that Tarla's voice? He thought so. He hoped so. But he did not look back. Instead, he ran harder than ever.

He bore down on the ball with such ferocity that the last boy who was nearer to it dove out of the way to keep from being trampled. Conan guided the ball forward with the side of his foot. One more boy stood between him and the goal, which was no more than the space between two rocks plopped down in the mud of the street. The boy set himself, but his face said he had no hope of stopping the hurtling missile that would momentarily fly his way.

And yet the goal was never scored. In the same instant as Conan drew back his foot for the last kick, a rider on horseback trotted into Duthil: a rider on a horse so astonishing, the blacksmith's son skidded to a stop and simply stared, all but unable to believe his eyes.

Horses in Cimmeria were few and far between. This great snorting monster was almost man-high at the shoulder, which put its rider high as a god above the ground. That rider stared down at Conan from an elevation even his tall father had been unable to match since the boy was much younger.

The Aquilonian horseman had a long, pale, big-nosed face with a receding chin partly concealed by a thin fringe of beard and with eyes set too close together. When he spoke, he startled Conan by using Cimmerian: "Get out of my way, boy."

He urged the horse forward. Conan's surprise and that huge beast bearing down on him made him jump aside. Had he not, the Aquilonian would have ridden him down. He was as sure of that as of his own name. Even so, shame at giving way brought fire to his cheeks. He hurried after the rider—the knight, Aquilonians called such armored horsemen—and spoke in the invaders' language: "Who are you? What you do here?"

Hearing Aquilonian made the man on horseback rein in. He gave Conan a second glance—gave him, in fact, what was almost a first glance, for he had paid him little heed up until then. "I am Count Stercus, commander of all the Aquilonians in Cimmeria, and I have come to see how the village of Duthil prospers under the rule of the great and good King Numedides," he answered, and paused to find out whether Conan understood. Conan did—well enough, anyhow. Seeing as much, Stercus asked, "And who are you, and how did you learn this speech?"

"Conan, son of Mordec the blacksmith." To Conan, his father's trade was at least as important as Stercus' noble blood. With a shrug, he went on, "How I learn? I hear, I listen, I talk. How you learn Cimmerian?"

A civilized man, even a civilized boy, would have known better than to challenge thus the leader of the host that had subjected his folk, but Conan was familiar with only the rude frankness of the barbarian. And his candor seemed to amuse Count Stercus, whose smile illuminated every part of his face but those dark, fathomless eyes. "How do I learn?" he echoed in Cimmerian considerably more fluent than Conan's all but grammarless Aquilonian. "I also hear and listen and speak. And I have had most excellent, most lovely, most charming teachers. You may be sure of that."

Although Conan was anything but sure of precisely what Stercus meant, he did get the feeling hidden meanings lurked in the Aquilonian's words. That in itself was plenty to rouse his easily kindled temper: why could the man not come straight out and say whatever was in his mind? Roughly, Conan asked, "When are you people going to leave Cimmeria? This not your country."

Again, that was forthrightness no civilized man would have shown. Again, it but amused Stercus, who threw back his head and laughed uproariously. "Leave, boy? We shall never leave. I told you, this is King Numedides' land now."

He rode down the street; his horse's hooves, almost as big as dinner plates, clopped and squelched through the mud.

Conan spied a fist-sized stone near a house. He could take it and hurl it and perhaps lay even an armored man low with it—but what if he did? The soldiers in the encampment outside of Duthil would wreak a fearful vengeance, and his own people lacked the warriors to hope to withstand them. Hate smoldering in his heart, Conan followed Stercus.

The Aquilonian continued along the street at a slow walk, an expression of disdain on his face. None of the other boys who had been kicking the ball dared impede him, even for a moment. Conan stayed close to Stercus until the knight reined in once more, in front of the home of Balarg the weaver.

He bowed in the saddle there, something Conan had not only never seen but never imagined. "Hello, my pretty," he murmured in Cimmerian suddenly sweet as honey. "What is your name?"

"Tarla," answered the girl still standing in the doorway. She stared at the horse, too, and stared even more at the man atop it.

"Tarla," repeated Count Stercus. In his mouth, it might have been a caress. "What a lovely name."

Conan discovered he had only thought he hated the Aquilonian nobleman. Now, with jealousy tearing at him like acid venom, he would gladly have stuffed Stercus into his father's forge and worked the bellows for a hotter fire with a will he had never shown while helping Mordec to forge a sword or an andiron.

Tarla murmured in confusion and what was obviously pleasure. No one in the rude village of Duthil had ever paid her such a compliment before. Conan knew too well he had not, and wondered why. The answer was not hard to find: he had no more imagined such candied words than he had a bow from horseback. What the folk who had it called civilization knew wiles subtler and more clinging and perhaps more deadly than a spider's web.

With another seated bow, Stercus continued, "I had not

looked for so fair a flower in these parts, even in springtime. I must come back again soon, to see how you bloom."

Tarla murmured again, in even more confusion. Stercus urged his horse forward. As he rode on through Duthil, he turned and waved to the weaver's daughter. Tarla started to raise her hand to return the gesture. A panther might have sunk its fangs into Conan's vitals. Tarla let her hand fall without completing the gesture, but that she had so much as begun it was a lash of scorpions to the blacksmith's son. He watched Stercus leave the village. That the Aquilonian commander failed to fall over dead proved beyond any possible doubt that looks do not, cannot, kill.

One of the slightly younger boys, to whom the byplay between Stercus and Tarla had meant nothing, kicked the ball again. It spun straight past Conan, but he heeded it not. With Stercus gone, his gaze had returned to Tarla's. He had had his share—perhaps more than his share—of a youth's half-formed longings for a maid, and had dared hope Tarla harbored half-formed longings for him as well. But Count Stercus had crashed in upon his dreams like a stone crashing into an earthenware jug. Stercus' longings were anything but half-formed; the Aquilonian knew exactly what he wanted—and, very plainly, how to go about getting it.

"That is a foreign dog," snarled Conan.

Had Tarla been truly ensnared by Stercus, that outburst against him would have cost Conan the game on the spot. As things were, she shook herself like someone coming out of deep water. She nodded, but said, "No doubt he is. Still, he speaks very gently, doesn't he?"

Conan had no answer to that, or none that would not have involved the vilest curses he knew. From across the street, though, a gray-haired woman called, "Why should he speak a young girl so fair, with him a man full grown?"

Another woman said, "You know why as well as I do, Gruoch." They both cackled—there was no other word for it.

The shrill sound filled Conan with almost as much horror as Count Stercus' irruption into Duthil had done. Tarla's cheeks went red as ripe apples. That horrified Conan, too. The weaver's daughter drew back into her house, closing the door behind her. Her embarrassment only made the women cackle more. Conan had not fled from serpent or wolves or Aquilonian knight. The women of his own village were another matter. They went on laughing and clucking, hardly noticing his retreat.

His father was sharpening a knifeblade against the grinding wheel when Conan came into the smithy. Sparks flew from the edge of the blade. Without looking away from what he was doing, Mordec said, "I'm glad you're back, son. We've got some firewood behind the house that needs chopping."

Firewood was the furthest thing from Conan's mind. "We have to slay all the damned Aquilonians who've come into our land!" he burst out.

"I expect we'll do our best one of these days." Now Mordec did lift the blade away from the grinding wheel. He also stopped pumping the foot pedal, so the wheel groaned to a stop. Eyeing Conan, he asked, "And what has set you to eating raw meat and breathing fire like a dragon from out of the trackless north?"

"Didn't you see him, Father?" demanded Conan in angry amazement. "Didn't you see that cursed Count Stercus ride past our doorway?"

Mordec's gaze narrowed and sharpened. "I saw an Aquilonian knight go by, yes. Do you mean to tell me that was their commander?"

Conan nodded. "I do. It was."

His father scowled. "I hope you did not make him notice you. Remember, even the Aquilonian captain at the camp nearby warned us against this man."

"He knows I speak a little of his language. Past that, no," said Conan.

"I do not suppose that will put you in any particular danger," said Mordec. "A few of use have learned some Aquilonian, and some of the invaders can speak a bit of Cimmerian now."

"This Stercus does—more than a bit, in fact. He knows it well," said Conan.

"I am not sure this is good news," said his father. "Those people commonly use our tongue when they want to take something from us."

"He spoke—" The words did not want to come after that, but Conan forced them out one by one: "He spoke to the weaver's daughter." He did not wish to name Tarla. If he did not, he would not need to admit, either to himself or to his father, that he cared more about her than he might have about some other girl in Duthil.

"Did he, by Crom?" said his father, and his scowl got deeper. By the way he looked at Conan, what the boy felt was no secret to him. After a moment, Mordec went on, "If Stercus spoke to Tarla, I am going to have to speak to Balarg. That man has made a name for debauching young girls— though despite what Captain Treviranus said I did not think his gaze would light on one so young as she. But who can know? Once a man goes into the swamp, is he not likely to mire himself ever deeper?"

Conan did not follow all of that. He had only the vaguest notion of what debauching meant. All he knew was that he had not liked the way the Aquilonian looked at Tarla, and had liked the way Stercus spoke to her even less. He said, "Do you think Balarg will make her stay away from him?"

"I hope so," answered Mordec. "I would, were she my daughter. Still, Balarg is a free man—or as free a man as any of us can be, living under Numedides' yoke. He must choose for himself. To choose well, he must know the truth." He looked down at the knife blade he had laid on the frame of the wheel. It still needed more work. Even so, shrugging, he went down the street toward the weaver's house.

He came back in less than half an hour. To Conan, the wait had seemed like an eternity. "Well?" asked the boy eagerly.

"He says he will do what he can," answered Mordec. "I do not know just what this means. I do not think Balarg knows, either. He cannot keep Tarla inside his house all day and all night. She was work to do, like anyone else in Duthil."

Had Conan had his way, he would have had Balarg wrap Tarla in a blanket and stick her in a storeroom so Stercus' eye could never fall on her again. Or would he? If she were hidden away like that, his own eye could never fall on her again, either. In murky, misty Cimmeria, he spied the sun seldom enough as things were. Losing sight of Tarla would be like having it torn from the sky.

Mordec set a large, hard hand on his shoulder. "We may be fretting over nothing," the blacksmith said. "Tomorrow, Stercus may find another girl in a different village, or even some Aquilonian wench, and trouble us no more."

"If he troubles Tarla, I will kill him myself," said Conan fiercely.

"If he troubles Tarla, every man in the village will want to kill him," said Mordec. "If you see clearly he has come for that—strike quick, or someone else will snatch the prize from you."

"If he comes for that," said Conan, "he is mine."

Whenever Conan went into the woods to hunt these days, whenever he loosed an arrow, he imagined he was aiming at Count Stercus' neatly bearded face. Imagining the shaft going home in the narrow space between the Aquilonian's dark eyes made him send it with special care.

Songbirds twittered on the branches of firs and pines and spruces. Here and there in the forest, Conan had smeared birdlime on some of those branches. He hoped for grouse, but would take whatever he caught. Food was food; he approached hunting with a barbarian's complete pragmatism and lack of sentimentality.

He had not called on Melcer's farm since Stercus rode through Duthil. He did not care to admit, even to himself, that he had formed something of a liking for the Gunderman; the mere idea of liking any of the invaders was abhorrent to him. But it took Stercus' visit to the village to remind him that there could be, there should be, no meeting between those who had come into Cimmeria and those who rightfully belonged here. In his own country, Melcer would have been a good enough fellow. In Conan's country, what was he but a marauder and a thief?

Conan was gliding through the forest, not on a game track but not far from one, either, when he heard a twig snap on the track a hundred yards behind him. In an instant, he silently slipped behind the bole of a great, towering fir. He had an arrow nocked and ready to shoot. Deer were not usually so careless as to announce themselves.

A moment's listening convinced him that this was no deer. It was no Cimmerian, either; no one from Conan's people could possibly have been so inept among the trees. The blacksmith's son grinned a wide and ferocious grin. What better sport than tracking one of the Aquilonians through the forest? Actually, Conan could think of one better: tracking the Aquilonian and then slaying him. But his father had forbidden that, and no doubt wisely, for it would cost the folk of Duthil dear.

Through gaps in the trees, Conan soon saw who the blunderer was—a squat, heavyset Gunderman named Hondren. Conan's lip curled scornfully. He did not care for Hondren, and had trouble thinking of anyone who could. The soldier roared and cursed whenever he came into Duthil, and had been known to cuff boys out of his path when they did not step aside fast enough to suit him. He had not tried cuffing

Conan, but Conan had never got in his way, either. Trailing him, dogging him, would be a pleasure.

On through the woods Hondren stumbled. Of course he found nothing worth pursuing; he could hardly have spread a better warning of his presence had he gone along the trail beating a drum. Conan followed, quiet as a shadow.

For most of an hour, Conan had all he could do not to laugh out loud at Hondren's blundering. He could have shot the Gunderman a hundred different times, and Hondren would have died never knowing why, or who had slain him. He had to work hard to remember his village would suffer if anything befell this miserable lump of a man.

Hondren began cursing ever louder and more foully at his lack of luck. That his own incompetence had brought that bad fortune never seemed to have crossed his mind. Conan got bored with trailing him through the forest and began showing himself. He wondered how long Hondren would take to notice him. The Gunderman needed even longer than he had expected.

At last, though, Hondren realized he was not alone in the woods. "Who's there?" he growled. "Come out, you dog, or you'll be sorry."

Out Conan came, laughing. "You not catch anything?" he jeered in his bad Aquilonian.

"No, by Mitra, I didn't catch anything." Fury on his face, Hondren advanced on the young Cimmerian. "And now I know why, too: I had a stinking barbarian close by, scaring off the game."

Conan laughed louder than ever. "I not scare game. I follow you long time. You scare plenty all by self."

"Liar!" Hondren slapped him in the face, as he might have done with a small boy on the main street in Duthil.

But they were far from the main street in Duthil, and Conan, though a boy, was far from small. His ears rang from the blow. It did not cow him, though—far from it. Red rage

ripped through him. He struck back with all his strength, not
with a slap but with his closed fist. Hondren's head snapped
back. Blood spurted from his nose. He blinked, clearing his
senses. A slow, vicious smile spread over his face.

"You'll pay for that, swine," he said, gloating anticipation
in his voice. He flung himself at Conan and bore him to the
ground by weight and momentum.

The blacksmith's son knew at once that Hondren did not
merely seek to punish him for presuming to answer one blow
with another. The Gunderman wanted his life, and would take
it unless he lost his own. Hondren's hands, hard as horn,
sought his throat. Conan tucked his chin down against his
chest to keep his enemy from gaining the grip he wanted.

A knee to the belly made the Gunderman grunt. But Hondren was still stronger and, most of all, heavier than Conan,
who had not yet got all the inches or thews that would one
day be his. Hondren dealt out a savage buffet that made
Conan's senses spin, and his weight was a dreadful burden
that seemed as if it would crush the life from the Cimmerian
even if his foe failed to find the stranglehold he sought.

Scrabbling wildly and more than a little desperately, Conan
felt his hand close on a rock that fit it nicely. In a mad par-
oxysm of fury, he tore the stone from the ground and brought
it smashing down on the back of Hondren's head. The Gunderman's eyes opened very wide. A shudder ran through his
body; his hands lost their cunning and ferocity. With a savage
cry of triumph, Conan struck again, and then again and again,
until blood poured onto him from Hondren's torn scalp and
smashed skull, and until the man from the south stopped
moving altogether.

After making sure Hondren was dead, Conan stood a little
while in thought. If the deed were traced to him, ten from
Duthil would die. But if Hondren were to vanish in the forest—who could say for certain what had befallen him?

Decision came on the instant. Conan took hold of the Gunderman's boots and dragged his corpse to a stream that chuckled through the woods less than a hundred yards away. Before pushing the body into the stream, he went back and carefully erased every sign of its passage from the place where he and Hondren had fought to the streambank. By the time he was finished, he doubted even a Cimmerian hunter could have traced what he had done. From everything he had seen, the Aquilonians were far less woodswise than his own folk.

He stuffed stones into Hondren's breeches and tunic, to make sure the corpse did not rise once decay set in. Although he pushed it into the stream at the deepest point he could find, less than a yard of water covered it—not enough to suit him. An alert searcher might spy it, no matter how shadowed by tall trees its final resting place was. He gathered more stones, these larger and heavier, and set them on the body to weight it down and to break up its outline and make it harder to see. That done, he used moss and branches and pine needles to disguise the places from which he had taken the stones. Someone who knew the streambank well might notice something had changed; someone seeing it for the first time would spy nothing out of the ordinary.

By the time he finished his work, he was soaked from head to foot. That gave him yet another idea: he pulled his tunic off over his head and scrubbed it in the stream, cold water being best for taking bloodstains out of cloth. Having taken care of that last detail, he went on with the hunt.

Mordec looked up from his work when Conan came into the smithy carrying a brace of grouse and some songbirds. "Those will be tasty," said the blacksmith, and then he took a closer look at his son. "What happened to you? You're all wet."

"I—fell in a stream," answered Conan.

Hearing his hesitation, Mordec advanced on him, hammer

still in hand. "What happened to you?" he repeated, ominous thunder his his voice. "The truth this time, or you'll be sorry." He hefted the heavy hammer to show how sorry Conan might be.

His son did not flinch from the weapon. Looking Mordec in the eye, he said, "I killed a man in the woods."

"Crom!" exclaimed Mordec; whatever response he had expected, that was not it. Gathering himself, he asked, "Was he a man of this village, or a stranger from some other place? Will the blood feud take in our family alone, or all of Duthil?"

"He was an Aquilonian," said Conan: "that brute called Hondren."

"Crom!" repeated Mordec; surprises were coming too fast to suit him. He knew the man his son meant, and knew he was indeed a brute. But he also knew of the warning the invaders had laid down. If one of their men was murdered, ten Cimmerians were to escort his spirit out of the world. "Tell me what passed. Tell me all of it. Leave out nothing— nothing, do you hear?"

"Aye, Father." Conan did: a bald, straightforward account. He finished, "The lich is hidden as well as I could hide it. In the forest, the Aquilonians are all fumblefingered fools. I do not think they will come across it. They will decide he had a mishap in the woods—and so he did." Savage pride filled his voice.

Without hesitation, Mordec knocked him down. When he got up, the blacksmith flattened him again. Afterwards, Mordec helped him to his feet. "That was to remind you the Aquilonians will decide Hondren had a mishap in the woods—if you do not brag of what you did. It is a brave and bold thing, a boy beating a warrior trained. But it is your life and nine more if you ever breathe a word of it. Silence, or you die! This is no game. Do you understand?"

"I do, Father." Conan shook his head to clear it; Mordec

had not held back with either blow. "You have a hard hand with your lessons."

"And you have a thick skull to drive them through," said the blacksmith with rough affection. "I have to make sure they get home."

"I'll keep quiet," said Conan. "I know what I did. I don't have to shout it in the street—I'm not Balarg."

Mordec threw back his head and laughed. That was his opinion of the weaver, too, although Balarg, no doubt, also had a low opinion of him. Their rivalry did not keep them from working together when they had to. Since the coming of the Aquilonians, they had to ever more often.

But laughter quickly faded. Setting a hand on his son's shoulder, Mordec said, "You did well, son, as well as you could once he attacked you. Now we hope all the invaders are as woodsblind as you say. I think they may be." Even saying that, though, he wished Crom were the sort of god who hearkened to his worshipers' prayers.

chapter vii

The Weaver's Daughter

When the Aquilonian army advanced into Cimmeria, it had come through the woods. It had had to; without coming through the woods, it could not have penetrated the country. But pioneers with axes had widened the forest tracks so good-sized columns of men could advance along them, and all of the Gundermen and Bossonians could see one another and draw strength from seeing one another.

Now Granth son of Biemur picked his way along a game trail hardly wider than the spread of his shoulders. He clutched his pike with both hands, ready to impale anything that burst out from among the trees. Behind him tramped his cousin Vulth, who hung on to his pike just as tight. And behind them strode Benno the Bossonian, an arrow nocked in his bow. As far as Granth knew, no other Aquilonians were within a mile or two of his comrades and him.

"Hondren!" he called. "Hondren! You out there? You hear me?" In lower tones, he muttered, "If we do find the stinking dog, we ought to beat his brains in for making us go through this nonsense."

"What makes you think he's got any brains to beat in?"

asked Vulth. He too raised his voice: "Hondren! Where are you, you mangy hound?"

Benno spat. "Who cares if we find him or not? I can't stand that bad-tempered bastard, and I don't know anybody who can."

Granth wished the archer had not said that. He did not like Hondren, either, and also knew not a single man who did. Hondren was nothing but trouble for everyone around him. That had been true in the Aquilonian encampment next to Duthil. From things Granth had heard and others he had seen, it had been true in Duthil itself. And it was certainly true now that Hondren had gone missing in the woods.

"We're not looking for him for his sake—Mitra knows that's true," said Vulth. "We're trying to find out what the devil happened to him. If the Cimmerians knocked him over the head, they've got to pay for it or they'll think we're soft."

That only made Benno spit again. "If it were up to me, I would have paid them to get rid of him."

"He was a good man in a fight," said Granth: as much praise as Hondren was ever likely to get now. He had been missing for three days. None of the search parties had found any trace of him.

"He did like fights," agreed Vulth, but that was not the compliment it might have been, for he went on, "He liked them so well, he'd start them himself."

"If he started one out here, he didn't win it," said Benno. "Something's gnawing the meat off his bones right now." Somber satisfaction filled his voice.

"Something or somebody," said Vulth. "I wouldn't put it past these barbarians to eat man's-flesh."

"Anybody who ate Hondren would sick him up afterwards." Benno made horribly real-sounding retching noises.

After another hour's trudge through the dark, gloomy forest, Granth stopped caring what had happened to Hondren. All he cared about was making sure the same thing, whatever it had been, did not happen to him. He said, "We'll never prove the Cimmerians did him in."

"Maybe we'll kill ten of them anyway, just for the sport of it," said Benno. "We ought to start with the cursed smith in that village. You know the fellow I mean? Big, ugly bruiser, and his eyes measure you for a coffin every time you walk past his doorway. I wouldn't be surprised if he was the one who knocked Hondren over the head."

"He doesn't hunt much himself," said Granth. "He usually sticks close to the forge and sends his son out instead."

"Maybe the boy did for Hondren," suggested Vulth. "That lad will be bigger than the blacksmith when he's done."

"He's not small now," said Granth.

"His beard hasn't even begun to sprout," said Benno with a scornful laugh. "If he put paid to Hondren, to hell with me if Hondren didn't deserve to die." That was cruel, but not too far from what Granth was also thinking.

A goldfinch fluttered across the game trail, a bright splash of color against the endless dark greens of the Cimmerian forest: warm brown back, black and white head, crimson face, and broad yellow chevrons on black wings. Three or four others danced through the air behind it, calling sweetly. Then they were gone, and shadows and silence ruled once more.

No, not quite silence, for a stream murmured and splashed just on the edge of hearing. Granth cocked his head to one side, to gauge the direction. "Shall we go over there?" he asked, pointing. "My water bottle is about empty."

"Well, have a swig from mine." Vulth took it off his belt and held it out to Granth. "I don't want to waste any time with side trips, and Hondren won't be in that stream unless he went and drowned himself."

"He wouldn't do anything like that," said Benno. "Too many people would thank him if he did."

Granth raised his cousin's water bottle to his lips, tilted back his head, and drank. Sweet, strong Poitanian wine ran down his throat. He took a long pull, then gave the bottle back to Vulth, saying, "I made a good trade, for my bottle held nothing but water."

"Wine is sovereign against a flux of the bowels," said Vulth solemnly.

"No doubt," said Benno. "It also goes down smoother than water."

Laughing, the three Aquilonians went on down the track. Not a bowshot away, the stream chuckled to itself. Whatever secrets it held, secret they would stay.

Conan knew the invaders were beating the woods for their missing fellow. He saw search parties going into the forest every morning. He slipped in amongst the tall trees himself more than once, shadowing the Gundermen and Bossonians as he had shadowed Hondren. Here, though, he remained but a shadow. Had he revealed himself to the blundering Aquilonians, they might have wondered if he had done the same to their missing soldier.

He wanted to brag about what he had done. He wanted to clamber up on his rooftop and shout out the news to all of Duthil—no, to all of Cimmeria. Making himself keep silent might have been harder than slaying Hondren. But the thought of what the invaders would do to his village—and, even more, the thought of what his father would do to him— held his lips sealed.

Mordec noticed how much trouble he had keeping quiet. After a few days, Conan's father asked, "How would you like to go and spend some time with Nectan, boy? If you're helping him watch his sheep, you'll be keeping your secret from only one man, not from the whole village. Maybe that will be easier for you."

"All right, Father. I'll go," said Conan, who was always eager to give the shepherd a hand. Then he hesitated. "Will

Mother be all right with just you here to take care of her?"

"I was taking care of your mother before you were born, you know," said Mordec. "I'll go on doing it as long as we both live. Don't you worry about that. I know she snaps at me. Don't you worry about that, either. It's her way; she's short-tempered because of her sickness. But we understand each other well enough."

Reassured, Conan threw a loaf of brown bread and some smoked mutton into a leather sack and hurried out to the meadows to join Nectan. The shepherd seemed not at all surprised to see him. Only later did he wonder if his father had come this way before speaking to him.

"Good to have an extra pair of hands and an extra set of eyes with me," said Nectan. "It's lambing time now, and I don't deny I can use you here."

He did not set Conan to helping him help the ewes who had trouble giving birth. Conan had no idea how much good Nectan's ministrations did the ewes. As always, the blacksmith's son marveled at how quickly the newborn lambs could start gamboling across the grass after their mothers — and how quickly they could go gamboling off straight into trouble.

He pulled them out of a creek that ran through the hilly meadow. He watched some of them tumble down the hillsides and then get up again, apparently unharmed. And he watched one tumble down a hillside and then not get up, for it had broken a hind leg. Nectan stooped beside that one and cut its throat, and he and Conan ate roast lamb that night.

"Happens every year," said the shepherd as he cooked a chunk of meat over the campfire. "Seems a shame, but it can't be helped. Hand me a few of those mint leaves, will you?" Eaten along with the lamb, they made the savory meat taste even sweeter.

Lambing season also brought wolves and eagles down on the flock, for they found newborn lamb every bit as savory as did Nectan and Conan. The shepherd and the blacksmith's son drove them off with showers of stones. Conan knocked down one great hawk on the wing. He thought he had killed it, but it fought its way into the air once more and flew off, screeching in pain and fear.

"Bravely done," said Nectan. "The way you throw, I'd not want to get in the way of a stone from your hand."

"I wanted it dead." Defeating a foe did not satisfy Conan; he craved nothing less than his enemies' utter destruction.

Nectan only shrugged. "I wouldn't want to kill off all the eagles. They're rare bold birds. Wolves, now—if your stones could smash in the skull of every cursed wolf ever born, I'd not shed a tear. Only reason the wolves go after lambs instead of me is that I put up a tougher fight—and I daresay the lambs are tastier, too." He chuckled.

Despite all they could do, the shepherd and his helper lost some lambs. Without Conan's help, the shepherd would surely have lost many more. Conan did shoot one wolf through the heart as it was about to leap on a lamb. Nectan skinned the beast and presented him with the hide.

"You keep it. I have others," said Conan, remembering his fight for life with the pack of wolves in the snow.

But Nectan would not hear of it. "A wolfskin for me?" He laughed at the very idea. "By Crom, the sheep would love me for that, wouldn't they, if I draped it round my shoulders for a rain cape? They'd flee me fast as they could run. If anyone is to get any use from it, that had best be you."

Seeing the shepherd's stubbornness, Conan could only nod. "I thank you," he said. "If you have a need, come to the smithy. My father or I will do your work for you."

"I don't use much in the way of ironmongery, though I thank you for your kindness," said Nectan. "Arrowheads now and again, for I will lose shafts, same as any other archer. If I'm out here and can't come into Duthil, I'll chip the heads out of flint. I'm not so good as the cursed Picts, who do it all the time, but I manage."

"Picts," muttered Conan, and he scowled ferociously. In Cimmeria, the Aquilonians were enemies because they were neighbors and, at the moment, because they were invaders. Enmity between Picts and Cimmerians, though, was in the blood of both folk, and went back to the days when lost Atlantis still rose above the waves. As long as Cimmerians and Picts both survived, that enmity would also endure.

"I didn't say I loved 'em, boy, for I don't," responded Nectan. "But they do know how to chip stone. And they had better, for in working metal they may as well be so many helpless babes."

When Conan thought of Picts, he thought of killing Picts. No Cimmerian could think of Picts any other way. And when he thought of killing Picts, he thought less of the Gunderman he had actually slain. Little by little, as time went by, he grew less likely to brag about what he had done. The unending vigilance a herdsman needed also played its part in that: he was too busy to dwell excessively on what he had done.

His father let him stay with Nectan almost a month. By the time Mordec came out to reclaim him, he had for all practical purposes become a shepherd himself. "Do I have to go back to Duthil?" he asked. The prospect of dealing with people rather than sheep seemed distinctly unattractive.

"I was beginning to hope you would let me keep him, Mordec," added Nectan. "He's as good here as anyone could hope to be."

"Glad to hear it," said Mordec. "But I have need of him, too, and so does the smithy." He nodded to Conan. "Come along, son."

His tone and his looming physical presence brooked no argument. However regretfully, Conan turned away from Nectan. "Aye, Father." He did not look back toward the shepherd until he and Mordec were at the edge of the meadow and about to plunge into the dominant Cimmerian forest.

Then he waved once. Nectan waved back just as Conan and Mordec plunged in amongst the trees.

They walked on for a while, their footfalls almost silent on the pine needles carpeting the forest floor. A red fox ran across the game trail they were using. The fox stared in astonishment; the breeze blew from it toward them, so it had not taken their scent, and not even its keen ears let it know they were near. With a flirt of its brush, it vanished behind a fir. Conan had started to nock an arrow. Without a target, he slid the shaft back into its quiver.

High overhead, a hawk screeched shrilly. Again, Conan reached for an arrow. Again, he left the motion incomplete. Nodding, Mordec said, "If it's after a lamb, it's Nectan's worry now."

"Soon the lambs will be too big for any bird to carry off," said Conan. "But the wolves are a different story. They will steal from the flock at any season of the year." He carried on his back the roughly tanned hide of the wolf he had killed. "Miserable, thieving creatures."

"They might as well be men," remarked his father. After another minute or so, Mordec asked, "You liked it there, then?"

"I did, Father," said Conan, with an enthusiastic nod of his own. "Things are—simpler than they are in Duthil."

"No doubt." Mordec walked on once more before continuing. "Things in the village are less simple than when you left, too."

"Oh?" Conan did not care for the way his father said that. "What's gone on? And how is Mother?"

"Your mother is about the same as she always is," answered Mordec. "She is not well—I do not think she will ever be well—but she is no worse, or not much worse, than she was when you saw her last."

"All right," said Conan. His mother had been sickly for as long as he could remember. He always hoped she would get well, but he would have been amazed—so amazed, he might not have known what to do—if she actually had. He asked, "What about the village, then?"

"Ah. The village." Mordec did not seem eager to talk about it. At last, unwillingly, he said, "Well, Count Stercus has come back again."

"He has?" cried Conan. He grabbed for an arrow once more, though the gesture was even more useless than it had been with the fox or the hawk. "What is he doing there? Why won't he leave us alone?"

"Well, he said he came because of the Aquilonian soldier who disappeared near Duthil," answered Mordec. "The first time he said that, I feared he was going to punish us even if his men never found the fellow's body. But I think that just gave him the excuse he needed to come back anyhow."

"The excuse?" echoed Conan, his voice rising in puzzlement. But then a sudden, horrid certainty blazed in him, fueling fury fierce as his father's forge. "Tarla!" he burst out.

"It seems so, yes," said Mordec unhappily. "He sniffs around her, sniffs around Balarg's house like a hungry hound after meat."

"I'll kill him!" raged Conan. "I'll cut his heart out and feed it to swine. I'll drape his guts over the roofpole. I'll—"

His father shook him, hard. Conan's teeth clicked together on his tongue. Pain lanced through him. He tasted blood in his mouth. When he spat, he spat red. He said no more. Seeing that he was going to say no more, Mordec nodded in somber approval. "Good," said the blacksmith. "Maybe I've shaken some sense into you. Can you imagine what would happen to Duthil if you were mad enough to murder the Aquilonian commander? Can you?"

"He deserves death," said Conan sullenly.

"Yes, no doubt," said Mordec. "I told you once you might kill him if he aims to debauch Balarg's daughter the way he did that other Cimmerian girl. But think on it. Wouldn't you say it's truly Balarg's first duty to defend her honor?"

"I—" Conan broke off in confusion.

Laughing, Mordec finished for him: "You like the shape of Tarla's nose and her pretty little ankles, and so you think you can do what her father really should."

Conan walked on for a long time without saying another word. His cheeks and ears felt as if they were on fire. Like most boys first setting eyes on a girl they fancied, he had been too shy, too much afraid of making a fool of himself, to say much to the one who was the object of his affection. Like most boys, also, he had fondly believed his grand passion went unobserved by those around him. Finding himself so badly mistaken could be nothing less than mortifying.

"Don't fret, lad," said Mordec, not unkindly. "Maybe there will be a match between the two of you, and maybe there won't. It could happen. Seeing where Balarg and I stand in the village, joining our two houses might prove wise. We've even spoken of it, once or twice. But I will tell you this: whether the match comes or not, the world will go on. Do you understand me?" Still not trusting himself to speak, Conan grudged a nod. His father went on, "And I will tell you one thing more, no matter how little you care to hear it—no one dies of a broken heart, even if people often wish they could. Do you understand that?"

Since Conan was convinced his father was raving like a lunatic, he could not very well nod again. Yet to shake his head would have been to deny the plain import of his father's words. With both choices bad, he walked on, pretending he had not heard. Mordec's rumbling chuckle said the pretense was imperfectly convincing. Conan flushed once more.

They walked into Duthil side by side, Conan matching his father's long, tireless strides. Villagers and two or three soldiers from the camp not far away were on the main street. Conan, who had had no company save Nectan and a flock for the past month, stared in wonder at so many people all together.

A ball came rolling his way. Before he could do anything about it, his father leaped forward, kicked it with all his might, and sent it flying far down the street. The usual shouting pack of boys chased after it. "I *liked* that," said Mordec, more cheerfully than Conan was used to hearing him speak. "When you grow up, you don't get the chance for such things so often, and that's a cursed shame." He pointed to the boys. "Do you want to get into the game? Do it while you can."

But Conan shook his head. After a month tending sheep, kicking a ball seemed a childish pursuit. He had been playing games all his life. If his father enjoyed them so much, he was welcome to them.

And then Conan forgot Mordec, forgot the ball, forgot everything around him, for up the street toward him came Tarla, a brass-bound wooden water bucket on her hip. He hurried toward her. "Are you all right?" he demanded.

Though she had no more years then he, she knew what to do with them. Her cool gray eyes measured him with womanly precision. Her gaze made him realize how seldom he had washed, how seldom he had run a bone comb through his hair, in all the time he had spent with Nectan. The shepherd cared nothing for such fripperies, and Conan had cared for them no more. Now, too late, he did. He stared down at the mud under his boots.

"Of course I'm all right," answered Tarla. In Conan's ears, her voice might have been the chiming of silver bells, even though she continued, "Why wouldn't I be?"

"Why? Because of that—that blackguard Stercus." Conan had learned some fine new curses from Nectan, and wanted to tar the Aquilonian nobleman's name with all of them. Somehow, though, he did not think that would improve his standing with Balarg's daughter, and so he swallowed most of what he might have said.

Tarla tossed her pretty head. Sable curls flew. "Oh, he's not so bad," she said, and sniffed. "At least he bathes now and again."

Even a few weeks earlier, that sally would have sent Conan off in headlong retreat. As much as anything else, what made him stand his ground was the loathing he felt for Stercus. Once more in lieu of worse, he said, "He's nothing but a damned invader."

The weaver's daughter tossed her head again. "And what business is it of yours, Conan, who I see or what I do?"

His father had reminded him such things were Balarg's business first, and not his own. From Mordec, those were only words, words to be evaded or ignored. From Tarla, they were a thrust through the heart. Again, though, he did not flee. "What business is it of mine?" he repeated. "The business of someone who —" He broke off. He did not flee, no, but he could not go on, either.

Yet what he managed to say was enough to draw Tarla's notice in a way nothing that came before had done. She leaned forward, and had to make a hasty grab at the water bucket to keep it from slipping from its place. "Someone who what?" she asked softly.

"Someone who thinks you should have nothing to do with the stinking Aquilonian, that's what!" blurted Conan.

Tarla's gaze went hard as flint, cold as ice. "You would know more about stinking than Stercus does," she said, and pushed past the blacksmith's son, walking on toward her father's house with angry, determined steps.

Conan stared helplessly after her. He knew he had blundered. He even knew what he should have said — not that that did him any good now. He kicked at the dirt and snarled some of the things he had wanted to call Stercus, bringing the curses down on his own head instead.

"Come on, son," said Mordec. Conan started; he had almost forgotten his father. The blacksmith added, "Maybe time will mend it. That often chances."

"It's ruined," said Conan. If something was wrong now, it would stay a disaster forever. That was a law of nature, especially when one was thirteen.

"We lost the fight against the cursed Aquilonians," said his father. "Do you suppose we'll stay quiet under their heels forever? Things have a way of changing."

"What's that got to do with Tarla?" stormed Conan: there is none blinder than he who will not see. He hurried away from Mordec and stormed on to the smithy. The boys kicking the ball hastily got out of the way, wanting no part of the storm clouds that darkened his features. More than one grown man stepped aside, too; had the whole world had but a single neck, he would gladly have brought a sword down on it, and his face showed as much.

Only after he crossed the threshold did his expression soften. He hurried past the forge, back into the part of the building where his family dwelt. His mother sat up in bed, propped on cushions, knitting a vest for him or for Mordec. Conan nodded to her. "I'm home," he said.

Verina smiled. "It's so good to see you, Conan. I've missed you." Her voice seemed even weaker and more rasping than Conan remembered it.

"How do you feel?" he asked anxiously.

She shrugged. "Every day is another day. But I know I will be better, now that you are here again."

He hoped she was right, but he could not help wondering whether she was trying to reassure herself or him. "Is there anything I can get for you?" he asked.

"No, no, no." Verina waved away the question with a flutter of thin fingers. "I have everything I need, now that you are here again."

"I was doing something I needed to do," said Conan.

"So your father told me." Verina made a sour face. "I wish you wouldn't get into so much trouble."

"If I hadn't fought back, that—Aquilonian would have killed me," said Conan, not wanting to describe Hondren to his mother in any more detail than that.

Mordec came up behind Conan. "The boy is right," said the blacksmith. "He had to be strong, or he would have gone under. Life is hard. Life is cruel. All we can do is hold off death as long as we can."

Verina looked at her husband. "I know something of holding off death," she said. Mordec coughed—not the long, dreadful, racking coughs that tore at Verina, but a short one full of embarrassment. Verina went on, "And I know how hard and cruel life can be, too. Do you think I would stay in my bed day after day, year after year, if I did not?"

Although Mordec had fought the Aquilonians for as long as he could, Verina drove him off in headlong retreat. Conan stayed; she had not turned her sharp tongue on him, and seldom did. "Are you sure there's nothing I can do for you, Mother?" he asked.

"Stay safe," she answered. "Past that, nothing matters. Too many I hold dear have died on one field or another. I don't want you to fall that way."

"I won't," declared Conan. His hand folded into a formidable fist. "I'll make the other fellow fall instead." He did not doubt he spoke the truth, and wondered why his mother began to weep.

In his first full growing year on Cimmerian soil, Melcer discovered both the good and the bad about the land where he had chosen to settle. The soil itself was splendid: as rich as any in Gunderland, and here he had a farm large enough to be worth working, not the tiny fragment of a family plot that would have been his portion in the country where he was born.

The weather, on the other hand—well, the less said about the weather, the better. He thanked Mitra he had not put wheat in the ground; no variety he knew would have reached maturity in the short Cimmerian growing season. Even barley was risky; he tried not to dwell on how risky it might be. The barbarians here raised rye and oats, which ripened more quickly still. Melcer did not mind rye bread, but, as far as he was concerned, oats made better animal fodder than food for human beings.

The vegetables in the garden by the cabin flourished—until a late frost wreaked havoc upon them. Fortunately, the barley sprouted the day after that frost. Had it come up the day before, he would have lost the whole crop, and he did not have the seed grain to withstand such a catastrophe.

Evlea's belly began to bulge with their second child. This seemed a healthier place to raise children than Gunderland, perhaps because it was less crowded. He heard of many babies of Aquilonian blood being born on nearby farms, and of hardly any dying. Families were large down in the land whence he had come, but practically all of them had the sorrow of losing a young child, or more than one. Loving something as vulnerable as a baby meant casting the dice with fate, but few mothers or fathers were so cold as to refuse the challenge.

Though he had other Aquilonians for neighbors, Melcer still carried his pike wherever he went, on the farm or off it. He seldom saw a Cimmerian, and not seeing the natives suited him fine. They seemed cowed for the time being, but how long would that last? How long could it last? The barbarians were fierce and proud. Would they not seek revenge for their defeat one day? If they did, Melcer intended to be no easy meat.

He did not think all the Cimmerians lusted for his blood,

even if some of his fellow settlers seemed to take that view. The odd half friendship he had forged with the boy named Conan helped dissuade him from believing any such thing. But then the whole winter and much of the spring went by without his seeing Conan. He began to wonder whether some misfortune had befallen him.

When Conan did reappear, he came out from behind a tree at the edge of Melcer's farm with such silent grace, he might have been standing there for some little while before the Gunderman noticed him. And when Melcer did, he needed a moment to be sure the newcomer was indeed the boy he had known. Conan had added a couple of inches and at least twenty pounds, and, despite already being more than good-sized, still gave the impression of a puppy who had not yet grown into his feet.

"Hail," said Melcer, and then, cautiously, "Is there peace between us?" The pike was thrust into the ground close by, but not close enough to suit him. Conan looked devilishly quick and dangerous.

But the Cimmerian did not shake his head. "No war between us, anyhow," he said. His Aquilonian was still bad, but better than it had been the last time he visited Melcer's farm. He had plainly kept company with some of the settler's countrymen, even if he had not come here for some time. In an odd way, that made Melcer jealous. Conan went on, "No have special quarrel with you."

"No special quarrel, eh?" Melcer unobtrusively shifted closer to the pike. Now he could grab it in a hurry if he had to. "And do you have a general quarrel with me?"

"Of course." Conan seemed surprised at the question. "You are Aquilonian. You are invader. Not love you, not—" He blew Melcer a kiss to show what he did not feel about him.

You are an invader. You are an Aquilonian. Melcer wondered whether every Cimmerian stored that hatred in his heart, whether it merely awaited the opportunity to burst forth. That was a worrisome thought, for the natives still far outnumbered the settlers. It would take years of immigration—probably years of out-and-out expulsion, too—before southern Cimmeria took on a fully Aquilonian character.

And yet Conan had said, with the rude frankness of the barbarian, that he had no special quarrel here. Melcer saw no reason not to believe him, not when he so openly declared his hates. The Gunderman asked, "Where have you been? Why didn't you come here for so long?"

"In my village, and hunting," answered Conan. "And some time with Nectan the shepherd." He stood even taller and straighter than usual. "I kill wolf."

"Good for you," said Melcer, and meant it. Cimmeria had far more wolves than he had ever known in Gunderland. Their howling had kept him awake through many long winter nights, and he had lost livestock despite his best efforts to stand watch over the animals every moment. "I have killed wolves, too," he told the Cimmerian.

"A man's work," said Conan. Melcer took that in the spirit in which it was offered: as praise for him and not bragging on Conan's part about his own manhood. But then the youngster added, "I want all wolves in Cimmeria dead." He was not looking at Melcer, but he was staring south toward Venarium, the heart of Aquilonian rule in the conquered province.

When Melcer thought of wolves that went on two legs rather than four, he did not look in the direction of Venarium. Instead, barbarians such as the youngster standing before him sprang to mind. He did not think the Cimmerians would give warning by howling before they began to hunt.

And then Conan surprised him by asking, "You know Count Stercus?" He pronounced the unfamiliar name with great care, obviously not wanting to be misunderstood.

"Do I know him? By Mitra, no!" said Melcer. "But I know of him. Everyone who comes here knows of him."

So intent was Conan on his own thoughts, he did not even snarl at the idea of Aquilonian settlers coming into a land he reckoned his. He simply asked, "What do you know of him?"

"That he is the governor of this province," began Melcer, but the young Cimmerian waved impatiently: that was not the sort of thing he wanted to hear. Melcer went on, "Of the man I know not so much, and not so much of what I know is good."

Conan said something in his own language then. Melcer had learned not a word of Cimmerian, nor did he care to, but the curses bursting from the young barbarian's lips sounded fiery enough to make him wish he knew what they meant. Somewhere off behind Conan, a bird sang sweetly, offering an odd counterpoint to his impassioned oaths.

At length, the youngster had vented his spleen to the point where he could abandon his own tongue and attempt to speak in a civilized language once more: "You tell what you know."

Melcer began to obey before reflecting that Conan had not the slightest right to command him. By then, he had already said, "I hear that Stercus is a lecher of no small fame—that if he weren't a lecher, he would have been able to stay in Tarantia and wouldn't have had to command the army that came up into this country."

"A lecher." Again, Conan pronounced a word strange to him with care. "What means this?"

"He chases women—and young girls, too, by what folk say, though I know not if that be true—more than is proper for a man."

"Crom!" Conan whispered. The next moment, he was gone, as suddenly and silently as he had appeared. A bush shook for a moment, giving some small hint of the direction in which he had gone, but Melcer heard not a sound. The Gunderman shrugged broad shoulders and then went back to work; on a farm, especially a new farm, there was always plenty to do. For a little while, he wondered why a barbarian boy should care about the highest-ranking Aquilonian hereabouts. But in the unending round of labor, he forgot Conan's concerns soon afterwards.

chapter viii

The Wandering Seer

As spring passed into summer, Mordec at last began to believe the Aquilonians would not take revenge on Duthil for Hondren's disappearance, and that Conan had hidden the soldier's body well enough to foil detection. He had not thought that Captain Treviranus would seize hostages and slay them without good reason; the commander of the local garrison impressed him as a decent enough fellow within the limits of his position and situation. But Count Stercus — Count Stercus was a different story. Whenever Mordec saw the Aquilonian commander, he thought of a serpent, and serpents were all too likely to strike without warning.

And Mordec saw Stercus far more often than he wished he would. The Aquilonian nobleman kept riding into Duthil on one pretext or another. And, whenever he came into the village, he always made a point of seeing, or of trying to see, Balarg's daughter Tarla.

After three or four such visits, there could be little doubt of Stercus' intentions. Conan, in his jealous rage, had seen through them from the first. Mordec was loath to believe that his son could be right, that the Aquilonian had conceived an unhealthy passion for a girl so young. When the blacksmith could no longer escape the truth, the hatred he conceived for Stercus, though colder than Conan's, was no less savage. He wanted to crush King Numedides' governor under the sole of his boot, to wipe him off the face of the earth. And what was worst of all was that Stercus behaved so smoothly, he gave no provable cause for offense, no matter how plain he made his interest in Tarla. Worse still, she seemed as much flattered as repelled by it; Mordec wondered if she were using the Aquilonian nobleman to lacerate Conan's feelings.

He soon discovered he was far from alone in his reaction to Stercus, for the Gundermen and Bossonians of the nearby garrison loved the count hardly better than did he. Nor were they shy about saying so over a stoup of ale at the smithy.

"Oh, aye, he's a piece of work, he is," declared one of them with drunken sincerity. "Ready for aught—if it's pretty and not quite ripe."

"Why put up with such a man?" asked Mordec. "In Cimmeria, he would not last long. His first crime would be his last."

The Gunderman stared at him owlishly. "You haven't got noblemen in Cimmeria, have you?"

"Noblemen?" Mordec shook his head. "We have clan chiefs, but a man is a chief because of what he has done, not because of what his great-great-grandfather did."

"I thought so. That explains it," said the Gunderman. "We put up with bad nobles, you see, for the sake of good nobles—and there are some. If you know who's on top right from the start, you don't need to fight about it all the time. You can get on with the rest of your business."

That made more sense than Mordec wished it did. Tiny, pointless wars between clans or, even more often, within clans had plagued Cimmeria for centuries uncounted. What Cimmerian would ever admit he was any other man's inferior? Not even the edge of a sword against his throat was sure to make him say such a craven thing; he was as likely to lash out against the swordbearer, conquer or die. Mordec wondered whether the invaders from the south fully grasped the difference between their land and the one in which they now found themselves. He doubted it. Getting on with the rest of your business had never been a great worry in Cimmeria.

"Besides," added the Gunderman, "who knows what we'd get for a commander if we did knock Stercus over the head? No matter what else you say about him, he's a brave fighter. We might be stuck with some other fellow in bad odor with the King who'd run away if a hawfinch chirped at him."

"I thought you spoke of good nobles," said Mordec.

"I did, and there are," said the soldier, draining his mug. Mordec poured it full again. "I thank you," the Gunderman told him. "There are plenty of good nobles—in places like Tarantia. But you'll not see many of that sort here, by Mitra. A man comes to a place like this without a reputation or at best to try to repair one. If his is already good, he can do better."

Had he spoken with contempt, he would have infuriated Mordec. But he did not: he simply told the blacksmith how he saw the world. Mordec judged that worth knowing. He did not believe any of the Aquilonians cared to learn how the folk whose lands they had invaded looked at them. Learning such a thing would have proved instructive for the men from the south, had they attempted it.

The Gunderman heaved himself to his feet. "I'd best get back to the camp," he said. "I thank you again for your ale and for your company. You're a good Cimmerian, you are." Off he went, wobbling slightly as he walked.

He might have called Mordec a good dog in the same tone of voice. The blacksmith's great, hard hands folded into fists. "A good Cimmerian, am I?" he whispered. "One of these days, you will see how good I am."

Conan spent as much time as he could either in his father's smithy or in the forests far from Duthil. If he did not wander the now dusty, now muddy streets of the village, he ran no risk of bumping into Tarla—and he did not have to see Count Stercus coming to Balarg's house for yet another visit. Conan would cheerfully have murdered the Aquilonian noble. Fear of Stercus' armor and weapons deterred him not at all. Not even the fear of his father held him back, for he sensed Mordec would not have minded in the least seeing Stercus stretched lifeless and bleeding in the dirt. Only fear of what the invaders would do to Duthil in reprisal stayed his hand.

Every so often, while pumping the bellows or changing a quenching bath or doing such other work as his father set him, he would see Count Stercus riding past. Then he wanted nothing more than to take up Mordec's heaviest hammer and smash Stercus' skull as he had broken Hondren's. When his father let him shape simple tools, he pounded at them in a perfect passion of fury.

Escaping Duthil altogether suited him better. Then he did not have to boil with rage at spying Stercus or flinch with mortification and jealousy whenever he set eyes on the weaver's daughter. In the woods he saw no one, spoke to no one. And if he looked back on his last unfortunate conversation with Tarla and wished that conversation might have gone otherwise—if he did that out there among the pines and fragrant spruces, who but he would know?

He perched on a great gray granite boulder one noon, eating a frugal lunch of oatcakes and cheese, when a man said, "Might I share somewhat of that?"

Conan started. He had neither seen nor heard the stranger approach, a fact that should have been impossible. His hand closed round the shaft of a javelin he had plunged into the ground by the boulder. "Who are you?" he demanded roughly. "What do you want?"

"My name is mere rubbish. If you would have it, though,

it is Rhiderch." The stranger bowed. "A wandering seer, I." He bowed again. He looked the part. He was about sixty, his hair gone gray, his beard—nearly white—reaching halfway down his chest. His garments were of colorless homespun set off by a necklace and bracelets of honey-gold amber. "As for what I want, well, after far travel a bite of food is welcome."

"Share what I have, then," said Conan, and gave him some of the oatcakes and half the chunk of cheese. The old man ate with good appetite. Conan watched him for a while, then burst out, "How did you come upon me without my being the wiser? By Crom, you could have slit my throat and taken everything I had, and I would not have known you were there until too late."

Rhiderch's eyes, gray as the granite upon which Conan sat, twinkled. "I am no robber, lad. I seek what's free-given, and thank you for your kindness."

"You did not answer me. How did you come upon me unawares? I thought no wolf nor panther could do the like, let alone a man."

The seer chuckled. "There are ways, lad. Indeed there are. I know but the minor mysteries. Many others are wiser by far."

"Teach me!" said Conan.

At that, the laughter faded from Rhiderch's face. Now he had come upon something he took seriously. "Why, perhaps I shall, if it be your fate to learn such things. Give me your hand, that I may learn whether it is permitted me."

Conan held it out. Rhiderch clasped it in his own. The two hands were a study in contrasts: Conan's square and scarred and callused, with short, grimy nails on thick, strong fingers; Rhiderch's long and thin and pale and spidery, his palm narrow, his fingernails fastidiously groomed. Conan had seen palm readers before, but Rhiderch did not examine the lines on his hand. Instead, the seer closed his eyes and murmured a charm in a language whose cadences were like those of Cimmerian but which the blacksmith's son could not understand. Suddenly and without warning, Rhiderch's hand closed tight on Conan's. At the same time, the seer's eyes opened very wide. Thinking it a trial of strength, Conan squeezed back as hard as he could. He was twice as thick through the shoulders and arms as the scrawny Rhiderch. But, for all the impression his grip made on the long-bearded wanderer, he might as well not have bothered responding to what he took to be the challenge. Rhiderch's hand clenched tighter and tighter, at last with crushing force.

As abruptly as the seer had begun to squeeze, he relaxed the pressure. Sweat poured down his forehead and cheeks; a drop dangled at the end of his long, pointed nose. He swiped a sleeve across his face. "Crom!" he muttered: the ejaculation of a man shaken to the core.

"Well?" demanded Conan. "Am I fit to learn your tricks for sliding through the trees without a sound?"

"You are fit for—" Rhiderch broke off and mopped his brow again. "What you are fit for, son of Mordec, is more than I can say. Never have I seen—" He stopped once more, shaking his head. "Truly, I wonder whether I read you aright."

"How do you know my father's name?" asked Conan, for he was sure he had not spoken it.

"I know a good many things," said Rhiderch, but after a moment he shivered, though the day was mild. "One of the things I know is that yours is the strangest destiny of any ever to come into my ken."

"How so?" asked Conan, but the seer would not answer him. He tried a different question: "If you saw my destiny, did you see the Aquilonian called Stercus in it?" He did not say that Stercus commanded the Aquilonians in Cimmeria; this, from him, passed for cleverness and caution.

Rhiderch looked at him—looked through him. "Speak not

of slicing saplings when the tall tree towers. Speak not of slaying sparrows when the hawk hovers."

"I spoke of slicing nothing. I spoke of slaying no one." Conan knew some of his countrymen collaborated with the invaders. He could not fathom it, but he knew it to be true. He would not admit his lust for Stercus' gore to a man he had not met before this moment.

But what he admitted, what he denied, seemed to mean nothing to Rhiderch. "Your mouth spoke no words," said the seer. "Your spirit cried aloud—though the greater cry all but drowned the smaller."

"Will you speak sense?" asked Conan testily. "All your words go round and round, reflecting back on one another with no meaning left behind."

"If you will not hear, you shall surely see." Rhiderch remained cryptic. "Like a migrating bird, your fate flies high and far. Where you will end your days, and in what estate, I cannot say, but no Cimmerian's weird is stranger."

"Lies and foolishness. You make me sorry I fed you instead of driving you away," said Conan.

He hoped to anger Rhiderch, but the seer only smiled. "No mean feat for me, for few will ever make you sorry for anything you do."

That did it. Anger sparked in the blacksmith's son. "Get you gone," he growled. "Get you gone, or I shall not answer for what will come next." Now he reached for the javelin he always kept close at hand.

"As you say it, so shall it be." Rhiderch vanished with the same unnerving speed and silence he had used in appearing. One instant, he stood beside Conan; the next, the blacksmith's son might have been—was—alone on his boulder.

Too late, Conan remembered that he had wanted Rhiderch to teach him that trick of silent appearances and disappearances. "Come back!" he shouted. "Come back, you stinking old fraud!" But Rhiderch, however obscure he might have been, was no fraud, not in the way Conan meant it. He did not come back, nor did Conan ever ask him about it again— and if the young Cimmerian ever mastered the art of silently and unexpectedly entering or leaving a scene, as many in times to come were to find he had done, he did it by himself and on his own.

For the time being, Conan sat there muttering curses and regretting the waste of the oatcakes and cheese. They could have kept him well fed for another meal out here in the woods, which meant they could have kept him away from Duthil for another half a day, maybe longer. Away from Duthil, and especially away from Balarg's house, was where he most longed to be.

But later that day he knocked down a stag. It was perhaps the cleanest kill he had ever made: his arrow pierced the stag's heart, and the animal fell over dead after only a handful of stumbling steps. Conan wanted to roar in triumph like a great hunting cat. Only the knowledge that such a cry would surely draw scavengers, whether of the two-legged or four-legged sort, held him back.

Still, to the hunter went the rewards. Conan kindled a small, almost smokeless fire and roasted the stag's kidneys and mountain oysters and slices of its liver over the flames. Eaten with mushrooms he found nearby and washed down with pure, cold water from a chuckling brook, the repast was as fine as any he had ever enjoyed. He buried the offal and wedged the rest of the meat, wrapped in the deer's hide, in the crutch of two branches, too high up for wolves to reach. He slept nearby; also up a tree.

Waking before sunrise the next morning, he hurried back to the pine where he had secured the meat. He found wolf tracks in the soft ground by the base of the tree and claw marks in the bark on the tree trunk as high as his head. The beasts had done all they could to despoil him, but their best had not been good enough.

After starting up the fire again, he breakfasted on more liver and a chunk of the stag's heart. He wished he could keep the rest of the meat fresh longer. Since he could not, he put the remainder of the carcass on his back and started off to Duthil.

Count Stercus rode out of Fort Venarium and through the brawling streets of the little town that had come to bear the same name. Many Aquilonians took the existence of the town of Venarium to mean that civilization had come to southern Cimmeria. To Stercus' way of thinking, by contrast, the town of Venarium was proof that civilization would never come here.

He escaped the smells and the clamor of the place with a sigh of relief. Once out in the countryside, he was at least in territory honestly barbarous: Venarium wore a tawdry mask and aped its betters. He tried to imagine King Numedides or some other truly cultured man finding pleasure here on the wild frontier, tried and felt himself failing. A truly sophisticated taste would recoil in horror from what was available hereabouts.

"But even so—" murmured Stercus, and urged his horse up from a walk to a trot. Some of the raw material to be found here, though often very raw indeed, did hold a certain promise. That girl in that stinking Cimmerian village might prove very enjoyable indeed, once he broke her to his will—and breaking her would be enjoyable, too, in its way.

He wondered if he simply ought to take her back to the fortress and get on with the business of turning her into his pliant slave. Some of the barbarians had grumbled about the other girl with whom he had so amused himself, but that was not his principal reason for holding back here. Showing himself too eager had ended up disgracing him down in Tarantia; if not for that, he never would have had to come to this accursed frontier at the edge of the world. Restraint, then, might serve better—and might also be amusing.

In one way, though, Stercus showed no restraint whatever. He rode with his sword naked across his knees, ready to use at a heartbeat's notice. It would be years before Aquilonians could travel through this country without a weapon to hand. Stercus muttered to himself, wishing his officers had not persuaded him to refrain from avenging the disappearance of that Gunderman near Duthil. He remained convinced the man had not vanished all on his own. If he had, would his body—or at least his bones—not have come to light? Stercus thought so.

The road was narrow, not a great deal broader than the game track it had been before the Aquilonians first came to this miserable land. Dark, frowning firs pressed close on either side. It made ideal country for an ambush. Much of Cimmeria, in fact, made ideal country for an ambush. That was another reason why Stercus doubted whether the soldier named Hondren had gone missing all on his own. "Damned skulking barbarians," he muttered.

But the barbarian he met when he guided his horse around the next bend in the road did not skulk. The fellow strode along boldly, as if he had as much right to the roadway as any civilized man. His hair and beard had gone gray. The only ornaments he wore were a necklace and bracelets of amber.

Stercus nearly rode him down then and there. In truth, the nobleman could hardly have said what held him back. He reined in and pointed an accusing finger at the Cimmerian, saying, "Stand aside, you!" He did not bother with Cimmerian. He had no idea whether the other man knew Aquilonian, nor did he care: that pointing finger and a loud, commanding voice more than sufficed to make his meaning plain.

As it happened, the barbarian proved to understand his lan-

guage, and even to speak it himself. "Soon, soon," he said
soothingly. "First I would know something of the manner of
man you are."

"By Mitra, I will tell you what manner of man I am,"
snapped Stercus, brandishing his blade. "I am a man with
scant patience for any who would let or hinder me."

He hoped to put the barbarian in fear, but found himself
disappointed. The man came up to him and said, "But give
me your hand for a moment, and I will speak to what lies
ahead for you."

That piqued Count Stercus' interest. "A seer, are you?" he
asked, and the Cimmerian nodded. Stercus lowered the
sword, but only partway. He held out his left hand, at the
same time saying, "Come ahead, then. But I warn you, dog,
any treachery and you die the death."

"You may trust me as you would your own father," said
the barbarian, at which Stercus laughed raucously. He would
not have trusted his father with his gold, nor with his wine,
nor with any woman he chanced to meet. He thought that
meant the barbarian knew not the first thing whereof he
spoke. That the man might have known more than Stercus
guessed never once crossed his mind.

"Here," said Stercus, extending his hand farther yet in a
gesture he copied from King Numedides.

The Cimmerian took it. His own grip was warm and hard.
He nodded to himself, once, twice, three times. "You are measured," he said. "You are measured, and you are found wanting. You shall not endure. Twist as you will, turn as you will,
nothing you do shall stand. The old serpent dies. The young
wolf endures."

"Take your lies and nonsense elsewhere," snarled Stercus,
snatching his hand away. "Not even one word of truth do
you speak, and you should praise Mitra in his mercy that I
do not take your life."

"You laugh now. You jeer now," said the Cimmerian.

"Come the day, see who laughs. Come the time, see who jeers."

"Get you gone, or I will stretch your carcass lifeless in the dust," said Stercus. "I have slain stouter men for smaller insults."

"I go," said the barbarian. "I go, but I know what I am talking about. I have seen the wolf. I have counted his teeth. You are but a morsel, if you draw consolation from that."

Stercus swung up the sword with a shout of rage. The Cimmerian who called himself a seer skipped back between two tree trunks that grew too close together to let Stercus follow unless he dismounted. Not reckoning the barbarian worth his while to pursue, he rode on toward Duthil.

By the time the Aquilonian got to the village, he had all but forgotten the warning, if that was what it was, the barbarian had given him. He looked ahead, toward seeing Tarla, toward tempting her into wanting for herself all the things he wanted for her. He sometimes thought the temptation the greatest sport of all, even finer than the fulfillment.

When Stercus came into Duthil, he saw the blacksmith's son walking up the street with the evidence of a successful hunt on his shoulders. The Aquilonian noble reined in and waved. "Hail, Conan," he called. "How are you today?"

The boy's face flushed with anger. Stercus knew Conan loved him not; that knowledge only piqued his desire to annoy the young Cimmerian. He suspected that Conan held some childish affection of his own for Tarla, which would do him no good at all when set against the full-blooded and refined passion of a sensual adult.

"How are you, I say?" Stercus' voice grew sharper.

"Well, till now," answered Conan in thickly accented Aquilonian—though somewhat less so than when Stercus began coming to Duthil. Like a parrot, the boy could mimic the sounds his betters made.

And, as Stercus realized after a moment, Conan could also ape, or try to ape, the studied insults a grown man might offer. Had a grown man, one of his own countrymen, offered Stercus such an insult, he would have wiped it clean with blood. The *code duello* was ancient and much revered in Aquilonia. Dirtying his sword with the blood of a barbarous blacksmith's boy never once occurred to Stercus. But he did suddenly spur his horse forward, and the destrier would have trampled Conan if the youngster had not sprung to one side with an agility that belied his loutish size. Laughing, Stercus rode on to the house of Balarg the weaver, the house of Tarla, the house of what he conceived to be his affection.

Conan found his mother up and about, filling a pot from a great water jar and hanging it to boil above the hearth. "You should rest," he told her reproachfully.

"Oh? And if I rest, who will cook our food? I see no slave in the house," replied Verina. "And what's the point of rest? When your father begins to hammer, every stroke seems to go straight through my head." She raised a hand to press it to her temple.

"I'm sorry," said Conan, who could have slept sound and undisturbed were Mordec beating a sword blade into shape six inches from his ear. He set down the burden he had brought from the forest. "See the fine venison we'll have?"

His mother looked at it, sniffed, and coughed. To Conan's relief, the cough did not begin one of her spasms. "This will do for tomorrow, I suppose," she said indifferently. "For stew today, I killed the black hen who'd stopped laying. We may as well get some use out of her."

"Ah," said Conan, and then, a moment later, "All right." He did his best to make himself believe it was.

"If you want to be useful, you can cut up these turnips and

parsnips and onions for the stew — and chop up this head of cabbage, too — not too fine, mind you, or it will cook too fast when I put it in," said his mother.

"Of course," said Conan. As the knife tore through the vegetables, he wished it were tearing through Count Stercus' flesh instead. He imagined blood spurting from every cut, not colorless turnip juice. The picture pleased him, so much that he sliced harder than ever.

"Easy, easy," said Verina. "These are not heads to be set above the doorposts of our house, you know. No need for murder here."

"Oh, but there is," said Conan. "If ever a man wanted killing, that damned Aquilonian is the one."

"I doubt he's any worse than the rest of them," said Verina.

"He is," insisted Conan. "The way he sniffs around — around this village is nothing but a disgrace." He felt uncomfortable mentioning Tarla to his mother.

She understood what he was talking about even when he did not talk about it. With a toss of the head, she answered, "That one is a little hussy. If she weren't, the accursed Aquilonian wouldn't keep sniffing around her. I don't know why you worry about her. She isn't good enough for you."

Conan started chopping the vegetables even more savagely than before. His mother did not think anyone was good enough for him. Conan did not know what he thought. He only knew that, as he passed from boy to man, he cared less with each new day that went by whether a girl was good enough for him. Whether she was interested in him — that was another story, and one in which he had a burning interest.

"But don't mind me," said Verina. "After I'm dead and gone, you and your father will settle things to your own liking, I'm sure." She began to cough again, softly but steadily.

"Here. Drink some water, Mother." Conan hurried to dip some out of the jar and into a mug. He handed it to his mother and stood over her until she did drink. Not so long before, she had been taller than he; he remembered those days very well. Now he towered over her. Before too long, he would overtop his father, too. That was a truly dizzying thought. No one in Duthil could match Mordec's inches.

Mordec came back into the kitchen from the smithy, as if thinking of him were enough to conjure him up. Sweat ran down his fire-reddened face and forearms, washing clean rills through the soot that covered them. "I could do with some water, too, son," he rasped. "Fetch me a cup, if you'd be so kind."

"Aye, Father." Conan found a larger mug and dipped it full.

"My thanks." Mordec drained it in one long draught. Then he went to the water jar himself. He filled the mug again. Instead of drinking from it, he poured it over his head. "Ahhh!" he said: a long exhalation of pleasure. Water ran through his hair, ran through his beard, and dripped from the end of his nose.

"There you go, making part of my kitchen floor into mud," said Verina shrilly. As in the smithy, the floor here was only of rammed earth. When it got wet, it did turn muddy.

But Conan's father only shrugged. "Give it a little while and it will dry, Verina," he said. "As for me, though, I needed that, by Crom. I'm surprised I didn't hiss like hot iron quenched when I poured it over me."

"Did you see Count Stercus today, Father?" asked Conan.

Mordec's mouth thinned to a narrow line. "I saw him, all right. What if I did?"

Conan scowled blackly. "Is that not the face of a man who deserves death?"

"I've seen men I liked better at first glance," answered his father. "But my guess is, where he looks bothers you more than how he looks."

That shaft hit unpleasantly close to the center of the target. Conan flushed so hot that he longed for a mug of water to cool him. Stubborn as always, he said, "He's got no business here."

"He thinks otherwise," said Mordec.

"Well, I think he can—" But Conan broke off. He could not say what he wanted Count Stercus to do, not with his mother listening. He growled in frustration, down deep in his throat.

"What happens to him does not first depend on what you think," said his father. "We've been over this ground before. It depends on what Balarg thinks. He is the girl's father, after all." Verina tossed her head once more. Mordec took no notice of her.

"Why doesn't Balarg do something, then?" cried Conan.

His father frowned. "By now, I wish he would do more myself. And I wish Tarla would stop preening every time she sets eyes on the Aquilonian noble. Balarg should speak to her about that. But the world is as it is. It is not the way we wish it were. I suppose that's why Crom isn't the sort of god who makes a habit of granting prayers."

However earnestly he spoke, Conan hardly heard him. Mordec had presumed to criticize Tarla, which only served to infuriate his son. As far as Conan was concerned, Tarla could do no wrong—this despite the fact that she did not care to speak to him and showed Stercus far more sweetness, just as Mordec had said. Verina started to cough again. Conan scarcely noticed even that sound, which most of the time roused nothing but dread in him.

Mordec guided Verina back to the bedchamber. A glum frown on his heavy-featured face, the blacksmith returned to the kitchen and finished the supper his wife had begun.

At harvest time, almost everything in Duthil stopped. Even folk who did not farm went into the fields to help bring in the oats and rye. The ripe grain had to come in before bad weather could spoil it. On it depended the hopes of the village through the winter and into the following spring.

Conan and Mordec both swung scythes whose blades the blacksmith had forged. So did Balarg. Along with the other women of Duthil, Tarla helped gather the golden grain into sheaves. The Aquilonian soldiers watched the work from their encampment not far away. None of them came out to help the Cimmerians. The first autumn they had been here, and even the second, they had tried to join the villagers. Everyone in Duthil had pretended they did not exist. By now, the invaders had learned their lesson: they might be here, but they were not welcome.

Mordec stood up straight. He grunted and twisted and rubbed at the small of his back. "This is not my proper trade," he grumbled, "and every year my bones tell me so louder and louder." Conan worked on tirelessly. He might have been powered by the water that would turn the grindstones in the mill to make the grain into flour. With his fourteenth winter approaching, aches in the bones were as far from him as gray hair and a walking stick.

Like all the villagers, he did pause ever so often to glance anxiously up toward the sky. Mist and clouds floated across it even at high summer, and high summer was a long way behind them now. Rain at harvest time would be disastrous. Hail would be even worse. Hail at harvest time might mean old men and women and young children would never see another spring. As Mordec had said, Crom did not answer prayers, but more than a few went his way at this season even so.

Bend. Swing the scythe. Watch the grain fall. Straighten. Take a step forward. Bend. Swing again. That was Conan's life from first light of dawn until the last evening twilight leaked from the sky. Almost all the men in Duthil, and the boys old enough to do their fair share, took part; the chief exception was Nectan the shepherd, who did not leave his flock even for the harvest.

When the men came back to the village, they wolfed down food and ale, then fell into bed and slept like the dead. When morning came, they would munch oatcakes or porridge, then stuff more oatcakes and perhaps some cheese into their belt pouches and lurch out to the grainfields for another day's backbreaking labor.

At last, only a few gleaners were left in the fields, gathering up the last heads of grain the main harvest had missed. And then, with only stubble and dirt remaining, Duthil took one of its rare days of rest. Instead of rising before sunup, men—and women—slept late. When at last they rose, they did only the most essential things. Whatever was not essential would wait. A lot of families, Conan's among them, did heat water for baths, which had gone by the wayside along with so much else during the work-filled chaos of harvest time.

After the day of rest came a day of celebration. By age-old custom, the folk of Cimmeria celebrated whether the harvest was good or bad. If it was good, they celebrated because it deserved celebrating. If it was bad, they celebrated to cast defiance in the face of fate. Chickens stewed. Ducks and geese roasted, with thrifty housewives carefully catching the drippings. Slaughtered hogs turned on spits over trenches full of fire. Casks and jars of ale were broached.

Like any Cimmerian, Conan had been drinking ale since he stopped drinking his mother's milk. It was more filling and often more wholesome than water. He rarely drank to excess. A couple of thick heads had made him wary of that. Today, though, he recklessly poured down the ale, hoping to borrow enough courage from it to say some of the things he wanted to say to Tarla.

He had not said them by midafternoon, when Count Stercus rode into Duthil. The Aquilonian noble sat astride his charger and, unusually, led a pack horse with several stout casks tied to its back. Spotting Conan's father in the crowd of strangers, he pointed to him and spoke in Aquilonian, no doubt to make himself seem more important: "Translate for me, my good man."

Mordec nodded. "Say what you will."

"Tell your people I heard they would feast today. Tell them also that no feast is a true feast without wine." Stercus pointed to the pack horse. "I have brought your enough to prove the point."

He could not have bought himself popularity, or even toleration, with silver or with gold. Wine proved another story. The Cimmerians drank it when they could get it; Aquilonian traders had made it known in this land where no vineyard could prosper. But so much of the strong, sweet brew at harvest time—yes, sly Stercus had known what coin to spend.

And if he made sure Tarla drank several beakers of the red blood of the grape, if he laughed by her when her walk went clumsy and her speech got slurred, if he whirled her in a sprightly Aquilonian dance when pipes and drums began to play, who could hold it against him? No one at all—no one but Conan the blacksmith's son, who found himself upstaged again.

chapter ix

For Stercus' Sake?

Rhiderch the seer stayed in and around Duthil through the winter. He made himself useful now and again. Balarg's wife had lost a silver ring — work of the Æsir — and Rhiderch told her to slaughter a certain hen. Sure enough, she found it in the bird's gizzard. It must have slipped from her finger while she was scattering grain for her chickens. She valued the ring enough to feed the seer for a week afterwards — and she was not one usually given to fits of generosity.

And Rhiderch also found four sheep that had wandered away from Nectan during a snowstorm that covered their tracks as fast as they were made. He told the shepherd to look by a red rock beneath a tall spruce. Nectan knew a reddish boulder just in from the edge of the forest that fit the bill. When he went to the rock, there were the sheep. He gave Nectan one of them, reckoning it better to have three back than to have lost them all.

The seer's powers came and went. They did not always serve him as he would have wished. He also did odd jobs to keep himself fed and sheltered. Except for his erratic gift, he did nothing better than everyone else. But he did a lot of things better than most people, and so found ways to make himself useful.

One morning in early spring, Conan came upon him repairing the wall of a neighbor's house. Wherever he had learned to work with wattle and daub, he took pains to do a proper job, using plenty of sticks and twigs to anchor the mud. Nodding to the blacksmith's son, he said, "A good day to you. Next I'll put more thatch on the roof, to keep the rain from dripping through and marring the wall again."

"That will keep the house sound, sure enough." Conan hesitated, then asked, "How do you see what you see?"

Rhiderch did him the courtesy of taking the question seriously. "I know not, lad," he answered. "All I know is that I see. Sometimes it will be as clear as if it were before my eyes, the way I see you now. Sometimes what I see will mean nothing or next to nothing to me, yet seem plain enough to the person to whom I tell it. And sometimes neither I nor he will know what a vision means."

"When you see something, are you ever wrong?" asked Conan.

"Wrong?" Again, Rhiderch paused to think before replying. "Well, as I say, there are times when I cannot tell you what will come from things I have seen. But that's not what you meant, is it?" Conan shook his head. Rhiderch thought a little longer, then said, "No, I don't believe I see falsely. If a meaning comes of it, it is the meaning I have seen."

"So it seemed to me," said Conan. "Tell me, then: what do you see about our folk and the Aquilonians?"

"So far, I have not seen anything, not in the way you mean," replied Rhiderch.

"Could you?" asked Conan eagerly.

"Could I bring on a vision instead of waiting for one to strike me?" The seer frowned. "I know not. I do not believe I have ever tried. For most visions, I would not try."

"But this one is important to all our people," protested Conan.

"Well, so it is," admitted Rhiderch. "All right, lad. I'll give it a go. Let no one say I fought shy of doing what we Cimmerians need."

He stood there at the edge of Duthil's main street: a lean old man with long, clever hands filthy from mud. His lips moved, at first silently and then in a soft, droning chant. Awe prickled through Conan. He realized the seer was gathering his mental powers to pierce the veil of the unknown as a sharp awl might pierce thick, resistant leather. Rhiderch's eyes met Conan's, but the blacksmith's son did not think the other man truly saw him. Whatever Rhiderch saw, it was not the little village where Conan had lived all his life.

The seer suddenly went stiff. His eyes opened very wide, so that white showed all around their irises. "Crom!" he muttered, whether calling on the grim northern god or simply in astonishment Conan could not have said. In a voice that might have come from the other side of the grave, Rhiderch went on, "Gore and guts and grief and glory! War and woe and fire and flame! Death and doom and dire deeds! War, aye, war to the knife, war without mercy, war without pity, battle till the last falls still fighting!"

Conan shuddered. He had got more in the way of a vision than he had bargained for. Rhiderch twitched like a man in the throes of an epileptic fit. Hoarsely, Conan asked, "But who will win?" Nothing else mattered to him. "Who will win?"

Now Rhiderch's gaze thrust through him like a sword. "War and woe!" repeated the seer. "Duthil dies a dismal death. The golden lion—" He twitched again. "Aye, the golden lion flaps above your head."

"No!" howled Conan, a long wail of misery. Bitterly he repented of his own curiosity. Repentance, as usual, came too late. "No! Let it not be so! Tell me not that accursed Aquilonia triumphs."

Rhiderch blinked several times. Only after the fact did Conan notice the seer's eyes had stayed open every moment while he was prophesying. With reason on his face once more, Rhiderch inquired, "What said I?"

"You do not know?" exclaimed Conan. Rhiderch shook his head. Although he had manifestly returned to the mundane plane, he still seemed pale and drawn, as though he had just shaken off a nearly killing fever. As best Conan could, he recounted Rhiderch's baleful words.

The seer heard him out in silence. Rhiderch looked down at the daub on his hands as if it were dripping blood. "I know not what to say to you, lad," he said at last, "save this alone: the foretelling and the event are not the same. The event is the thing, the foretelling but a shadow. Like any shadow, it shifts and grows and shrinks in response to the light that casts it."

"Cold comfort, by Crom!" jeered Conan. "You have seen my village dead. How shall the shadow of that shift? You are nothing but a stinking carrion crow with corpse meat in your mouth!"

Rhiderch bowed his head. "If you blame the messenger for the message, strike now," he said.

Instead of striking, Conan swore. He spun on his heel and stormed out of Duthil. Slaying Rhiderch would solve nothing, for how could he slay the seer's words? They would echo inside him until the unfolding of time revealed their fulfillment—and he was all too sure it would. Rhiderch had been a man inspired; however shadowy his words might have been, he had spoken truth.

Air spicy with the sap of conifers surrounded Conan as he rushed into the woods. Leaving behind the stinks of Duthil— the dung, the animals, the smoke, the unbathed bodies, the tanning hides—was easy. Leaving behind Rhiderch's prophecy came harder. That followed Conan: indeed, try as he would, he took it with him. Escape was what he wanted most, and what he could not have.

A raven croaked at him from a tall spruce. He shook his fist at the big, black bird. "Begone, cruel corbie!" he cried. "You'll not take the flesh from my bones to feed your nestlings." He stooped to pick up a stone.

Wise and wary in the ways of men, the raven leaped into the air with a great rustle of wings. Conan hurled the stone anyway, as much from sheer rage as for any other reason. It just grazed the outermost feather on the raven's left wing. The bird gave another hoarse cry and vanished into the forest.

"And take your ill-luck with you, accursed thing!" shouted Conan after it. The woods seemed to swallow his words. He wondered if they reached the raven. He could only hope. Had curses stuck as readily as they were given, all the Aquilonians would long since have vanished from Cimmeria.

Conan realized he had only an eating knife at his belt, for he had rushed out of the village in a passion, with not the slightest thought for what he would do next. Now that his temper began to cool, he keenly felt the lack of either bow or javelin. A knife was no weapon to wield against wolf, let alone panther. He took two steps toward Duthil, but then abruptly checked himself. What would the villagers do if he came stumbling back after rushing away so furiously? Would they not laugh at him, whether to his face or behind his back? Of a certainty, they would.

Pride is a terrible thing. For pride's sake, the blacksmith's son would sooner have risked his life than risked the laughter of friends and neighbors. And, had any other man of Duthil stood where Conan stood, he would have made the same choice. What the Cimmerians lacked in material goods, they made up for in a superabundance of pride. If not for pride, they would have fought less amongst themselves, and would have made a harder nut for the Aquilonians to crack. None of that crossed Conan's mind. He knew only that he would rather have faced wolves than his fellow villagers.

A twig breaking underfoot froze him into animal immobility. The oaths that followed were in Aquilonian. Conan would not be laughed at, but he mocked the shortcomings of others readily enough. The invaders blundering along the trail there could hardly have made more noise had they been a herd of cattle.

As Conan had amused himself by doing before, he began to trail these Aquilonians. The closer he could come to them without their being aware he was anywhere nearby, the happier he would be. They ambled along, loudly announcing their presence to anyone with ears to hear. Conan almost gave himself away at their antics; only by biting down hard on the inside of his lower lip did he defeat the urge to guffaw.

Someone else stepped on a stick. "You clumsy idiot," said a Bossonian. "How are we supposed to catch anything when you do that?"

"Oh, and it wasn't you the last time, eh?" retorted a Gunderman. "You walk like you've got rocks in your boots."

"And you talk like you've got rocks in your head, so devils eat you," said the Bossonian. He cupped a hand behind his ears. "And if you listen, you can hear all the animals in the forest running away from us."

"Not in this forest." The Gunderman shook his head. "Half the things in this forest want to kill us."

Conan nodded. He wanted to kill all the invaders who tramped through the woods that had been his ever since he grew old enough to venture into them for the first time. He was close enough to smash in a couple of the hunters' skulls with hurled rocks, too. But he did not think he could slay every one of them, and even if he did he would only bring a savage vengeance down on Duthil. He cast no stones, then, but hung close to the Aquilonians and listened.

Another Gunderman spoke for the first time: "Everything in this whole country wants to kill us." Conan nodded again; so did the Gunderman's hunting companions. The yellow-haired soldier continued, "I'll tell you something else, too— our beloved count isn't making things any better for us, the way he's prowling around that girl in the village."

That astonished Conan. Even the Aquilonians realized Stercus had no business doing what he was doing? The blacksmith's son had not dreamt that could be so. Why did they not restrain him, then?

The Bossonian archer laughed. "And if you tell him so, Vulth, you'll get it in the neck. In fact, if you even talk about it with anybody you can't trust, you're liable to get it in the neck anyway. Stercus doesn't like people telling him what he can do and what he can't."

"King Numedides told him," said the Gunderman who wasn't Vulth: a younger man, with a merry smile. "That's why he's up here, not still down in the capital prowling after young girls there."

"Ah, but there's a difference," the Bossonian replied. "Numedides can tell anybody anything. That's what being king is all about. You damned well can't. You're just a miserable, no-account pikeman with dung on your boots. Nobody wants to hear what you've got to say."

Had anyone spoken so to Conan, the blacksmith's son would have done his best to murder the offender. No Cimmerian would stand for the notion that his word was not as good as any other man's. Clan chiefs won their places not thanks to their fancy bloodlines but by virtue of the strength and wisdom they displayed. Anyone might challenge them, and men frequently did. If being frozen in place from fear of a wicked nobleman's status was what went into civilization, then Conan wanted no part of it, vastly preferring the barbarism in which he had been raised. His father had seen that benefits also accrued from a social system more highly structured than Cimmeria's, but he was blind to those.

The Gunderman, instead of taking the archer's words as a deadly insult, only laughed. "And you've got dung on your tongue, Benno," he said. "That's why everybody loves you so much."

Benno's reply taught Conan several new Aquilonian curses. He was not completely sure what all of them meant, but they sounded splendid, rolling off the Bossonian's tongue with a fine, sonorous obscenity. The Gunderman at whom they were aimed laughed some more. That Conan did understand. Friends could take such liberties.

For a little while, he forgot about murdering all the invaders. Following them, spying on them, made sport enough.

Granth hated the Cimmerian forest. Even with comrades along, he always felt like a flea making its way through the matted fur of the biggest, shaggiest dog in the world. He did not offer up that conceit to Vulth and Benno. He knew too well that his cousin and the Bossonian would make the most of it.

When he stopped for a moment, the other two soldiers also halted. "What is it?" asked Vulth. "Did you see something? Did you hear something?" He sounded edgier than usual himself; perhaps the damp, silent immensity of the woods had begun to get under his skin, too.

However reluctantly, Granth shook his head. "No," he admitted. "But half the Cimmerians in the world could be within fifty feet of us, and we'd never notice, not in woods like these."

"By Mitra, we would!" Benno laughed and mimed taking an arrow in the chest. "We'd notice pretty damned quick, too."

That had a horrid feeling of probability to Granth. It also made him stop, look, and listen again. But he saw nothing, heard nothing, sensed nothing—except the hair-prickling feeling at the nape of his neck that not all was as it should be. He muttered to himself.

"Still jumpy?" said Vulth.

"Not—jumpy." Granth tried to put the feeling into words: "More as though a goose just walked over my grave."

"You're a goose—a silly one," said his cousin. Granth scowled; he might have known Vulth would make him pay for careless words like those.

"And if anything walks over your grave in this country, it's likelier to be a panther or a dragon—something with long, sharp claws, anyway—than a goose," added Benno. "Geese are the least of what we've got to worry about here."

That only served to reinforce Granth's feeling on unease. Try as he would, he could find no rational reason for it. Telling himself as much, though, did not make it go away. He leaned against the rough bark of a fir that might have sprouted before the kingdom of Aquilonia coalesced out of the wandering Hyborian tribes that had shattered the ancient, sorcery-steeped land of Acheron. Even then, this forest had belonged to Cimmeria.

Thinking of the land naturally made him think also of the dour folk who dwelt upon it. But thinking of the Cimmerians only added to his unease. Again, he groped for words: "They aren't acting so—so beaten as they did just after we came up here."

Neither Vulth nor Benno had to ask who they were. Frowning, Vulth said, "They've had a couple of years to lick their wounds and to take our measure. What's the old saw? Familiarity breeds contempt, that's it. They've seen us drinking ale and standing around scratching ourselves. They haven't seen us fight for a while."

"We should have gone on," said Benno. "We should have bitten off a bigger chunk of this cursed country than we did."

"If you ask me, we're lucky we bit off any—if you want to

call it luck," said Granth. "They could have beaten us there by Fort Venarium. Hell, they almost did."

"And they know it, too," agreed Vulth. "You can see it in their faces when you go into Duthil. Like I said, they've licked their wounds. They're pretty much healed. Now they're getting to want another crack at us."

This time, Benno did pull an arrow from his quiver and set it to his bowstring. "If they want one, I'll give it to them."

"More of us now than there were when the army first came up into Cimmeria," observed Granth. "Every settler who's started a farm can wield a spear or a sword or a bow or an axe at a pinch."

"I still wish we'd conquered more of Cimmeria," said Benno stubbornly.

To Granth's annoyance, Vulth nodded. What was he doing, backing a Bossonian against his own cousin? But then he looked to the north and said, "So do I. How many Cimmerians are there that we didn't beat? How many of them can fight at a pinch? And how many of them are feeling the pinch now?"

Yes, Granth had always hated the Cimmerian forests. They stretched across the landscape like a great mantling cloak. And just how many savage barbarians sheltered beneath that cloak? He did not know. He hoped he—and all the Aquilonians in these parts—would not have to find out.

A fireplace poker was one of the simplest bits of smithery Mordec did: a long iron bar with one end twisted back on itself to make a handle. It had neither edge nor temper, and needed neither. Taking the hot metal off the anvil with his tongs, the blacksmith simply set it aside to let it cool.

He set down the tongs, too, then walked back into his bedchamber to see how his wife fared. Verina had fallen into a fitful sleep. Her face was thinner and paler than it had been even when the Aquilonians invaded Cimmeria; the bluish cast to her lips was more pronounced. Mordec's great shoulders heaved in a hopeless sigh. How long could she go on? How could he go on—and, especially, how could Conan go on—when she lost her protracted struggle with mortality?

He sighed again, then straightened. For the time being, she did not need him. With Conan out hunting, he had wanted to be sure of that before stepping away from the smithy for a little while. Nodding to himself, he turned and walked out into Duthil's narrow, muddy main street.

Boys yelled and ran, kicking at their leather ball. Chickens clucked indignantly. They flapped their all but useless wings to help them scurry out of the way of the boys. Dogs, by contrast, ran joyously with the children. They might not know what the sport was, but they were ready to play. A brindled cat yawned from a doorway, every line of its sleek body declaring that it had better things to do with its energy than waste it so prodigally.

Mordec strode through the noisy chaos as if it did not exist. Boys and dogs and even chickens made way for him. The cat, unimpressed, yawned again, flipped the tip of its fluffy tail up over its eyes to keep out the sun, and fell asleep. Mordec had not far to go. He ducked his way into the house of Balarg the weaver.

Balarg was busy at the loom. He worked on for a few moments, then nodded to the blacksmith. "Good day," he said, civilly enough. "You look to have somewhat on your mind."

"I do. I do indeed." Mordec had little lightness in him at any time. His nod now was as somber and jerky as if he were made of the iron he worked.

"Say your say, then," Balarg told him. The weaver gestured toward another stool. "And sit, if you care to."

"I'd sooner stand," said Mordec. Shrugging, Balarg got to his feet, too. He was not so thick through the shoulders and chest as the blacksmith, but came closer than any other man in Duthil to matching him in height. By rising, he might as well have warned Mordec he would not suffer himself to be loomed over. Ignoring such subtleties, Mordec bulled ahead: "This has to do with your daughter."

"With Tarla?" Balarg's eyebrows rose in surprise or a good simulation of it. "We've walked this track before, but you look bound and determined to do it again, so go on, by all means."

"She draws that accursed Aquilonian noble the way spilled honey draws flies," said Mordec bluntly. "We'd all be better off if he stopped coming to Duthil, and you know it as well as I do."

Now the weaver's brows came down, though even frowning he lacked Mordec's gloomy intensity. Still, his voice had no give in it as he replied, "Tell me just what you mean. You need to be careful about what you say, too. If you claim she has done anything improper with the Aquilonian—anything at all, mind you—then we can step out into the street and settle that directly. You once said our quarrels could wait while the men from the south were in our country, and I thought that fair enough. Still, Mordec, some things cannot be borne."

The blacksmith exhaled angrily. "I do not say she has done anything—not the way you mean. But when that stinking Stercus comes to call on her, she—she smiles at him."

Balarg threw back his head and laughed. "Plain to see you have a son and not a daughter. That is the way of girls—the way of women—and has been for as long as they have had to try to deal with us men."

"Oh, I know a girl's smiles are sweet, and I know the sweetest of smiles need not mean a thing. I am not a fool, Balarg, and you make a mistake if you reckon me one," said Mordec. "But I also know some things you seem to forget. Does the tale of poor Ugaine mean nothing to you?"

"Ugaine was Stercus' plaything, in the town the Aquilonians have built," said Balarg. "Tarla stays here in Duthil, and

Stercus has not laid a finger—not so much as a finger—upon her. Do you deny it? Do you, damn your stiff neck?"

"I do not," said Mordec. "But do you deny that even his own officer warned us against Stercus? Do you deny he has given her more attention than is her due? What he has done is no guide to what he will do, or to what he would do. And you will also have heard the stories the Aquilonian soldiers tel, that he was cast forth from their capital, cast forth from their kingdom, for liking young girls too well? He has done these things, Balarg. Given the chance, he will do them again."

"You are the one who speaks Aquilonian, so you would know better than I," said Balarg. Mordec glowered and flushed; the weaver might have accused him of friendship with the invaders. Sensing his advantage, Balarg went on, "Besides, if we listened to everything the soldiers said, we would never have time for anything else. I think your quibbles spring from a different seed, myself."

"What nonsense are you spewing now?" rumbled Mordec irritably.

"Nonsense? I doubt it." Balarg was a clever man, and, like most clever men, pleased with his own cleverness, and with showing it off. "You complain about the Aquilonian because you aim to match Tarla with your own great gowk of a son. I've seen him casting sheep's eyes at her often enough."

Mordec scowled, for at least part of what the weaver said was true. "He'd make a better match for her than any other you'd find in Duthil, and you know it."

"In Duthil? Aye, likely enough." But Balarg spoke as if Duthil were a very small place indeed. "Tarla, though, Tarla might find a match in any of the villages of Cimmeria, and pick and choose from among her suitors."

"What if—" But Mordec broke off with that question unspoken. If he asked Balarg whether Tarla would entertain a suitor from Venarium, he would mortally insult the other villager, and their feud would burst into flame whether he wanted it to or not. Or, worse, Balarg might make it plain that he would entertain a suit from Stercus, in which case Mordec did not see how he could keep from inflaming the feud himself.

Being a clever man, Balarg saw much of that, if not all, regardless of whether Mordec finished the question. "I think you have said enough," growled the weaver. "I think you have said too much. And I think you had better go, or one of our wives will be a widow before the sun sets tonight."

"Oh, I'll leave," said Mordec. "But I will tell you one thing more, Balarg: you are no blacksmith, and you know nothing of the fire you play with." He turned on his heel and tramped out into the street.

The boys' ball came bounding toward him. Before he thought, he drew back his foot, then shot it forward. His toe met the ball squarely and sent it flying over the houses of Duthil and far out into the fields beyond. The boys skidded to a stop, their necks craning comically as they turned in unison to follow the flight of the ball. When at last it thudded to earth, some of them ran after it. Others stared in awe at Mordec.

"Nobody can kick like that," said one.

"He just did, Wirp," said another. Wirp shook his head, manifestly disbelieving what he had just seen.

Mordec said not a word. He slowly walked back to the smithy, wishing he could boot sense into Balarg as readily as he had vented his spleen on a harmless ball.

On sentry-go outside the Aquilonian camp by Duthil, Granth son of Biemur watched Count Stercus ride south toward Venarium. Turning to his cousin, he said, "I wish he'd find some other village to visit."

Nodding, Vulth answered, "You aren't the only one. The more he comes here, the more trouble I see down the road."

Out of the side of his mouth, Benno said, "Here comes trouble closer than down the road."

Sergeant Nopel emerged from the fortified encampment and bore down on the sentries. Granth tried to straighten up, and also tried not to be too noticeable as he straightened: that might have made Nopel see he'd been slouching. Nopel noticed almost everything; noticing was part of what made him a sergeant. But he only waved now, a world-weary flap of the arm that said he had larger things to fret about than whether his sentries slouched. "As you were, boys," he called.

Despite that, Granth did not relax from the brace he had taken. "What's up, Sergeant?" he asked.

Nopel did not answer right away. He looked toward Duthil. After a moment, Granth realized he was looking beyond Duthil toward the trackless wilderness still inhabited by wild, unsubdued Cimmerians. He said, "The tribes are stirring."

Granth and Vulth and Benno and Daverio stared at one another in consternation. "How do you know that?" asked Daverio.

"How do I know?" said Nopel. "How do I know? By Mitra, I'll tell you how I know. I've just come from talking with Captain Treviranus, and he told me. That's how I know." By the way he spoke, he might have had the news from the gods themselves.

Granth was not prepared to disagree with him. As far as the Gunderman was concerned, Treviranus made as good a garrison commander as anyone could want. If he said a thing was so, so it was likely to be. But cynical Daverio asked the question that had barely occurred to Granth: "Well, how does the captain know?"

"How does he know?" Sergeant Nopel sounded as if he could not believe his ears. But the Bossonian bowman nodded. Nopel's frown was fearsome. "Why, because he's heard, that's how."

"Well, who told him?" persisted Daverio. "It wasn't anybody from here, or we'd all have heard about it by now."

And Granth could hardly disagree with that, either. Anything anyone in the garrison knew, everyone in the garrison knew in a matter of minutes. The Gundermen and Bossonians, a tiny island in a vast, hostile sea, had no secrets from one another.

"I don't know who told him. I only know what he told me," said Nopel. He fixed Daverio with a challenging stare. "You want to go tell him he's wrong? You want to tell him you know better, and we can all relax? He'll be glad to hear that. You bet he will."

Daverio was a hard and stubborn man, but no common soldier would have been so rash as to beard Captain Treviranus in his den. He shook his head now, saying, "I'm trying to find out what's going on, that's all. If the tribes are stirring out there somewhere, what are we supposed to do about it?"

Exactly how vast was Cimmeria? Granth did not know, not in any detail; he knew only that the corner of it Count Stercus' army had worried off was just that—a corner. Countless clans of barbarians—clans assuredly uncounted by any Aquilonian, at all odds—still prowled the dark woods in squalid freedom. If they were to band together against the soldiers and settlers from the south— "Aye, Sergeant," said Granth. "What are we supposed to do about it?"

"I was coming to that," said Nopel portentously. "Did you think I wasn't? We've got to push scouts up to the north and see with our own eyes what the damned barbarians are up to."

"We can send scouts north, all right," said Vulth. "We can send 'em, but will we ever see 'em again if we do?"

"And why wouldn't we?" demanded Nopel.

All the sentries laughed. The laughs were not pleasant. "Why, Sergeant?" said Granth. "On account of the damned Cimmerians will do for them, that's why. Do you think we can kill ten for one for what happens up there?"

Nopel grunted. He turned and tramped away without answering. Vulth clapped Granth on the back. "Well done, cousin," said Vulth. "You made the sergeant shut up, and not everybody can boast of that."

Benno had a more practical way of congratulating Granth. He took his water bottle off his belt and offered it to him. When Granth tilted back his head and drank, he wasn't too surprised to find sweet, strong wine running down his throat. He took another pull at the bottle, and then another, until at last Benno snatched it out of his hand.

Granth wiped his mouth on his sleeve. Benno glowered. Vulth chuckled. "You see?" he said to the archer. "He's figuring out what it's all about."

"It's about him being greedy, that's what," said Benno. But even the touchy Bossonian seemed not too put out.

For his part, Granth looked to the north. He had seen one swarm of Cimmerians bearing down on the army of which he was a small part. In his mind's eye, he saw another, this one bigger, fiercer, more ferocious. Until that moment, he had not imagined anything more ferocious than the onslaught he and his countrymen had so narrowly survived. Now he discovered his imagination was stronger than he had thought possible.

"What do we do if the barbarians come down on us, the way Nopel and the captain say they might?" he asked, worry in his voice.

"Kill 'em," Vulth answered stolidly. "Kill 'em till they're piled so high, they have to climb over their cousins to jump down onto our pikes."

When Granth looked toward the village of Duthil, everything seemed tranquil enough. Women carried water from the stream back to their homes. Wood smoke rose from the smoke holes in their roofs. A couple of men stood talking. Neither of them paid the least attention to the Aquilonian encampment. Two years after the fight at Fort Venarium—now the citadel at the heart of the town of Venarium—the villagers might have accepted the camp as part of the land-scape. A dog nosed at a mound of garbage. He ignored the encampment, too. He might have been sincere. Granth had his doubts about the Cimmerians.

If more barbarians swarmed down out of the north, what would the folk of Duthil do? Would they take up arms and fight alongside the Aquilonians against the new invaders? Would they sit quietly and wait to see how the other Cimmerians fared against the men from the south? Or would they grab whatever weapon came to hand and try to murder every Gunderman and Bossonian they could find?

Granth did not know, of course. Only a god could know the future. But the pikeman had a good idea which way he would bet.

He said, "We ought to haul some of the villagers out of that place and squeeze them. To hell with me if they don't know more than they're letting on."

"Not a bad notion," agreed Vulth. "Some of the women seem plenty squeezable—or they would, if you didn't think they'd knife you for touching them."

"They act that way when others are around to see, sure enough," said Benno. "But some of them are friendly enough if you can get them off by themselves."

"Braggart," said Granth. Benno preened.

"Braggart and liar both," said Vulth. "Before I believe a word he says, I want to know who he means, and I want to know how he knows."

"Who? The miller's wife, for one." Benno looked toward Duthil and licked his chops. "And how do I know? When the millstones start grinding, the Cimmerian who runs them has to make sure they behave, and then he can't make sure his lady behaves. And the stones are so noisy, he can't hear a thing that goes on anywhere close by."

After looking at each other, Granth and his cousin both shook their heads. "Braggart," said the one. "Liar," said the other. Benno protested, but not, Granth judged, in the way he would have it he really had done the things he claimed to have done. Soldiers, of course, had been telling lies about women ever since Mitra first let there be soldiers and women.

Then something else occurred to Granth. "Maybe the young one Count Stercus keeps coming back for will stick a knife in him one of these days, and maybe we'll all be better off if she does."

"No." Vulth shook his head. "Think of the vengeance we'd have to wreak. Have you got the stomach for massacring a whole village?"

"For Stercus' sake? For him doing what he's got no business doing, with somebody he's got no business doing it with?" Granth did not need to think that over; he knew the answer at once. "Not a bit of it." But then he hesitated. "To save our own necks, though? That's a different story." None of the other Aquilonian soldiers argued with him.

chapter x

For Tarla's Sake

Few would have called Count Stercus a patient man. In the matter of the weaver's daughter in Duthil, though, he had been more patient than most of the debauched rogues who had known him down in Aquilonia would have dreamt possible. For one thing, he reckoned the game with Tarla worth the candle. And, for another, he still painfully remembered the consequences of his impatience in Tarantia. If not for that, he never would have found himself reduced to pursuing a chit of a barbarian girl here at the misty northern edge of the world.

And so, patience—patience to a point, at any rate. But Stercus was no Stygian priest, no mystic from the distant, legendary land of Khitai, to practice patience for its own dusty sake. He was an Aquilonian to the core: a man of action, a man of deeds. He could bide his time—he had bided his time—with some definite end in view, but if the end remained in view, remained close enough to reach out and touch, he would, sooner or later, reach out and touch it.

That time, at last, had come.

He rode forth from Venarium in helm and back-and-breast, more to make a brave show when he came to Duthil than for any other reason. These days, the country north of what had become a booming little town put him more in mind of the Bossonian Marches or Gunderland than of the dark, brooding wilderness Cimmeria had been before the coming of the gold lion on black.

Fair-haired men and women worked in fields and garden plots carved from primeval wilderness. Smoke rose from the chimneys of sturdy cabins. Garrisons overawed surviving Cimmerian villages. Some of those forts might grow into towns, as Venarium had. The barbarians themselves would surely go to the wall, overwhelmed by the strength and majesty of advancing Aquilonian civilization. Contemplating their fate, Stercus allowed himself a certain delicate melancholy. It was a pity, but the count did not see how it could be helped.

Even now, so soon after the initial conquest, most of the traffic on the road was Aquilonian: more settlers' wagons coming into this new land; soldiers who helped keep the settlers safe; merchants and peddlers of all sorts, intent on taking what profit they could from the land in which they found themselves. And, coming the other way, down toward Venarium, farmers who had more closely followed the army were bringing first fruits and vegetables to market. An oxcart full of onions might not seem such a wonderful thing at first glance, but Stercus smiled as he rode past it, for those were Aquilonian onions.

Only a handful of Cimmerians were on the road. Except for the sake of a drunken carouse or luxuries they could not make for themselves, the barbarians seldom went to Venarium. They wanted little to do with the Aquilonian presence swelling in their midst. That they wanted little to do with it was in Stercus' eyes yet another harbinger of their eventual extinction. If they could not see they were in the presence of something greater than themselves, that went a long way toward proving they did not deserve to survive.

Axes rang in the forest. Trees fell. More cabins full of settlers from Gunderland rose every day. Stercus smiled to himself, for it was good.

But, by the time he got most of the way to Duthil, the road had become a track once more, and the woods pressed close on either side. This far north, few settlers had yet come. The land remained in its state of primitive barbarism.

Another horseman on the track, this one riding south, caused Stercus to rein in. The roadway was especially narrow here; they would have to go slowly as they edged past each other. By the crimson crest on his helm, the other man was a captain. "Your Excellency!" he called, recognizing Stercus. "Well met, by Mitra! I was on my way to Venarium to bring word to you."

"Word of what, Treviranus?" asked Stercus, his voice a little chilly; his mind was on other things than duty.

The commander of the garrison by Duthil pointed back over his shoulder to the village and beyond. "The tribes are stirring, your Excellency. Out beyond where our arms have reached, Cimmeria begins to bubble and boil like a pot of stew left too long over too hot a fire."

Stercus' laugh was loud and long and scornful. "If the barbarians want another go at us, they are welcome to it, as far as I am concerned. We smashed them once. We can do it again."

"Sir, we smashed three or four clans," said Treviranus worriedly. "If three or four more rise against us, we'll smash them again, aye. But Cimmeria has clans by the score. If thirty or forty rise against us, that is a very different business. How could we throw back such a swarm of men?"

"If you have not the courage for the work, Captain, belike I can find a man who has," said Stercus.

Treviranus flushed angrily. "You misunderstand me, your Excellency."

"Good. I hoped I did," said Stercus. "Have you got any true notion how many barbarians may be in motion against our frontier? With the way the Cimmerians squabble among themselves, isn't it likelier to be three or four clans than thirty or forty?"

"Most of the time, your Excellency, I would say yes to that," replied Treviranus. "But not now."

"Oh? And why not?" Again, Stercus laced his voice with scorn.

The junior officer said, "Why not, sir? Because most of the time, as you say, Cimmerians fight Cimmerians, and they break up into factions. But we know one thing about them: they all hate us. I worry that they will sink all their own feuds until they have driven us from their soil."

Count Stercus yawned. "You grow tedious, Captain. If you want to keep an eye on the barbarians beyond the border, you may do so. But if you start at shadows like a brat waking up in its crib in the middle of the night, then you do yourself no good, you do King Numedides no good, and you do Aquilonia no good. Do you understand me?"

"Yes, sir," said Treviranus tonelessly. He saluted with mechanical precision, then yanked his horse's head around and rode back up the track toward Duthil. He did not look over his shoulder to see whether Stercus followed. By his stiff, outraged posture, he was doing his best to pretend Stercus did not exist.

Laughing, the Aquilonian nobleman urged his own mount into motion once more. Thirty or forty clans of Cimmerians getting together for any reason, any reason whatsoever? Count Stercus laughed again. The notion was absurd on the face of it. He would have had trouble believing even three or four clans could unite, if not for the fight at Fort Venarium. If three or four more clans came, he had no doubt the Aquilonians would indeed crush them and send them off howling.

No doubt because of his outrage, Captain Treviranus rode faster than Stercus. The garrison commander had already gone back into his little fortress by the time Stercus emerged from the trees into the clearing surrounding Duthil. The count rode past the palisade toward the village. One of the Aquilonian sentries pointed his way. He saw as much out of the corner of his eye, but did not deign even to turn his head. That he was recognized gratified him. That he acknowledge being recognized never entered his mind. His notion of nobility did not include obliging.

When he came into Duthil, he did slow his horse so he would not trample any of the boys playing ball in the street. He cared nothing for them; seeing them go down under his horse's hooves would have made him rejoice. But it would have angered and grieved Tarla, and Stercus was not a man to frighten his quarry before he brought it down.

He did not see the blacksmith's son among the shouting boys. That left him oddly relieved. The hatred in Conan's blazing blue eyes could not be disguised. And the Cimmerian, though still smooth-cheeked, was already six feet tall, with powerful shoulders and chest a man twice his age might have envied. When thinking of Conan, Stercus was not at all sorry he rode a charger and wore armor.

And here was the house of Balarg the weaver. Count Stercus swung down off his steed, and his armor clattered about him. Then, feeling foolish, he mounted again, for he saw Tarla coming up the street carrying a bucket of water from the stream that ran by the village. He rode up to her, saying, "Good day, my sweet."

"Good day," she answered, and looked down at the ground.

Eyeing her, Stercus wondered how he had contented himself with Ugaine even for a moment. This was what he really wanted: unspoiled, lovely, and young, so young. But he had been patient for a long time—a very, very long time, to his way of thinking. Every heartbeat left Tarla older. Soon, too soon, she would no longer be his image of perfection, only what might have been.

Thinking of that made all Stercus' hard-kept patience blow away like the mist. "We've already waited too long, my darling," he said urgently. "Come away with me now."

She shook her head. "I cannot. I will not. I belong here."

Rage rose up like black smoke from the fire that burned inside Stercus. Had she been playing him along all this time, playing him for a fool? She would be sorry—sorrier—if she had. "You belong with me," the nobleman said. "You belong to me."

At that. Tarla's chin came up in defiance. She shook her head again, more firmly this time. "No. I belong to myself, and to no one else," she declared, as full of native love of freedom as any other Cimmerian ever born.

Count Stercus cared nothing for the freedom of Cimmerians. "By Mitra, you are mine!" he cried, and, leaning down, snatched her up onto his saddlebow. The bucket went flying, water splattering the already muddy street. Tarla shrieked. Stercus cuffed her. She shrieked again. He hit her once more, harder this time.

One of the boys playing ball in the street threw a rock at Stercus. It clanged off his backplate and did him no harm. Another youngster ran toward Count Stercus with a stick of firewood—the first weapon he could find—in his hand. Stercus' sword sprang free. He swung it in a shining arc of death. The Cimmerian boy tried to block it with the wood, but to no avail. The blade bit. The boy fell, spouting blood, his head all but severed from his body.

"Wirp!" cried Tarla. But Wirp would never answer.

The rest of the barbarians in the street roared. They ran not away from Stercus but toward him, intent on pulling him from the saddle. He set spurs to the destrier. Snorting, the great horse sprang forward. Lashing out with its hooves, it stretched another boy dead in the street, his skull smashed. Left arm encircling Tarla's supple waist, Stercus thundered out of Duthil and into the woods.

Granth son of Biemur knelt on one knee in a soldiers' hut. The dice had been going his way—he was up twelve lunas, and hoped to make it more on his next cast. Before he could throw, though, a trumpeter blew the assembly call. "Damnation!" he said, scooping up the silver he had won. "Why did the captain have to decide to hold a drill now?"

"We'll get back to the game soon enough," said Vulth, "and then I'll clean you out."

"Ha!" said Granth. He got to his feet. "Come on—let's get it over with."

Gundermen and Bossonians hurried out to the open space between huts and palisade. They clapped helms on their heads, fastened mailshirts, and had pikes and bows ready. If by some accident this were no drill, they were ready for war.

"Foolishness," grumbled Benno. But his bow was strung and his quiver full.

"No doubt," said Granth. Then Captain Treviranus strode out in front of the Aquilonians. Seeing his grim countenance, Granth began to wonder how foolish the horn call was.

"Something's gone wrong in Duthil," said Treviranus bluntly. "Count Stercus rode into the village a while ago, and he hasn't come out—at least, not this way. And the barbarians in there have been whooping and hollering ever since he did ride in. We'd better find out why they're in an uproar and calm them down—if we can."

"What if we can't?" called someone. Granth could not see who it was, but the same question had crossed his mind. What would he and his friends have to do to pull Stercus' chestnuts out of the fire?

Treviranus faced the question squarely. "If they want trouble, we'll give them all they want and more. We can't let them think they can rise up against us. If they do, the whole countryside is liable to boil over." He waited to see if any more questions would come. When none did, he nodded. "All right, then. Let's go."

He led the Bossonians and Gundermen—the whole garrison except for a handful of men left behind to hold the camp—toward Duthil. That he led made the archers and pikemen follow willingly. Some officers would simply have sent the soldiers forth, but Treviranus was not one of that stripe.

Even before leaving the fortified encampment, Granth could hear the Cimmerians shouting and their women keening. A man came out of Duthil and strode straight at the oncoming Aquilonians. One man against a company of soldiers—but such was his fury that Granth almost halted and did tighten his grip on his pikestaff.

"Two!" shouted the Cimmerian in bad but understandable Aquilonian. "He kill two boys, steal girl. He pay! You all pay!"

"Count Stercus did this?" demanded Treviranus.

"Aye, he do! Dog and son of dog!" the Cimmerian said. "We catch, we kill."

Granth knew Captain Treviranus had no more love for Stercus than any other Aquilonian did. Treviranus might have been able to soothe the villagers—except that they did not want to be soothed. The man who had advanced on the soldiers stopped, picked up a stone, and flung it at them.

The stone thudded off a pikeman's buckler. The response of the Bossonian archers was altogether automatic. Bowstrings thrummed. Half a dozen shafts whistled through the air. They all pierced the Cimmerian. He took a couple of staggering steps toward the men from the south, as if still intending to assail them, then slowly crumpled.

"Damnation," said Treviranus quietly. "I wish that hadn't happened. Well, no help for it now. Forward, men. Battle line—pikemen in front of the archers. We're likely going to have a fight on our hands now."

He proved a good prophet. No sooner had the Cimmerian fallen than more stones began flying at the Aquilonians from Duthil. At least two archers also began shooting from the village. A Bossonian cried out and sat down hard with an arrow through his thigh.

Vulth reached up and settled his conical helm more firmly on his head. "We're going to have to clean the place out now," he said, "and the barbarians in there are going to try to clean us out, too." Granth nodded. His cousin struck him as a good prophet, too.

Along with his comrades, Granth pressed on into Duthil. He saw no one on the street—but, down at the far end of it, two bodies sprawled in ugly death. The Cimmerian had not lied. Granth had not really thought he had.

A door flew open. A barbarian charged out swinging an axe. He chopped down one Bossonian and left another bow-man pouring blood from a great gash in his leg. The pikemen turned on the barbarian then and stretched him lifeless in the mud, but not before he had taken more from the Aquilonians than they could ever take from him.

An arrow from the house next to the blacksmith's caught a pikeman three soldiers down from Granth in the throat. The other Gunderman clawed at the shaft that drank his life. He fell to his knees and then over on to his side. "Dever!" cried Granth, but Dever would never hear him again.

"Now we have to crush them," Captain Treviranus said. "One house at a time, if we must, but crush them we will!"

Even after the battle in front of Fort Venarium, Granth had never imagined work like this. Men fought to the death with whatever weapons they had. Women snatched up kitchen knives and flung themselves at pikemen and archers. More often than not, they would plunge the blades into their own breasts rather than risk capture. The Aquilonians spared children—until a boy who could not have been eight years old stabbed a Bossonian in the back. He had to reach up to get the knife between the bowman's ribs, but it found his heart. After that, the soldiers behaved as if they were destroying a nest of serpents.

Serpents, though, never stung back so savagely. Granth was one of the Gundermen who used a log to batter down the door to the smithy. The only person they found inside was a skeletally skinny woman whose gray eyes blazed in a face ghost-pale. She came at them not with a kitchen knife but with a long, heavy sword. She wounded two men, one of them badly, and fought with such ferocity that she made the Gundermen slay her.

"Mitra!" said Granth. "These aren't barbarians—they're demons, demons straight from hell!"

"Mitra carry Count Stercus straight down to hell," panted Vulth. "If not for him, everything would be quiet here. Now—"

Now the Cimmerians of Duthil, making their final stand, thought of nothing but taking as many of their foes with them as they could. Wounded barbarians feigned death, lying quiet until they could spring up and strike one last telling blow. The shrieks of the sorely hurt and the dying on both sides rose up into the uncaring sky.

At last, all the Cimmerians in Duthil above the age of five or so lay unmoving. Granth's pikestaff was scarlet along half its length. Gore splashed his mailshirt. He no longer hesitated about spearing Cimmerians on the ground to make sure they would not rise again—he had seen too many of them do just that. Vulth had a bandage on his right arm. Benno had taken an arrow through his left hand. Daverio was dead, his head smashed in by a Cimmerian despite his helm.

Captain Treviranus limped with a leg wound. "You're bleeding," he told Granth.

"Am I?" said Granth foolishly. He found he was, and that a chunk was missing from his left earlobe. He had no memory of getting hurt. Waving at the carnage all around, he asked, "What now, Captain?"

"Now I'd like to roast Stercus over a slow fire," answered Treviranus. "The whole countryside will rise up against us on account of this—and for nothing! Nothing!"

Vulth prowled the wreckage of the village. The carrion birds that had already begun to settle flew up again, croaking in annoyance, when he walked past. They came fluttering down again after he went by. When he came back to Granth and Treviranus, his face bore a worried expression. "What's wrong?" asked Granth.

"I've been looking for the blacksmith's body," said his cousin. "He's big as a bear—he shouldn't be hard to spot. But he's not here."

"Are you sure?" asked Treviranus. Vulth nodded. Granth could not remember seeing the smith in the brief, bloody, uneven battle. By Captain Treviranus' frown, neither could he. The garrison commander said, "Where is he, then?" In Duthil, the Aquilonians found no answers.

Mordec and Balarg and Nectan the shepherd tramped north—farther north than they were used to going. Nectan laughed and grinned at Mordec. "For one so grim, you've got a rare sneaky streak in you. Setting your son to guard the sheep is the best way I know to keep him from coming with us."

"I told him he could fight when war came again," answered Mordec. "Soon we'll know if it is here. That will be time enough to blood the boy in battle." He did not say that Conan was already blooded. The time for battle might not yet be at hand. If it were not, what point to spilling his son's secret and risking betrayal? Two had some small hope of keeping silent. Four, as far as he could see, had none—especially when he had brought Balarg with him not least to make sure the weaver spoke to no Bossonians or Gundermen. Maybe he did the man an injustice. If he did, he would apologize when the time came. Meanwhile—

Balarg pointed ahead, past the next line of evergreen-clad hills on the northern horizon. "Do you think they will be there?" he asked.

"Crom! They had better be there!" exclaimed Nectan.

"Even the invaders have begun to get wind of them," said Mordec. "If the accursed Aquilonians think they're there, there they're likely to be." He tossed his head, dismissing the question. "No point fretting about it, not now. Sooner or later, one way or the other, we'll know."

The most widely traveled of the men from Duthil, the blacksmith led the weaver and the shepherd along a winding trail over the side of one of those steep hills to the north. A broader, easier path went through a valley below, but Mordec steered his comrades away from it. They had already evaded two or three Aquilonian patrols. Being so obvious even ignorant foreigners could not miss it, the track in the valley was a logical place to find another.

Evade the Aquilonians they did. But the hill had not yet begun sloping down toward the north before a Cimmerian voice came out of nowhere: "Halt, dogs! Halt or you die!"

"We are of your own folk," said Mordec. But he halted, a step in front of Balarg and Nectan.

A harsh laugh answered him. "I've already slain three Aquilonians trying to sneak up this way. The last one wore a black wig and spoke our language as well as I do. He died anyway— and he died hard."

"Come and see who we are," said Mordec calmly. "We seek Herth's men, if they be near." He stood ready to spring into the woods if the first arrow missed him—and if it did, he aimed to avenge himself on the man who shot it, regardless of whether that man sprang from Aquilonia or Cimmeria.

After a moment, the Cimmerian came out into the track. He had a lean, pantherish build, and held a sword ready to use. His breeks were woven in the same checked pattern as Herth's had been. "I have friends behind me," he warned as he strode up to the men from Duthil. He prowled around them, then grudgingly nodded. "You're of my folk, all right. But how do you come to have Herth's name in your mouth, when the clan he heads dwells far from these parts?"

Balarg swelled with indignation. "Did I not guest him in my own house? Did these my comrades not speak with him there?"

"I don't know. Did you? Did they?" The Cimmerian scout was unmoved. "If you did, say your names, and maybe I will know them." One by one, Mordec, Balarg, and Nectan told him who they were. At that, for the first time, the scout stopped sneering. "Aye, he spoke of you. Come with me, then, and I'll take you to him." He ducked back into the woods, to return a moment later carrying a yew-wood long-bow almost as tall as he was. Without looking back, he hurried north. The three men from Duthil matched him stride for stride.

After a while, Mordec asked. "Did you truly have friends back there?"

That made the man from Herth's clan stop and grin. "You'll never know, will you?"

Not too much later, the blacksmith realized he was heading downhill: he and his comrades had reached the north-facing slope at last. But the trees were so thick around him that he could not see very far. He tramped on. Sooner or later, he would learn what he needed to know.

About two thirds of the way down the hillside, the forest abruptly gave way to meadow. The Cimmerian scout pressed on. Mordec stopped dead in his tracks. So did Balarg and Nectan. Their eyes were wide with astonishment. After a moment, Mordec realized his were, too.

The encampment sprawled over more than a mile of land, tents and lean-tos thrown up in the wildest disorder and men picking their way between them. The disciplined Aquilonians would have laughed themselves sick at the chaos. But they would have laughed out of the other side of their mouths at the great swarm of Cimmerians mustered here. Mordec had never dreamt so many of his countrymen could come together in one place without starting to murder one another. "Crom!" murmured Nectan, at least as astonished.

That soft exclamation made the scout realize he had lost the men he was supposed to be guiding. He looked back over his shoulder and saw them staring at the ragged but huge gathering of the clans. "Not bad, eh?"

"No." At the sight of such a host, Mordec's weariness fell from him like a discarded cloak. "Not bad at all."

Conan did not mind watching Nectan's sheep. As it often did, getting out of Duthil for a while appealed to him. If he did not have to see Tarla—and, most especially, if he did not have to see Count Stercus—he did not have so great a need to brood about what might have passed between them.

Keeping an eye on the new year's lambs pleased him better. They were too large now for any eagle to hope to carry off, but they wandered farther from their mothers than they had when they were smaller. That made them easier for wolves to take—or so it would have, at any rate, had the blacksmith's son not been vigilant.

On the little hillcrest from which he watched the flock, the air was crisp and clean and clear. It smelled of the meadow, and of the forests that were never far away in Cimmeria. The village stinks Conan was used to might have belonged to a different world. A slow smile stretched across his face. This was the life a man was meant to lead. If he could have spent the rest of his days herding sheep on the hillsides and meadows of his native land, he was sure he would have been happy.

He leaned back on the soft green grass, folded his hands behind his head, and smiled up at the sun, which had peeped out for a little while from behind the usually all-enshrouding Cimmerian mist. Some would have taken that pasture as an invitation to fall asleep, but Conan knew the sleeping shepherd was the one whose flock faced misfortune.

Regardless of what he knew, a yawn escaped his lips. He might have let himself doze, there in the fitful sunshine. He might have—but a sudden scream in the distance sent him scrambling to his feet.

The cry rang out again. It had to have burst from a woman's throat—and from the throat of a woman who knew herself to be in desperate peril. Conan snatched up his bow and quiver and began to run. He spared the sheep one brief glance over his shoulder as he dashed into the forest. For the next little while, they would have to fend for themselves.

Yet another scream dinned in Conan's ears. He nearly cried out himself, to tell the woman to keep screaming. Each shriek gave him a clearer notion of where she was. But if what harried her was man, not beast, Conan knew he would only warn that rescue was on the way. He held his tongue, but ran harder than ever.

At that pace, not even such a woodswise hunter as Conan could hope to travel silently. He heard small animals bounding away in all directions. He even saw a fox turn tail and flee. He remembered as much later. At the time, the fox scarcely registered.

Before long, he paused, panting, and cocked his head to one side. He knew he was close now, and did not want to run too far. A squawking commotion among the jays off to his left sent him hurrying in that direction. A moment later, another scream told him he had guessed well.

When he burst into the little clearing, he saw a girl on the ground, her tunic torn off, her bare skin white and glowing in the sun, her hands cruelly tied behind her, one of her ankles bound to a sapling. Above her towered a man who, by his swarthy coloring and light brown hair, had never been born in Cimmeria. The fellow looked up in surprise at Conan's arrival.

"Stercus!" cried Conan. "Die like the beast you are, you filthy Aquilonian devil!" He nocked an arrow, raised the bow, and drew it with all the fury in him—drew it with too much fury, in fact, for the bowstring snapped and the arrow spun away uselessly.

Count Stercus' sword already had blood on it. He gave Conan a mocking bow. "You see how Mitra favors me," he said. "I had not thought to combine two pleasures here, but since you are kind enough to give me the chance—" He slid forward in a fencer's crouch.

"Run, Conan! Save yourself!" called the girl.

"Tarla!" said Conan. Her words had on him the effect opposite the one she had intended. As long as she was in danger, he would not, could not, dream of fleeing. Throwing aside the bow, which was no good to him now, he quickly stooped and grubbed two stones out of the dirt. He hurled one, the smaller, at Stercus' head.

The Aquilonian nobleman was swift and supple as a serpent. Laughing a mocking laugh, he ducked the flying stone. But even as he ducked, Conan flung the other stone at his right hand, and it stuck squarely. Stercus let out a sudden, startled howl of pain. His sword spun through the air, to land well out of reach. Roaring like a panther, Conan charged him.

Stercus matched the blacksmith's son in inches, but Conan was already wider through the shoulders than the invader. He thought to bear Stercus down and crush or choke the life from him. But what he thought was not what happened, for the nobleman was wise in ways of wrestling he had never imagined. Conan found himself lifted and flipped and slammed to the ground, the arrows flying out of his quiver to land all around him.

"However you like, Conan," said Stercus, smiling a twisted smile. "For any way you like, I am your master." He lashed out at Conan with a booted foot. But the blacksmith's son had expected that. He grabbed the boot with both hands and yanked. With a startled squawk, Stercus toppled. But he kicked Conan away when the Cimmerian would have sprung on top of him. The two of them grappled, rolling and pummeling and cursing each other as foully as they could.

Stercus soon found the fight warmer than he really wanted. He tried to knee Conan in the groin. More by luck than by Conan's design, Stercus caught him in the hipbone instead: a painful blow but not a disabling one. Conan seized a fallen arrow and scored the back of Stercus' hand with the point. Stercus' laugh was more than half snarl. "You'll have to do better than that, barbarian!" he said.

The Aquilonian brought his knee up again, this time into the pit of Conan's stomach. The air whooshed out of the blacksmith's son. He writhed on the ground struggling to breathe, all else forgotten. Tarla wailed in despair. Count Stercus laughed once more, this time triumphantly.

But even as he rose to finish Conan, he suddenly gasped in horror. "I burn!" he whispered. "Oh, I burn! Poison!" He shook all over, like a man with an ague. His eyes rolled up in his head. Foam started from his mouth. He let out a bubbling shriek of supernal agony. The foam gave way to blood. Now Stercus was the one whose breath failed, and his failed forever. Tearing at his own throat for the air that would not pass, he fell over, dead.

When Conan got his breath back, he looked at the arrow that had slain Count Stercus. Sure enough, it had a greenish discoloration on the head and several inches down the length of the shaft: it was one of those he had envenomed from the fangs of the serpent he slew in the temple out of time. He had not known that when he grabbed it and used it. But who had proved mightier here, Mitra or Crom?

He scrambled to his feet, shaking off the battering that Stercus had given him as a dog coming out of a stream might shake off cold water. And then he snatched up Stercus' sword and hurried over to Tarla.

"Conan!" she said. The sound of his name in her mouth just then was worth more to him than the rubies of Vendhya, the gold of distant Khitai. And the look of her—Conan realized, more slowly than he might have, that she likely wished he would look away rather than staring at all Stercus had uncovered. And look away he did, but only after he had seen his fill.

"Here," he said roughly, stooping beside her. "I'll get you loose. Hold still, now, or you're liable to get cut."

Freeing her ankle was the work of a moment. He had to take more care with the thongs that bound her hands, but soon they too troubled her no more. As soon as the job was done, she turned lithely, flung her arms around him, and covered his face with kisses. "I thought he'd kill you!" she exclaimed. "Oh, Conan, sweet Conan, I was so afraid!"

He hardly heard a word she said. That she held him was miracle enough. Of themselves, his arms tightened around her as well. At the pressure of his hands against her bare, smooth flesh, she squeaked in surprise—surprise, perhaps, not altogether unmixed with pleasure. A heartbeat later, though, she twisted away and snatched up the tunic Count Stercus had stripped from her. But even after she donned it once more, it scarcely covered her, for Stercus had torn it in taking it away.

"I'd better bring you back to the village," said Conan. He cast a longing glance toward Stercus' great horse, which was tied to a young pine at the far edge of the clearing. He would have liked nothing better than to return to Duthil aboard the nobleman's charger. But he had never been on horseback, and bringing the destrier back to Duthil would have told the nearby garrison that Stercus had come to grief. Regretfully, he shook his head. Even more regretfully, he realized he had to leave behind Stercus' armor, which lay discarded beside the horse. The back-and-breast would be too small for him, but the helm might well fit. Even so—no. Better to sneak back and get them under cover of darkness. The sword he would keep now.

"Duthil will be all in an uproar," predicted Tarla. "That—that wretch killed Wirp and another boy who tried to keep him from stealing me. He cut one of them down, and the horse struck the other with its hoof." She shuddered at the memory and interlaced her fingers with Conan's.

He squeezed her hand, several different excitements warring in his breast. "Our folk will not bear an outrage like that," he said. "If there is to be an uprising against the Aquilonians at last, let the bards sing that it began in Duthil."

"Aye," said Tarla softly. "I—I was wrong to let Stercus have anything to do with me. I did it partly to make you jealous. I'm—I'm sorry."

"It doesn't matter." Conan's voice was rough. "He got what he deserved. Now we'll get you home to your father, and we'll spread the word of what happened to you in Duthil, and then"—he brandished Stercus' blade—"then let Aquilonians look to their lives!" Hand in hand, he and Tarla started down the track toward the village.

chapter xi

The Rising

A trumpeter blew a long blast on a battered horn. Mordec, by then, had grown used to the bugle calls that rang out from the Aquilonian encampment by Duthil. Those were sweet and musical. This was only noise, and harsh, discordant noise at that. But the sweet, musical calls belonged to the invaders, while this was of Cimmeria. He did not need to wonder which he preferred.

Not far away from him, Herth scrambled onto a lichen-covered boulder that thrust its way up through the grass of the meadow. The trumpeter's call blared out again. All through the vast, disorderly Cimmerian encampment, fierce eyes—some gray, others piercing blue—swung toward the northern chieftain.

"Hear me, men of Cimmeria!" cried Herth in a great voice. "Hear me, men of valor! We have come, many of us, from afar to right a great wrong and to drive the foul invaders from the south out of our land forevermore." He pointed south-ward, over the hills Mordec and Balarg and Nectan had crossed not long before. "Well, warriors? Shall we set our brothers free?"

"Aye!" Like a wave, the answering shout swelled and

swelled, until at last it filled the great encampment. That one ferocious, indomitable word came echoing back from the hills, again and again: "Aye! Aye! Aye!"

Mordec turned to Nectan and Balarg, who stood beside him. "Now let Stercus reap what he has sown."

Both his fellow villagers nodded. Balarg's response in no way differed from Nectan's. Mordec also nodded, in sober satisfaction. Unless he was altogether mistaken, the weaver made as true and trusty a Cimmerian as any warrior here who had traveled far to spill Aquilonian blood.

Herth pointed toward the south once more. "Forward, then!" he shouted.

And forward the Cimmerians went. No Aquilonian army could have done the like. Aquilonians, civilized men, traveled with an elaborate baggage train. The Cimmerians simply abandoned everything they could not carry with them. They had briefly paused here to gather in full force. For that, lean-tos and tents had proved desirable. Now the Cimmerians forgot them. They would eat what they carried in belt pouches and wallets. They would sleep wrapped in wool blankets, or else on bare ground.

But they would march like men possessed. And they would fight like men insane. Past that, what else mattered?

They had no generals, no colonels, no captains. They had clan chiefs—and listened to them when they felt like it. In long, straggling columns, they followed several tracks that led into and through the hills separating them from the province the Aquilonians had carved out of their country. They had only the vaguest notion of what they would find there. They cared very little. If it was not of Cimmeria, they would slay it.

Mordec and his companions from Duthil had come a long way. Most of the warriors streaming south had come from farther still. If they did not need rest, Mordec sternly told himself he did not need it, either. He watched Nectan and

Balarg brace themselves With him, they began to retrace their steps.

How many men tramped toward the Aquilonian province? Mordec had no idea. Enough, though. He was pretty sure they would be enough.

This time, he and Balarg and Mordec took the straight road, the road through the valley, that led back toward Duthil. It was shorter and involved less climbing than the track they had followed to reach the great Cimmerian camp. Mordec thought he had earned that much relief. And the straight road had Aquilonian patrols on it. The blacksmith carried an axe whose head he had forged himself. He intended to blood that axe again. It had been thirsty too long.

He pushed the pace, wanting to be among the first who came upon the Gundermen and Bossonians. His fellow villagers kept up with him, though they lacked his iron endurance and had to force themselves along. They were not at the very forefront when Cimmerians met Aquilonians, but they were close enough to join in the fight.

That fight was short and savage. The Aquilonians put up the best struggle they could, but before long Cimmerian numbers simply overwhelmed them. Mordec did indeed blood his axe—a Gunderman's head stared up glassily beside his body. Someone said, "A couple of the devils got away."

"Not good," said Mordec. "They'll warn their countrymen."

The other Cimmerian shrugged. "Let them. We'll be upon them soon enough, come what may."

"But—" Mordec gave it up. He had spent too much time in the company of the civilized Aquilonians. The future would be what it was, warning or no. He nodded. "Aye. We'll be upon them soon enough."

Conan and Tarla walked hand in hand down the track toward Duthil. In his other hand Conan clutched Count Stercus' sword. He had plunged it into the ground again and again to cleanse it of the blood of his fellow villager. Soon enough, he hoped, it would drip with Aquilonian gore. It was a rich weapon, the blade chased with gold and the hilt wrapped in gold wire. Conan cared little for the richness. That the sword was long and sharp mattered more.

"You saved me," said Tarla for perhaps the dozenth time. Her eyes glowed.

He squeezed her hand. He had no words to show her what he felt; pretty speeches were not in him. But he knew, and he thought Tarla knew, too. Nothing else made any difference.

"Almost there now," said Tarla.

Conan nodded; he knew the landmarks on the trail as well as he knew the backs of his own hands. He fretted about Nectan's sheep, for he knew they might fall into danger without him there to watch over them. But Tarla was more important. Once he brought her back to Balarg's house, he would hurry back to the meadow and resume the duty his father had set him.

Suddenly he halted, the inborn alertness of one who lived close to nature warning him something ahead was amiss. Tarla would have walked on, but his grip on her hand checked her. "Something's not right," he said, cocking his head to one side to listen.

After imitating his gesture, Tarla frowned in pretty confusion. "I don't hear anything," she said.

"Nor do I," answered Conan. "And we should—we're close enough to Duthil by now. Where's all the usual village noise? Too quiet by half, if you ask me."

"It's not always noisy there," said Tarla.

"No, but—" Conan broke off. He let himself be persuaded. If the girl he cared about more than anything in the world—at least for the moment—thought everything was all right, then all right everything was likely to be, merely because she thought so. Squeezing her hand again, he went forward once more.

In back of Duthil, the woods grew close to the village. He and Tarla were no more than ten or twenty yards from the closest houses when they came out into the open. They both stared in astonished horror at what they saw. Blood and bodies were everywhere. The stench of all that blood, a heavy iron stink that might almost have come from the smithy, filled Conan's nostrils. More ravens and vultures and carrion crows spiraled down by the moment.

But scavenger birds were not all that moved in Duthil. A pair of Bossonian archers spotted Conan and Tarla as they came forth from the forest. "Mitra!" exclaimed one. "We missed a couple of these damned barbarians."

"Well, we'll get them now," answered the other. Both reached over their shoulders for arrows, nocked them, and, in the same instant, let fly.

Both Bossonians aimed for Conan. He was plainly the more dangerous of the two—and, if they shot him, they might have better sport with Tarla. The bowmen were well trained and long practiced in what they did. Both shafts flew straight and true—but Tarla sprang in front of the blacksmith's son and took them full in the breast.

"A life for a life, Conan," she said. "Make us free." If she knew any pain, she did not show it. She fell with a smile on her face.

"No!" howled Conan. But as he stooped beside her, two more arrows hissed over his head. He turned then, and ran for the woods. Had Tarla not said those last three words, he would have thrown his life away charging the Bossonians. Now he could not, not when he had her last wish—no, her last command—ringing in his ears. He had to live. He had to avenge.

Yet another arrow thudded into the trunk of a pine by the

side of the track, while the fletching of one more brushed his shoulder as the shaft flew ever so slightly high. Then he was out of sight of the Bossonians. If they came after him, he intended to double back and ambush them. He paused to listen. When he heard the clink of mailshirts, he cursed and began running hard again. That meant they had pikemen with them, in numbers too great for one to assail.

"My own bow, then," muttered Conan as he pounded up the track. Fitting a new string would be but a minute's work. His own bow—and Count Stercus' head. No symbol would be more likely to rouse Cimmeria to rebellion against the invaders from the south than proof the hated governor was dead. But Conan would gladly have given even the abominable Stercus his life back again in exchange for Tarla's if Crom but granted such bargains.

Only after he was well away from Duthil did he stop again, cursing as foully as he knew how. If the Aquilonians had worked a massacre in his home village, what of his father? What of his mother? That last thought almost sent him running back down the track, straight toward the Gundermen and Bossonians. But no—they demanded a greater vengeance than he alone could wreak.

He found the clearing in which he had rescued Tarla. Count Stercus lay where he had fallen, an expression of anguish and horror still imprinted upon his dead features. Grimly, Conan hewed the head from the Aquilonian's body. Stercus' narrow blade was not the ideal tool for the job; a Cimmerian claymore would have been better. But the blacksmith's son did what he had to do.

Even as he lifted Stercus' head by the hair, a man called to him from the far edge of the clearing: "A fine prize, that. Whose would it be?"

He whirled, Stercus' head in his left hand, Stercus' sword in his right. The newcomer was another Cimmerian, but not a man he had seen before. He said, "It is the head of Stercus himself, the Aquilonians' accursed commander. However great a prize it may be, it was far too dearly won."

"Count Stercus' head? Crom!" exclaimed the stranger, who was lean and strong and worn from much travel. He wore an iron cap on his head and carried a formidable pike. Gathering himself, he went on, "This is great news, if true. Bring it straightaway to Herth, for he has with him men from the south who will know if you lie."

Conan raised his sword. "If you say I lie, you will lie yourself—lie stark and dead," he growled. "Take me to Herth." By the way he spoke, he might have been a chief himself.

And the other Cimmerian nodded, accepting and even honoring his touchy pride. The fellow pointed to Stercus' charger and back-and-breast and helm. "Did those belong to the Aquilonian wretch?"

"They did," said Conan indifferently. "Take the horse and the corselet, if they suit you. They are of no use to me. Let me try the helmet first." When he found it fit, he laughed grimly. "It will do better on my head now than on Stercus'." He shook his ghastly trophy.

"You give with both hands, like the leader of a clan," said the other Cimmerian.

"I am not. I am only a blacksmith's son," said Conan. "Take me to Herth. If he has men from the south in his company, they will know I am no liar."

When they came upon the meadow where Conan had warded Nectan's flock, he found more strangers taking charge of the sheep. "We must eat," said the man with him. "We have come far and traveled hard."

Though Conan would have liked to protest, he found he could not. "Better you than the Aquilonians," he said.

"You speak truth. Ah, there." His new companion pointed. "There is Herth, coming out of the forest. He has the southern men with him. Do you know any of them?"

"The biggest is my father," answered Conan. He ran toward Herth and Mordec. Dread clogged his heart when he saw Balarg with then, but he kept going.

"Conan!" cried Mordec, who lumbered forward to greet him. "What have you got there?" An amazed smile of pure delight spread over his father's face. "That is Stercus' head, Stercus' and no one else's." He turned back to shout at Herth: "Here's the Aquilonian leader dead, slain by my son. What wonderful news!"

But Conan shook his head. "No. Everything else I have to say is bad. Let Balarg only come up to hear, and I will tell it all."

Balarg recognized the head as quickly as Mordec had. "This is bravely done," he said. "Most bravely done indeed. If you seek Tarla's hand, how can I say no now?"

"I cannot seek Tarla's hand, however much I might want to," said Conan, and he went on to tell how he and Tarla had gone back to Duthil, and what they had seen there, and how Tarla had met her end. He looked at his father. "Had I known that you and Balarg were away from the village, I would have taken her north, not south, and then she might yet breathe."

Mordec's face might have been a mask of suffering cut from stone. "So she might. Not all my choices have turned out well, however much I wish they would have. I fear for your mother, lad."

"So do I," said Conan. "I came away for the sake of revenge alone, for Tarla and for her. Without that to think of, I would gladly have died there."

"No. It is for the Aquilonians to die," said Balarg in a voice like iron. Conan had never heard the like from him. "If they will slaughter innocents, they have sealed their fate. Blood and death and ruin to them!" Tears ran down his cheeks, though Conan did not think he knew he shed them.

Herth stepped forward and nodded to Conan. The clan chief and the blacksmith's son were much of a height. Herth said, "Lead us to this Duthil place, boy, and you'll have your vengeance. I promise you that."

"With my father and Balarg and Nectan, I would go back to Duthil whether you and your men come or not," said Conan. "But come if you care to. The Aquilonians have a fortified camp beyond the village with enough archers and pikemen in it to glut you all on gore."

"Forward, then," said Herth, and forward they went.

Sickened by the sights and stinks of death all around him, Granth son of Biemur finally threw up his hands in disgust. "Enough!" he said. "Plundering a battlefield after a fight is one thing. Plundering a place like this—" He shook his head. "If only these folk had a little more, we might be robbing the houses we grew up in. It makes me want to retch."

"Then go away," said Benno the archer, who had no such qualms. "More for the rest of us."

Maybe he thought he would shame Granth into going after booty with the other soldiers from the garrison. If he did, he was wrong. Granth turned and strode back toward the palisaded camp just south of Duthil. Benno had been pulling the wool stuffing out of a mattress in the hopes the Cimmerians who had slept on it had also secreted some of their valuables inside it. So far, his hope looked likely to be disappointed.

Granth almost ran into Vulth, who came out of the blacksmith's house carrying a heavy hammer. "What good is that?" demanded Granth.

"Not much, probably," admitted his cousin. "You look sour enough to spit vinegar. What's your trouble?"

"This." Granth's wave encompassed it all. "Are we a pack of ghouls out of the desert, to batten on the dead?"

"The Cimmerians won't miss it any more," said Vulth. "None of them left alive except maybe the blacksmith's son."

"He shouldn't have got away, either," said Granth gloom-
ily. "He'll cause trouble for us."

"What can one boy do?" asked Vulth with a dismissive
shrug.

Before Granth could even begin to answer, the soldiers at
the northern edge of the village, the edge closest to the endless
forest, cried out in surprise and alarm. And other cries mingled with those of the Bossonians and Gundermen: fierce
shouts in a language Granth had never bothered to learn.
They filled the pikeman's ears, and seemed to swell like approaching thunder.

"Cimmerians!" yelled someone, and then the storm fell on
Captain Treviranus' men.

More barbarians than Granth had imagined there were in
the world came loping out of the woods. As had the northern
men in the fight at Fort Venarium, they wielded a wild variety
of weapons. Here, though, they took the Aquilonians altogether by surprise—and here, too, no knights would come to
the rescue of the pikemen and archers. One of the barbarians
brandished Stercus' staring head.

"Form up, men! Form up!" shouted Treviranus desperately. "If we fight them all together, we still may win!"

But the Aquilonians never got the chance to follow their
commander's good advice. The enemy was upon them too
suddenly and in numbers too great, while they themselves
were scattered all through Duthil and not looking for battle.
But whether they sought it or not, it found them, and they
had to do what they could. Many of them, beset from front
and rear and sides all at the same time, simply fell. Others
gathered in struggling knots, islands in a sea of Cimmerians,
islands bloodily overwhelmed one by one.

Granth and Vulth, near the southern edge of the village,
had a few moments longer to ready themselves for the onslaught than most of their comrades. "Side by side and back

to back to the palisade," said Vulth. "It's the only hope we've got, and it's a long one."

Side by side and back to back it was: a savage business, but somehow less so than Granth had expected. In point of fact, he had never expected to reach the palisade at all. But after he and Vulth stretched a couple of Cimmerians lifeless on the grass of the meadow, most of the barbarians ran past them rather than attacking. Had they seemed cowards, they would have been quickly dragged down and killed. The appearance of courage meant they soon required less of the genuine article.

But by the time they reached the palisade, reaching it did them no good. Cimmerians were already boosting one another up to the top and dropping down into the fortress that had held down Duthil and the surrounding countryside for the past two years. With the whole garrison inside, the fortified encampment might have put up a stout defense. With only a few men within, it would not last long.

"What do we do? Where do we go?" asked Granth, seeing that the fortress would not save them.

"Into the woods," said Vulth. "They're our only hope. If we can get to a settler's farm, we may hold out against these howling devils."

Granth laughed wildly. "We'll make them pay for hunting us down, anyhow."

Into the woods they plunged.

More blood flooded Duthil's muddy main street. Here, though, Conan watched in delight, not horror, for these were Aquilonians who fell. And the blacksmith's son used Count Stercus' sword to wicked effect, bringing down a pair of Bossonian archers and a Gunderman who relied on the length of his pike to hold foes at bay but who fatally underestimated his foe's pantherish quickness.

Before long, the only Aquilonians left in Duthil lay dead in the street. Few of the invaders had tried to surrender; none had succeeded. Cimmerians plundered the corpses, taking for their own weapons and armor finer than what they had brought south with them.

Herth strode along the street. The clan chief bled from a cut on his forehead and another on his leg. He said, "They are men after all. When I saw they'd put a village to the sword, I took them for cowards and murderers and nothing more. But they are warriors as well, and they did not flee."

"They are brave enough," said Mordec. "They beat us in battle once. And belike the village was roused against them after Stercus stole Balarg's daughter."

"He paid with his life, as he deserved to," said Conan.

Balarg nodded. "He did indeed. And yet I would have let him live, if only that would bring back Tarla with him."

"And I." Conan nodded, too.

"That cannot be now," said Herth. "Now there is vengeance, a great glut of vengeance, to take."

Mordec went into the smithy. When he came out, grief etched his harsh-featured face. His great shoulders slumped. As he strode toward Conan, fear suddenly filled the youth's heart—fear not of danger, nor of foes, but of the news he was about to hear. That fear must have shown on his face, for Mordec nodded heavily. "She's dead, boy. Your mother's dead," he said hoarsely. But a somber admiration also filled his voice: "She took up a sword and made them earn what they took. And there's blood on the blade, so they paid a price for it."

Herth set a hand on the blacksmith's shoulder. "Any warrior can take pride in such a wife."

"I do," said Mordec. He turned to Conan. "And so should you."

"Pride?" Conan shook his head. "After today, what care I for pride? After today, with my mother dead"—he did not

speak of Tarla, who was Balarg's to mourn, and whose place
in his affections was more recent—"what care I if I live or
die?"

"I will tell you, if you truly need telling," answered his
father. "Herth had the right of it: to be sure she did not die
for nothing, and to be sure the accursed Aquilonians will pay
dearly for robbing us of what they had no right to touch. Do
you suppose Crom would care to hear you snivel? You know
better, and so do I. We still have a job of work to do before
we can die content."

Conan considered. He looked down at the gold-chased,
gold-hilted blade he held in his hand. Slowly, he nodded. Stercus' sword had not yet slaked its full thirst for Aquilonian
blood. "Let it be as you say, Father. For vengeance's sake, I
will live. I will live, and the invaders shall die."

"Why else do you think I still walk and breathe?" returned
Mordec.

"Come, then." Herth pointed ahead. The gate to the palisaded Aquilonian encampment had come open. Cimmerians
poured in, although the mere fact that those gates had opened
argued that there was no need for more fighting men within
the palisade. The clan chief saw as much, saying, "Let us go
south. And wherever we meet them, death to the Aquilonians."

There was a war cry Conan would eagerly shout. He went
into the smithy. Mordec took a step toward him and reached
out as if to halt his progress, but Conan twisted past. The
blacksmith started to go after him, then checked himself. To
Herth, he said, "Best he should see, I suppose."

"Belike," said the clan chief. "If he needs one more reason
to fight, what better?" After a moment, as if reminding himself, Herth added, "I'm sorry, Mordec."

"So am I," answered Conan's father. "She did not fear
death, not when she'd been battling it for years. This might
have been quicker and cleaner than she would have got in the

natural course of things. Still, though, the invaders will pay for robbing her of the time she would have had left."

When Conan came out into the street once more, his face was as set and grim as Mordec's. His eyes burned with a dry, terrible fire. "Death to the Aquilonians," he said. In his mouth, it was not a war cry after all. It was simply a promise.

Two men burst out of the woods at the edge of Melcer's field of barley. The farmer threw down his hoe and snatched up his pike. The men were so ragged and haggard and dirty, he thought they had to be Cimmerians. But the hair peeping out from under their helmets was as blond as his own, which meant they were Gundermen like himself. He did not set down the pike even so. Gundermen too could be robbers and brigands.

"Who are you?" he asked sharply. "What are you doing on my land? Answer me right this minute, or by Mitra I'll run you off it."

They could not answer him immediately. They both stood there panting, as if they had run a long, long way. At last, the younger one, a fellow with formidably wide shoulders and a face friendly despite its weariness, managed to gasp out, "The Cimmerians are over the border."

To Melcer, that was the worst news in the world. "Are you sure?" he said. "How many of them?"

The newcomers carried pikes, too, the pikes of foot soldiers. They held them out, not threateningly but so that Melcer could see the fresh bloodstains on the spearshafts. "We're sure, all right," said the older one. "How many?" He turned to his comrade. "How many do you suppose, Granth?"

"Oh, about a million," answered Granth, the broad-shouldered one. "Maybe more."

"They ran us out of Duthil," added the other Gunderman. "To hell with me if I know whether anybody else from the garrison is left alive. Stercus is dead, not that he's any great loss. And those barbarian devils have been baying at our heels ever since. If you're going to save yourself, you'd better do it now, or you're a dead man. You may be a dead man anyhow."

Melcer looked around his farm. He saw all the work of the past two years: stout cabin, barn, garden, fields. Then he looked to the north. He knew where he was likely to see smoke rising, and how much. More fires were burning than could be accounted for by the settlers' usual business, and some of the columns of smoke rising from the accustomed places were thicker and blacker than they should have been, as if rising from buildings rather than chimneys. Melcer was not afraid to make a stand if that stand had some hope of success. Dying to no purpose was something else again.

He nodded to the two pikemen. "My thanks. Go on and warn more folk." Even as the words left his mouth, a south-bound horseman galloped past winding a horn and shouting out danger to all who would heed him. Melcer nodded again. Now he had confirmation, not that he truly needed it. "Aye, go on, both of you. I'll tend to my business here."

On the very edge of hearing came howls that might have burst from wolves' throats—that might have, but had not. Those were the war cries of barbarians, barbarians on the loose, such swarms of savages had no business running loose within the bounds of the province. They had no business running loose, but here they came.

"We're off, then," said the older pikeman. "We'll make for Fort Venarium, I expect. If we can throw back the Cimmerians anywhere, that will be the place. And what of you?"

"If things go ill, perhaps I'll see you there," said Melcer. Above the uproar of the barbarians, a bell began to ring, loudly and insistently. "That is the signal for the yeomen of the countryside to gather. You only garrisoned this land. We live on it, and we will not give it up."

"They'll smash you," said Granth. "You don't know their numbers."

Melcer answered with a shrug. "If they do, then they do. But if they take us down to hell, you had best believe we'll have a fine Cimmerian escort to lead the way."

The two pikemen began arguing. Melcer had no time for them. He ran back toward the farmhouse—and met his wife hurrying his way, with their baby daughter on one hip and Tarnus, their son, hurrying beside her. "The alarm bell!" exclaimed Evlea.

"Sure enough," said Melcer. "The Cimmerians are over the border—over the border in a great horde, all too likely. We can flee or we can fight. I aim to fight."

"What are the odds?" asked Evlea.

He shrugged again. "I know not. All I know is, this is my land. If I must die for it, then die I will, and be buried on it." He quickly kissed her. "Get out while you can, dear."

She shook her head. "If I can find someplace to leave the children, I'll fight beside you. This is not your land alone."

One of the pikemen came over to them. "Vulth thinks he has a better chance in Venarium," said Granth. "Me, I'd sooner make my stand as far north as I can. I'm with you, if you'll have me."

"Gladly," said Melcer. Evlea nodded. The bell tolled out its warning cry. Melcer went on, "We're to make for it when it rings, and do what needs doing once we're gathered there."

Melcer hoped he could find a place to leave his children— and his wife—in safety before they came to the bell. But he discovered none, none he would trust against an assault by more than a handful of barbarians. By all the signs, far more than a handful were loose in the land. The bell rang in front of the house of a farmer named Sciliax. Pointing to the cabin, a bigger, fancier, stronger building than Melcer's, Sciliax said, "Women and children in there. We'll defend it with all we have."

All they had, at the moment, consisted of about thirty farmers armed with the sort of weapons farmers carried, plus perhaps half a dozen real soldiers like Granth. More men were coming their way. Would they be enough? Melcer saw, recognized, and worried about the expression on Granth's face: the pikeman did not like the odds. Slowly, Melcer said, "Maybe we ought to serve out swords and spears and whatever else we've got to the women who will take them."

"Yes, by Mitra!" cried Evlea.

But Sciliax said, "What if they're taken?"

"What if we lose?" returned Melcer. "They'll surely be taken then, and they won't have us at their sides to save them."

Sciliax was older than most of the settlers who had come north out of Gunderland, and plainly set on old ways of doing things. But he glanced toward Granth, as if wondering what a real soldier thought of the question. Granth did not hesitate. "This fellow's right," he said, pointing Melcer's way. "Whatever you do—whatever we do, I should say—our chances are bad. The more fighters we have, the better we're likely to fare. I've seen Cimmerian women fight. Are ours weaker than theirs?"

Before Sciliax could answer, Evlea said, "I'll see to it, then." She rushed into the farmhouse. Women began spilling out of it, women tough enough to make a go of things beyond the frontier of Gunderland. They all clamored for weapons. Some were young, some not so young. Before long, most of them had spears and axes and swords. Some of the men who wore helms gave them to women. With a sort of bow, Granth presented his to Melcer's wife.

"Here they come!" Suddenly, the cry rose from a dozen throats. Melcer's gaze went to the woods north of Sciliax's farm. Black-haired Cimmerians loped out from among the trees. They saw the defenders mustered in front of the farmhouse, saw them and swarmed toward them. The barbarians advanced in no neat formation, but they were ready—more than ready—to fight.

"Form a line!" shouted Granth. "Everyone—help your neighbor. If you save him, he may save you next. No point in running. They'll just slay you from behind." No one had appointed him general of this little force. He simply took the job—and the embattled farmers and their wives obeyed him.

Here came a Cimmerian swinging a scythe. He was lean and dirty and looked weary, as if he had traveled a long way with nothing more in mind than murdering Melcer. He shouted something in his own language. Melcer could not understand it, but doubted it was a compliment. The Cimmerian swung back the scythe—and Melcer speared him in the belly.

The soft, heavy resistance of flesh tugged at the pike. For a moment, the barbarian simply looked very surprised. Then he opened his mouth wide and shrieked. Melcer felt like shrieking, too. He had never killed a man before. He had to kick out with his foot to clear the Cimmerian from his pike.

Another Cimmerian swung a two-handed sword, a stroke that would have taken off Melcer's head had it connected. But the weapon was as cumbersome as it was frightful, and he easily ducked under it. He had gone a lifetime without killing anyone, but claimed his second victim only moments after the first.

He had no time to look around and see how the fight as a whole was going. He could only do his best to stay alive himself and make sure any barbarian who came near him fell. Some of the screams and shouts on the battlefield in front of Sciliax's house came from women's throats. Melcer could not even look to see if Evlea remained hale. "Please, Mitra," he whispered, and fought on.

Cimmerians fell. So did Gundermen. Some lay still, and would never rise again. Others thrashed and wailed and moaned, crying out their torment to the uncaring sky. The wounded on both sides sounded much alike. At first, the sounds of anguish tore at Melcer; as the fight went on, though, he heard them less and less.

After what seemed like forever, the Cimmerians sullenly drew back. Melcer had a chance to lean on his pike and draw a breath and look around. Evlea still stood. The axe in her hands had blood on the head. Granth's helmet sat dented and askew on her head. Granth himself was also on his feet. And so was Sciliax, though a scalp wound left his face bloody.

But the fight, very likely, was not over. As Melcer watched in dismay, more barbarians emerged from the trees to the north. He looked around in growing despair. Where would his own side find reinforcements?

chapter xii

The Fall of Venarium

Panting, Conan glared at the stubborn Gundermen who defended a sturdy farmhouse with a ferocity he had not thought any folk but his own could display. Beside him, flanks also heaving, stood his father. Mordec said, "They'll have their wives and their brats in there. If anything will make them stand fast until we cut them down, that's it."

"I know a couple of them," said Conan. His father looked at him in surprise. He pointed. "That one pikeman is from the garrison by Duthil."

"Oh, him. Aye." Mordec nodded. "He almost did for me a little while ago."

"And that other fellow, the tall farmer near him, worked lands not far from here," continued Conan. "He's not a bad man, or he wouldn't be if only he'd stayed in his own country. That's his woman there, with the axe."

"I mislike killing women, but if they try to kill me—" Mordec broke off and looked over his shoulder. "We have more men coming, I see. But those accursed Aquilonians will still take a deal of killing."

Off to one side, Herth was wrapping a rag around his head. His helm had kept a blow from smashing his skull, but the rim, driven down by the dint, left him with a long cut on his forehead. Wiping blood away from his eyes, the clan chief said, "That's what we've come for—to kill them."

The Cimmerians mustered themselves in a ragged line out of the range of the hunting bows a few of the Gundermen carried. Several of the men who had been in the fight before bore minor wounds. This had been Conan's first real taste of battle. He had dealt hard blows. He burned to deal more.

Ranged in front of the farmhouse, the yellow-haired farmers and soldiers waited. They were badly outnumbered now, but still stood defiant. "Why don't they go inside?" asked Conan. "They could give us a harder fight that way."

"They could for a little while," said Mordec. "Then we'd fire the place, and they'd burn with their families."

Conan grimaced, then nodded. Burning foes from a fortress—yes, he could see the need. Burning foes and families alike—he could, perhaps, see the need for that as well, but it raised his gorge even so. The women and children had done nothing to deserve such a fate but accompany their men into this land. Was that enough? Maybe it was.

Herth pointed toward the Gundermen. "Come on, lads!" he called to the Cimmerians around him. "Let's finish the job!"

Roaring and shouting, the Cimmerians surged forward. Mordec and Conan trotted side by side. Conan noted that his father did not waste his breath on war cries. He simply scanned the enemy line until he chose an opponent. Then he pointed at the man and spoke two words to Conan: "That one."

"The tall one with the pitchfork?" asked Conan, wanting to be sure. His father nodded. The two of them had fought as a team in their first clash with the embattled farmers. Few men, no matter how doughty, lasted long when beset by such a pair.

Shouting in Aquilonian, the man with the pitchfork thrust

at Mordec. The blacksmith beat aside the makeshift weapon with his axe. Conan drove Stercus' sword deep into the Gunderman's vitals. Blood spurted; its iron stink filled his nostrils. The Gunderman howled. Even with his dreadful wound, he tried to skewer Conan with the pitchfork. Mordec's axe—not a tool for felling trees, but a broad-headed war axe for cutting down men—descended. The sound of the blow reminded Conan of those made when cutting up a pig's carcass. The pitchfork flew from the farmer's suddenly nerveless hands. The fellow crumpled, his head all but severed from his body.

Another Gunderman fell to the two of them, and another. The farmers' line wavered. They still fought bravely, but bravely did not serve when each had to face more than one foe. In a furious, cursing knot, they fell back toward the farmhouse door. The three or four pikemen in mailshirts still on their feet defended the door, while some of the farmers—and the handful of women who had not fallen—ran inside.

One of the pikemen—the one Conan had recognized—nodded in an almost friendly way to Mordec and him. "I knew the two of you were trouble," the soldier said. "Now I see how right I was."

Some of the Aquilonians at the camp by Duthil had been dreadful. Some had merely been hard. A few, this fellow among them, had been decent enough. "If you stand aside, Granth, we will spare you," said Mordec.

Granth shook his head. "No. These are my people. If you try to harm them, I'll kill you if I can."

"Honor to your courage." Mordec might have been a man passing sentence. The fight grew fierce again, the Cimmerians battling to push past the last few defenders. Granth went down. Conan did not see how. He only knew that he fought his way into the farmhouse.

That was worse than any of the fighting outside had been. Women and children screamed like lost souls. Egged on by the presence of their loved ones, the Gundermen battled with reckless disregard for their own lives. From outside came a shout: "Clear away, you Cimmerians! We'll burn the farmhouse over their heads!"

Conan, by then, was caught up in the struggle. The fury of battle upon him, he did not want to break it off. His father dragged him out of the farmhouse by main force. Mordec was the only man there who could have overmastered him. Conan came close to striking out at the blacksmith, too. "We'll find more fighting later, never you fear," said Mordec, which helped resign the boy to turning aside from this clash.

Cimmerian archers shot fire arrows at the wooden walls and thatched roof of the farmhouse. Before long, the flames caught and began to spread. But even as some of the Cimmerians exulted, others pointed to the trees on the far side of the house and exclaimed, "They're fleeing there!"

"How can they?" demanded Conan. "We've got them cordoned off."

His father shook his head in what could only be admiration. "That damned Aquilonian must have dug himself an escape tunnel. What a sneaky wretch he has to be. He thought of everything—except he didn't run it quite far enough from the house."

The Cimmerians pounded after their prey. The fighting in amongst the trees was more confused than the battle before the farmhouse—more confused, but no less savage. Here and there, two or three Gundermen would turn at bay and sell their lives dear, allowing their comrades and their wives and children to escape the catastrophe that had befallen the colony.

Along with his father, Conan helped smash down one of those rear-guard efforts. More Aquilonians blundered along ahead of them. Now the invaders had a taste of defeat, a taste of terror. Conan wanted them to drink that cup to the very dregs.

He and Mordec swiftly gained on the running family

ahead. The woman had a baby on her hip and held a boy by the hand. "Go on, Evlea!" said the man. "I'll hold them off. Go on, I tell you." Pike in hand, Melcer turned and set himself. "Come on, barbarians!" he snarled. But then he recognized Conan. "You!"

"Go right, lad. I'll go left," said Mordec. "We'll take him down."

But Conan found himself with no great hunger for the blood of a man he did not hate. "Wait," he told his father. Mordec eyed him in astonishment, but did not charge ahead, as he had been on the point of doing. Conan spoke to Melcer in Aquilonian: "You leave this land? You leave our land?"

"Aye, curse you," growled the farmer.

"You leave and never come back?" persisted Conan. "You swear you leave and never come here again?"

"By Mitra, Cimmerian, this land will never see me again if I get out of it," said Melcer, adding, "Damn you! Damn you all!"

Conan shrugged off the curse and nodded at the oath. "Then go," he said. He spoke with authority a grown man— indeed, a clan chief—might have envied. The farmer from Gunderland and his family hurried off to the south.

They had not gone far before more Cimmerians hard on the heels of Conan and Mordec came trotting up. The newcomers, by the weave of their breeks, were men from the far north. They pointed indignantly at Melcer and his wife and children. "Are you daft? They're getting away!" cried one.

"Let them go," said Conan. "They have sworn an oath by their god to leave this land and never return. The farmer is a good man. What he has promised, he will do. It is enough, I say."

"And who do you think you are?" howled the Cimmerian from the north. "The King of Aquilonia?" He brandished his sword, as if to go after Melcer and Evlea and the children regardless of the oath the Gunderman had given.

"I am Conan son of Mordec," answered Conan proudly, "of the village of Duthil." That gave the other Cimmerians pause; they knew what had happened in Duthil, what had happened to Duthil, Conan added, "And anyone who would slay those Aquilonians will have to slay me first."

"And me." Mordec ranged himself alongside his son. They stood there, alert and watchful, waiting to see whether their own countrymen would charge them.

"Madness!" said the Cimmerian with the sword. The angry black-haired men shouted at one another and nearly began to fight among themselves, some wanting to slay Conan and Mordec, others respecting their courage even when that courage came for the sake of a foe. At last, that second group prevailed without any blows being struck. "Madness!" repeated the swordsman, but he lowered his blade.

"Let us go on," sad Mordec. "Plenty of other invaders loose in the woods, even if we give this handful their lives." In a low voice, he asked Conan, "Would you really have fought your own folk for the sake of a few Aquilonians?"

"Of course," answered Conan in surprise. "The farmer gave his oath, and I my word. Would you make me out a liar?"

"Did I not stand with you?" said his father. "But that northern man may have had the right of it even so when he spoke of madness." He clapped his son on the back. "If so, it's a brave madness. When Stercus' soldiers came in, I did not think you were a warrior. By Crom, my son, a warrior you are now."

"As I have need to be," said Conan. "My mother still wants vengeance." He cursed. "I could murder every accursed Aquilonian from here to Tarantia, and it would not be vengeance enough."

"You slew Stercus," said Mordec. "Everyone who had to live under him will envy you for that. And Verina died with blood on her blade. I think she was gladder to fall so than to let her sickness kill her a thumb's breadth at a time."

"It could be," said Conan reluctantly, after considerable thought. "But even if it is, the Aquilonians deserve killing." His father did not quarrel with him.

Melcer did not know who had owned the horse he acquired before it came to him. It was an Aquilonian animal, bigger and smoother-coated than the Cimmerian ponies he had occasionally seen in these parts. He put Tarnus on the horse's back, and sometimes Evlea and the baby as well. That let him head south faster than he could have with his whole family afoot.

And speed was of the essence. As long as he and his loved ones stayed ahead of the wave of Cimmerian invaders, they kept some chance of escaping the land that had risen against the settlers. If that wave washed over them, if too many barbarians were ahead of them on the road to Gunderland, they were doomed.

Conan and his father could have killed them all. Melcer knew as much. That the young barbarian had chosen to spare them instead still amazed the farmer. He had not thought any Cimmerian knew the meaning of mercy.

When he said that aloud, his wife shook his head. "Mercy had nothing to do with it," maintained Evlea.

"What name would you use, then?" asked Melcer.

"Friendship," she said.

He thought it over. "You may be right," he said at last, "although whenever I asked Conan if we were friends, he always told me no."

"He did not want to admit it," said Evlea. "Like as not, he did not want to admit it even to himself. But when the time came, he found he did not have it in him to slay a woman and children if he knew and liked their man."

That last phrase, no doubt, held the key. Melcer wondered what had happened back at Sciliax's farmhouse after his family and he used the escape tunnel. The memory of that terrifying journey through pitch blackness would stay with him until the end of his days. Clumps of dirt had fallen down on the back of his neck and his shoulders between the support beams. He had banged the top of his head on more than one of those beams, too, once or twice almost knocking himself cold. Every step of the way, he had gone in fear that the tunnel would collapse, burying him and his family forever. And screams of hatred and despair and agony had echoed from behind, driving him on like strokes of the lash. Better not to know, perhaps, what had chanced after he got out.

The horse stumbled. He yanked at the lead rope. "Keep going, you cursed thing," he growled. "If you don't keep going, we're ruined."

"Will we travel all night?" asked his wife.

"Unless that animal falls down dead under you, we will," answered Melcer. Then he shook his head. "No, not so: even if it dies, we go on, except then we go on afoot." He muttered under his breath. "These past two years, I've welcomed the long days and short nights of this northern summer. Now, though, now I would thank Mitra for less light and for more darkness to cloak us."

"Mitra does as he pleases, not as we please," said Evlea.

"Don't I know it!" Melcer looked around. Columns and puffs of black smoke rose all along the northern horizon, pyre after pyre marking the memory of Aquilonian hopes. Even as he looked, a fresh plume of smoke went up west and a little north of him. But the Cimmerians had not yet begun burning forts and steadings to the south. Therein lay his hope.

As the day wore on, he saw ever more settlers placidly working in their fields, men who did not yet realize peace here lay forever shattered. He shouted out warnings to them. Some cursed. Others laughed and called him a liar, thinking he was playing a joke on them. He wished he were.

The sun set in blood. Melcer kept going. He intended to

keep going as long as breath was in him, for he was sure the Cimmerians would do the same. The moon rose two hours after the sun set. He rejoiced and cursed at the same time: it would light his way, but it would also let marauding barbarians spy him. Where were the mists, where were the fogs, of Cimmeria? If they were not here, all he could do was go on, and go on he did.

He came to Venarium as the sun was rising again after too brief a night. His wife and children nodded and half dozed on the back of the horse, which tramped along as if worn unto death. He wished he could have treated the luckless animal better, but that would have endangered his family and him. The horse had to pay the price.

"What are you doing?" asked Evlea when he took the horse off the road that led to Venarium. He made for the river upstream from the town.

"They must know there that the blow has fallen," answered Melcer. "If they see me, they'll dragoon me into the army to try to hold Venarium. I swore an oath to the Cimmerian to leave his land—and I don't think we'll hold the place. So I'll skirt it if I can."

His wife did not have to think long before nodding. Melcer let the horse drink and crop the grass when it got down to the riverbank. He looked for a ford. About a mile east of Venarium, he found one. The water came up to his midsection; it barely wet the horse's belly. After he led the horse up onto the south bank, he did not make for the road again. Instead, he went straight into the middle of a dense patch of woods. He tied the weary horse to a sapling, then lay down, careless of his wet clothes. "We can rest here," he said. "With Venarium behind us, now we can rest."

Conan scratched at the rag bound to his left arm. The cut itched, but no longer pained him much. The Aquilonian soldier who had given him the wound was dead; the palisaded camp the man defended had gone up in smoke. Along with the other Cimmerians on the southbound road, Conan topped a last hill and stared ahead. "That must be Venarium," he said.

"No doubt," agreed his father. Mordec yawned. For all his iron strength, the marching and fighting had cruelly told on him.

Fresher because he was younger, Conan kept on looking at the town, and at the fortress at its heart. "How will we take this place?" he asked. That they would take it he had no doubt.

"This band alone won't do it," said Mordec. "We'll need to wait until more men come up. Then I suppose we storm it. What else can we do? We know nothing of siegecraft, and the Aquilonians might bring a new army against us while we sit in front of their fort."

Nectan the shepherd scowled at the houses and shops as much as he did at the fortress. "We'll burn all of it," he said, "and so we should. This was prime forest before the Aquilonians came."

"If we burn the houses and shops, the soldiers in the fortress won't be able to see what we're doing because of the smoke," said Conan.

His father eyed him. "Spoken like a true war leader," said Mordec. "Take that notion straight to Herth and put it in his ear. He needs to hear it. By Crom, my son, you may make a chieftain yourself one day."

Conan cared nothing about being a chieftain. He cared nothing about what might happen one day. Vengeance was the only thing that burned in him. The road to vengeance ran through Venarium. Knowing that, he went in search of Herth. The war leader was not hard to find. He had stayed at the forefront of the Cimmerian host ever since it burst upon the province the Aquilonians had stolen.

Herth heard Conan out, then nodded. "Here is a thought with some weight behind it," he said. "We already have plenty of reasons to burn Venarium. What need have we for such a place in our midst? It would only make us more like accursed King Numedides' men. And now you have told me precisely when and where the fires should be set. For this, I thank you."

Not all the Cimmerians were firmly under Herth's control. Such was the way of life among the warriors of the north. So many of them did as they pleased, not as any chieftain told them. More than a few did as they pleased in despite of what any chieftain told them. Having fought to the outskirts of the Aquilonian stronghold, they saw no reason why they should not fight their way straight into it.

The Aquilonians inside Venarium gave them such a reason. The defenders were not yet inclined to withdraw to the fortress. Archers lurked among the buildings at the outskirts of the town. As soon as Cimmerians drew within range, the archers began to shoot. They killed several men and wounded even more before the Cimmerians sullenly drew back.

"Here is what we will do," said Herth after fresh troop of black-haired barbarians came down from the north to augment his force. "We will all charge together at one signal. That way, the enemy cannot shoot many of us before we gain a lodgement in the town. Once we have done that, we can hunt down the bowmen—and any others who stand against us—because we have far more men than the Aquilonians. Wait for the signal, mind you, and then everyone forward together."

For once, no one quarreled, as often chanced when a war chief tried to impose his will on the men he more or less led. The bodies lying in front of Venarium spoke eloquently of the folly of every man's going forward for himself. The Cimmerians gathered themselves, looking to their weapons and looking for their friends and kinsmen. They had never been in the habit of marching or attacking in neat lines, but they all moved up to where they could hear the signal.

A bugle blared. The Cimmerians roared. They swarmed forward toward Venarium. A great excitement seized Conan, as if he had poured down too much ale. Here at last was the enemy's great stronghold. If Venarium fell, the Aquilonian hold on southern Cimmeria would be broken forever. He looked at the host of his countrymen dashing along to either side of him. How could the town, how could the fortress, keep from falling under such a weight of warriors?

Arrows arced out from the town toward the attackers. Here and there, a man fell, to lie thrashing or to lie still. But Herth had known what he was about. Too many men went forward for all, or even very many, of them to fall. On they came, roaring out their hatred of the foreigners who had tried to subject their land. And as soon as they got in among the homes and shops, the fight for the town of Venarium was as good as won.

Not that the Aquilonians in the town believed as much. Archers kept shooting from inside buildings. Pikemen would rush out of doorways, spear passing Cimmerians, and then try to get back to defend the entrances before other Cimmerians could cut them down. Sometimes they succeeded; sometimes they fell. But Venarium had plenty of defenders, and they were stubborn enough to make it a tough nut to crack.

Conan rapidly discovered that a sword did not make the ideal weapon with which to assail a pikeman. The soldiers who carried pikes had a longer reach than he did; he almost spitted himself on a pike, trying to get at the Gunderman who wielded it. But when another Cimmerian distracted the foe, Conan leaped close and drove the blade into his neck. He fell, blood spurting from the ghastly wound. Another Gunderman sprang forward to try to keep Conan's countrymen out of a shop. Someone from the street flung a rock at the Gunderman. He shrieked and staggered, his face a gory mask. He did not suffer long; Conan's thrust pierced his heart.

Before long, a cry went up in both Cimmerian and Aqui-

Ionian: "Fire!" Conan wondered whether Herth was using the ploy he had suggested, or whether some Cimmerian had simply concluded that burning out Venarium's defenders was the easiest and least costly way to flush them from the fine cover the buildings in the town afforded. He also wondered whether he would ever know, and doubted it very much.

"Ha!" shouted a Cimmerian, savage glee filling his voice. "Here's how we roast Numedides' swine!"

Smoke quickly thickened the air. Fighting fires was hard, even hopeless, work in the best of circumstances. Fighting fires in the middle of a desperate battle was impossible. As wooden buildings began to burn, the Aquilonian defenders came forth, either to fight in the streets or to flee back toward the fortress of Venarium.

Open space separated the fortress from the town. Count Stercus had not permitted taverns and saddleries to encroach on the palisade. Whatever else he had been, he had made a competent military engineer. Bossonian archers on a walkway inside the palisade shot at any Cimmerian who ventured into the cleared area.

The archers also shot at Aquilonians who ventured into the cleared area. By then, the town's attackers and defenders were inextricably mixed. Realizing as much, the Aquilonian officer in command ordered the gates shut against his countrymen outside, lest those gates also admit Cimmerians who would bring ruin with them.

Forced to fight out in the open in front of the fortress, the Gundermen and Bossonians who had been defending the town of Venarium realized only one thing was left to them: to sell their lives as dearly as they could. They turned at bay against the Cimmerians, fighting with the mad courage of men with nothing left to lose. Wild to crush the invaders, the Cimmerians battled back as ferociously.

Quarter was neither asked nor given in that wild struggle. Little by little, the Cimmerians fought their way toward the palisade. They did not have greater courage than their foes. They did have more men to throw into the fight. In the end, that sufficed.

Not far from Conan, Mordec's axe rose and fell, rose and fell. Red drops flew from it as he cut down one Aquilonian after another. "To me!" he roared again and again. "To me, you wolves of the north!"

And then, to Conan's surprise, the gates of the fortress flew open once more. Out stormed the knights of Aquilonia, of whom he had heard so much. He had seen how fearsome Stercus seemed, riding into Duthil on his great horse in his helmet—the very helmet now topping Conan's head—and back-and-breast. Twoscore knights thundered forth now, their lances couched, their faces—what could be seen of them—grim. "Numedides!" they cried, and, "Aquilonia!"

But their charge now proved less than it might have. For one thing, many of the men in front of the gates were Gundermen and Bossonians; the knights had to ride them down or force them aside before they could get to the Cimmerians. And, for another, the open space in front of the fortress of Venarium was so tightly packed with men, any charge quickly lost its momentum.

That left the knights an armored island in the midst of a Cimmerian sea. Many of them quickly threw aside their lances. They drew their swords and slashed away at the barbarians hemming them in on every side. But they could not keep all the Cimmerians away from them and their horses. Stallions screamed as they were stabbed. Knights were dragged from the saddle. Swords and daggers found the joints in their armor. The Aquilonians exacted a fearful toll from their foes, but more Cimmerians kept coming forward. The knights were irreplaceable. Once they went down to death, the men inside the fortress could send out no other such force.

Conan hurled a rock at an archer up on the wall. His aim

had been true against Stercus, and his aim was true now. The Bossonian clapped both hands to his left eye. He screamed loud enough to be heard above the din of battle. Screaming still, he staggered backward and fell off the walkway.

Not far from him, another Bossonian also went down, struck in the chest by a shaft from a Cimmerian bow. That left a gap in the defense, a gap the Aquilonians, beset everywhere, could not set right at once. "Come on!" cried Conan. "Boost me up, you men! If we once gain the palisade, Venarium's ours!"

Willing hands heaved him aloft. His own hands gained a purchase at the top of the palisade. He pulled himself up. He pulled himself over. He swung down onto the walkway, the first Cimmerian inside the Aquilonian stronghold. Soldiers rushed toward him, desperate to cut him down. At their van came a skinny little Bossonian. He shot at Conan. The arrow kissed the sleeve of the Cimmerian's tunic and flew harmlessly past.

As the archer nocked another shaft, Conan sprang forward. With tigerish quickness, he seized the little man and used his body as a shield and a flail, battering other Aquilonians and knocking several of them to the ground a dozen feet below. Then, roaring, he flung the luckless Bossonian down with them.

He was not the only Cimmerian on the walkway for long. Where he had gone, his countrymen were quick to follow. Soon a knot of northern warriors stood up there, hacking and smiting. More Gundermen and Bossonians came to try to slay them. The enemy knew what would happen if they held their ground.

"Stand aside, by Crom!" That great bass roar could only have come from Mordec. The blacksmith shouldered his way forward, to stand side by side with Conan once more. The blade of his axe was dented and all over blood. A wider smile than Conan had ever seen on him wreathed his usually somber features. He pointed to the foe. "At them!" he shouted, and Conan was not slow to join his charge.

As they had outside the fortress, the Aquilonians on the walkway fought with desperate bravery. Conan had doubted their courage before this uprising broke out. He doubted it no more. What flesh and blood could do, the Gundermen and Bossonians did. But flesh and blood could do only so much. He and Mordec, fighting side by side, were a host in themselves. And they had ever-growing weight behind them. The top of a ladder cleared the palisade. Cimmerians swarmed up it and onto the walkway.

"There's a stair." Mordec pointed with his axe. "We'll get down into the courtyard. Then this whole fortress will be ours."

A Gunderman lunged at him with a pike. Light on his feet despite his bulk, he sidestepped. Conan's sword bit into the Gunderman's wrist. The soldier's severed hand fell to the planks of the walkway with his spear. The Gunderman screamed. Mordec pushed him off the walkway, then surged forward once more.

Conan hacked and slashed and thrust. He was bigger and stronger and quicker than most of the men he faced, even if only down grew on his cheeks. Step by gory step, the head of the stairs grew closer. An arrow shot from the ground hissed past him and thudded into the logs of the palisade. Another shaft struck a Cimmerian behind him. His country-man's yells of anguish differed little from those of the Gun-derman he had mutilated.

More of Numedides' soldiers rushed up the stairs to try to stem the Cimmerian tide. Mordec's axe swept the head from a Bossonian's shoulders, then took off a Gunderman's arm above the elbow. "Come on!" shouted the blacksmith in Aquilonian. "Who's next to die?"

However brave the enemy soldiers were, such carnage could not help but daunt them, at least momentarily. Conan still at his right hand, Mordec set foot on the first step leading down into the fortress of Venarium. A moment later, they gained another step, and then another. After that, their foes recovered some of their spirit, and nothing came easy any more.

Easy or not, though, they and the rest of the Cimmerians cleared the stairway of Bossonians and Gundermen one hard-fought step at a time. "Forward!" bellowed Mordec again and again. Forward the men of the north went, over the hacked and bleeding bodies of those who would stand in their way— and over not a few of the bodies of their own countrymen. With a deep-throated roar of triumph, Mordec leaped from the last stair down to the ground within the fortress. He shouted again, this time with words in the cry: "Venarium is fallen! Venarium is ours!"

An arrow smote him, just to the left of the middle of his chest.

He stood there for a moment, a look of absurd surprise on his face. Then he turned to Conan, as if remembering something important he needed to say. Whatever it was, it never passed his lips. His eyes rolled up in his head. Like a toppling tree, he crumpled, the axe falling from fingers that suddenly would not hold it.

"Noooo!" shouted Conan, a long howl of despair and fury. That his father should fall in the moment of victory— "Curse you, Crom!" he cried, and threw Stercus' sword in a startled Gunderman's face. Then he snatched up the axe Mordec had wielded so well.

He swung that axe with a madman's fury. No Aquilonian could stand against him. No one could come close enough even to engage him. And he wounded more than one Cimmerian he did not recognize as a countryman because of his berserk grief. The men with whom he had fought his way into Fort Venarium grew as wary of him as the Gundermen and Bossonians they opposed.

"He is fey," said one Cimmerian to another, and his comrade nodded, for it did seem as if Conan willfully sought his own death on the battlefield.

But whether he sought it or not, it did not meet him at Venarium. Others died there, Aquilonians and Cimmerians alike. A handful of Bossonians and Gundermen managed to escape the falling fortress by scrambling down over the south wall of the palisade and fleeing across the river, but most fell either in the courtyard or defending one barracks hall or another until the Cimmerians either battered down a door and forced an entrance or burned the building over their enemies' heads.

At last, as the sun sank in the northwest, the fighting dragged to a stop, for no more Aquilonians remained alive and unwounded to carry on. Cimmerians tended to their own injured men and cut the throats of the Bossonians and Gundermen who lay on the ground. "They did the same to us after the last fight here," said Nectan the shepherd, leaning wearily on a pikestaff. "As often as not, it's a kindness of sorts, putting somebody who won't live out of his pain."

Conan heard him as if from very far away. The blacksmith's son looked down at his hands, which still clutched his father's axe. When he took them off the axe handle, the place where his father and he had clenched it was the only part not drenched in gore. And his palms seemed the only part of him not soaked in it. His arms were crimson up past the elbows. Blood dyed his tunic and breeks in colors Balarg the weaver had never intended.

Balarg himself had come through the battle apparently unwounded. He stirred bodies not so much to see if they yet lived as to find out what sort of wealth they carried.

"How can you think of loot when everything that matters to us is dead or in ruins?" demanded Conan.

"I am not dead," answered Balarg. "I am not dead, and I am well and truly avenged on my foes. I shall have to find a home in a new village. I would sooner do that as a man with riches than as a man with none. You will face the same trouble. You should plunder, too."

"I have no stomach for it, not now. What I have won, I have bought too dear," said Conan. He looked around and shook his head. "I have no stomach for Cimmeria, not any more. My father is dead. My mother is dead, and I have not had time to mourn her." That was a knife of shame, twisting in his gut. He looked Balarg in the eye. "And Tarla is dead. What do I have left to hold me here?"

"Where would you go?" asked the weaver.

"I know not." Conan's shoulders ached when he shrugged. How many times had he swung Stercus' sword and his father's axe in battle? More than he could count. With another shrug, he went on, "Let those who still have something worth holding here dwell in this land. As for me—" He spat and shook his head.

chapter xiii

Aquilonia

Even the wild rush of the Cimmerians from the north faltered after the fight at Fort Venarium. Before moving south of the river, they paused to treat their wounded, to put their dead in the ground, and to take what plunder they could from the ruined fortress and from the gutted town around it.

Conan was among the first to cross the river, two or three days after the battle. All that had kept him from going south sooner, going south by himself, was the desire for a vengeance greater than he could hope to wreak alone. He had already punished the Aquilonians for his mother's murder, and for Tarla's. Now he owed them for his father, too.

Revenge for Mordec proved harder to come by than he had hoped. The pause in the Cimmerians' reconquest of their stolen land allowed word of their onslaught to spread widely among the Aquilonians who had settled south of Venarium. By the time the Cimmerians pushed on, they found many farms abandoned. Some of the folk from Gunderland had driven their livestock along with their wagons. Some had even burned the farmhouses they were abandoning, to make sure their foes got no use from them.

Gundermen and Bossonians also left most of the fortified

garrisons they had built to keep watch on nearby Cimmerian villages. Here and there, though, the soldiers who fought under Aquilonia's gold lion on black fought rear-guard actions to slow the Cimmerians' advance and to help the settlers escape.

They picked the best places to defend that they could: mostly valley mouths, where the attackers had to come straight at them on a narrow front. Conan hurled himself into one of those savage little fights after another. Stercus' fine blade was gone; on his hip, Conan now wore a shortsword he had taken from the corpse of a blond pikeman of Gunderland. For his principal weapon, however, he still carried his father's axe. He did not try to clean the handle of the bloodstains that marked it. As far as he was concerned, they were a badge of honor.

He eyed a line of pikemen posted across the road, and a squad of Bossonian bowmen behind them. He had begun to see what Mordec meant about the Aquilonians' order and discipline. Because Numedides' men knew their places and their roles, they hurt the Cimmerians worse than they would have otherwise. The barbarians gathering with Conan had no sort of order whatever.

But they did have a driving ferocity alien to the Aquilonians. When Herth shouted, "At them!" they went forward at an eager, ground-eating lope that said they wanted nothing more than to close with their foes. Their shouts were fierce and wordless. They might have been hunters pursuing a stag.

Unlike stags, the Bossonians and Gundermen fought back. Arrows, flight after flight, felled poorly armored invaders before they could close. But the archers could not kill all the barbarians, and the ones who lived came on. The pikemen set themselves. Conan, running toward them, readied his axe.

A Gunderman thrust at him. A lithe twist meant he slid past the spearpoint. "Oh, no, you don't!" cried the pikeman, and drew back his weapon for another jab. Too late—Conan's axe split his skull from crown to teeth. The Gunderman crashed to the ground, dead before he realized what had hit him.

The blacksmith's son slew the soldier beside him, too. "Come on!" called Conan to his countrymen. "Here's a gap I've made for you!" Cimmerians rushed forward and poured through it. They suffered one more volley of Bossonian arrows. But then the archers, protected no more from the warriors they had tormented, needed to turn and run if they were to survive. Some saved their gore by flight. The Cimmerians cut down others from behind. Most of the pikemen from Gunderland died where they stood, trying to the last to slow the barbarians' advance.

"Boldly done, son of Mordec," said Herth when the slaying stopped.

With a broad-shouldered shrug, Conan replied, "I could slaughter every Aquilonian soldier in the world, and it would hardly seem vengeance enough."

Herth eyed the crumpled bodies on the sward. He knew how many of them had gone down before Conan's axe. He looked back toward Venarium and Duthil, recalling how many soldiers the blacksmith's son had slain in the fights farther north. "Son of Mordec, I am not a soft man," he said at last. "I have seen wars and battles aplenty, against the Æsir and Vanir, against the Picts, aye, and among our own folk as well. This I tell you, and I speak truly: in the matter of vengeance, those who bore you can have naught over which to complain."

"It is not enough, I tell you." Conan stubbornly set his jaw.

"You could kill and kill and kill, and still you would say the same," observed the clan chief from the north, and Conan nodded, for he knew he could not deny the other man's words. Herth continued, "Killing alone will never sate you."

Nodding again, Conan said, "Like as not, you speak the truth once more. What then? Shall I reckon myself forever unavenged?"

"If you measure vengeance by killing alone, I do not see what other choice you have," said Herth. "But Aquilonians did not only kill here. They ruled here as well, and that is as hateful to freeborn Cimmerians. I know you are determined to quit your homeland."

"I could be more determined about nothing else," agreed Conan.

"Well and good," said Herth. "I have no quarrel with you there. Perhaps one day you will make a mercenary soldier down in the south, a sergeant or even a captain. Then you may well come to have Aquilonians under your command, and you will rule them as they have ruled here. If anything can, that may complete your revenge."

"By—" But Conan broke off with the oath incomplete, saying, "So it may. Time will tell."

"Time always tells. As you come to have more years, you will begin to wish it held its peace," said Herth. "You do not swear by Crom?"

"Not now," answered Conan. "One of these days, I daresay, I will once more. For now, though, I am as angry at the god as he has shown himself angry at me. If he has robbed me of my nearest and dearest, I will rob him of his name in my mouth. It is the only thing of his I can take."

Before replying, Herth glanced again at the Aquilonian corpses all around. "I am glad I am not your foe," he said. "Even were I a god myself, I should be glad I was not your foe."

"I know not what you mean," said Conan. Where Herth had looked to the north, he hungrily stared southward. "We should be off. The longer we delay, the more of our foes escape." He kicked at the dirt. "I wish I would have kept Stercus' head, that I might have thrown it across the border into Aquilonia as token of the reason for our rising. But it would have begun to rot and stink by now, and we had no chance to pack it in salt, so I flung it to the swine instead, before we got to Venarium."

"A good enough fate for the Aquilonian," said Herth. Conan grudged a nod, although fury still seethed in him. The chief went on, "A pity, what befell Duthil. Otherwise, you could have salt-cured the Aquilonian's head and hung it over your doorway."

"This past little while has seen the end of all I held dear," answered Conan. "My family, my village, her I would have loved—all gone, all dead. Do you wonder I would quit this accursed land?"

Herth shook his head. "I have already told you no. And the more I see of you, son of Mordec, the less I wonder at anything you might do."

"Onward, then," said Conan, and onward he went. If the war chief who, as much as any Cimmerian, had mustered the northern tribes and clans for war against King Numedides' men chose to follow, Conan did not mind. And if Herth and the other Cimmerians chose to stop where they were, Conan did not mind that, either. He would go on alone against Aquilonia, an army of one.

Herth did order his men forward once more. He wanted to do the Aquilonians as much harm as he could, and he had little time in which to do it. The summer campaigning season was brief in the north; before long, his men would begin drifting back toward their homes to help in the harvest. In the meantime—in the meantime, the Aquilonians would pay, and pay, and pay.

Horncalls and fire beacons sent word of danger all along the border. It had been a generation since the Cimmerians invaded Aquilonia, but men whose hair and beards were now

grizzled told tales of the last war to those who would fight
the next: such has been the way of it since time began.

Melcer escaped the fall of the Aquilonian province in southern Cimmeria only to be dragooned into the army that would
try to withstand the barbarians. Since he already had a pike,
they did not bother to issue him one. The shortsword they
gave him was pitted with rust; the helm they clapped on his
head seemed hardly sturdier. When he asked for a coat of
mail, they laughed in his face.

"Mitra! You'll want a charger and his caparison next!" said
a fat sergeant. "What have you done to deserve iron rings?"

"I have fought the Cimmerians, up in the north," answered
Melcer. "What have *you* done, that you say me nay?"

The sergeant's face darkened with anger. "Speak not so to
me, dunghill clod, or you'll wear stripes on your back in place
of chainmail."

"If you use all your soldiers this way, you are a fool to trust
them in the field behind you," said Melcer. "Any number of
ways a fellow who makes his men hate him can find an end."

He did not get the mailshirt, but the sergeant troubled him
no more. And he did see Evlea and his children off to the
south. The more ground they put between themselves and the
barbarian irruption, the happier he was.

Looking north, back into the province he'd had to leave,
made Melcer's blood boil. Whenever he did, he saw fresh fires
going up. He knew too well what they meant: more farms
and settlements burning. What had been civilization was going back to barbarism as fast as it could. Remembering the
time and effort he had put into his own farm, knowing how
many other settlers had worked just as hard, Melcer cursed
both the Cimmerians and Count Stercus, whose brutality had
fired their rebellion.

From what the Gunderman had heard, the Aquilonian
army had crossed into Cimmeria in one place, had advanced
together until it ran into the wild men, and then had beaten

them, opening the southern part of the land to settlement. The barbarians' entry into Aquilonian territory was a different business. They slipped across the river by ones and twos, by tens and twenties, and soon Melcer was seeing new fires not in Cimmeria alone, but also in the land Kings of Aquilonia had ruled for generations.

The hastily mustered defense forces rushed this way and that, trying to run the barbarians to earth before they did too much damage. Sometimes they succeeded. More often, the Cimmerians escaped to burn and plunder and kill somewhere else.

Melcer slept very little. His pikestaff acquired sinister red-brown stains. He found himself wearing a mailshirt before too long. The underofficer who had had the shirt would never need it again. Of that Melcer was sure. It did not fit him very well, but he stopped grumbling after it stopped an arrow that might have pierced his heart. He soon found himself doing a sergeant's job. He did not get a sergeant's pay—he got no pay at all, only food, and not enough of that—but men recruited after him, men who had not seen what he had seen or done what he had done, listened to what he said and obeyed his commands.

He wondered what he would do if he and his men hunted down Conan and his father. The Cimmerians could have slain him. Conan had not called letting him go an act of friendship or mercy or anything of the sort. But whether he had used the name or not, that was what it amounted to.

Maybe the boy—the youth, now—and the great, hulking man who had sired him had perished in the fight at Fort Venarium or one of the smaller skirmishes between Sciliax's farm and the border between Cimmeria and Aquilonia. For the sake of his own conscience, Melcer hoped they had.

He soon had other things to worry about. As more and more barbarians came over the border, the defenders had to split themselves up into smaller and smaller bands to try to deal with all of them. Sometimes a larger swarm of Cimmerians would fall on one of those bands, in which case the result would be massacre, but not massacre of the sort King Numedides' followers wanted.

Melcer and his men and some other soldiers from Gunderland had to clean up the results of one such miscalculation. For a little while, things went better than they had any business doing, for they found some of the Cimmerian sentries drunk asleep, got past them, and assailed the main body of enemy warriors before the barbarians knew they were anywhere close by. But the Cimmerians fought back with a grim, implacable ferocity that stalled the Aquilonian attack at the edge of an orchard.

The trees gave archers excellent cover. Melcer's byrnie turned another Cimmerian arrow. He wondered whether the sergeant who had not wanted to give him a coat of mail still lived. He also wondered whether that sergeant had got into the fighting himself, or whether he had fled south and let others try to hold the barbarians out of Aquilonia.

"Let's go!" shouted Melcer. "We can drive them back!" He rushed at a Cimmerian. The man carried only a shortsword and wore no armor, not even a helmet. He had no chance against a mailed pikeman, and he knew it. He gave ground to save his gore.

Seeing him draw back encouraged the Bossonians and Gundermen with Melcer. They followed the farmer, where they might not have if the Cimmerian had stood his ground. Here in this little brawl, the civilized soldiers outnumbered their barbarous foes.

Once the fighting got in amongst the apple and pear trees, it was every man for himself. "Numedides!" cried Melcer, and his men took up the cry. The Cimmerians yelled back, some using war cries in their own language, others calling down curses on Numedides' head in broken Aquilonian.

A Cimmerian threw a stone at Melcer. The chainmail kept

it from breaking ribs, but he knew he would wear a bruise despite the padding under the links of iron. He saw another Cimmerian with an axe hotly engaged against a Gunderman, and rushed over to help his countryman finish the enemy warrior.

Before he got there, the Cimmerian cut down the other pikeman. The fellow brought up his axe, ready to chop at Melcer, who set himself for a lunge at the barbarian. They both checked themselves in the same instant, exclaiming, "You!"

In that frozen moment, Melcer made his choice. He drew back and lowered his spear, saying, "Go your way, Conan. You spared me and mine when you might have slain. I can do no less for you. Is your father here as well?"

"No." The young barbarian shook his head. "He fell at Venarium. Stay safe, Melcer. Maybe some other Cimmerian will bring you down."

"We were invaders in your land," said Melcer. "You fought hard to drive us out. You are the invaders here. Do you think we will act differently?"

Conan shrugged broad shoulders: a man's shoulders, though he was not yet a man. "I care not. Find a new foe. I will do the same."

Melcer drew back another pace before looking for a different Cimmerian to fight, in case Conan meant trickery. He and his countrymen won the skirmish. They were happy enough to plunder the corpses of those who had stood against them. Melcer prowled the orchard to see if one of those corpses were Conan's.

He did not find the blacksmith's son's body. He never saw the Cimmerian again. But he had reason to remember him the rest of his days.

"We can't turn back," said a lean, gloomy young Cimmerian named Talorc as he and his comrades sprawled around a fire in the hills of Gunderland. "Too many of those accursed Aquilonian dogs between us and the border."

One of his comrades was Conan. "If we can't go back, we go on," he said, and swigged from a skin of wine taken from a tavern.

Most of their fellows had not penetrated so deeply into Numedides' kingdom. They were no longer part of an army. They were a bandit band, out for loot and out to stay alive in a land roused against them.

A howl came from off in the distance. In Cimmeria, it would have been a wolf's cry in the night. Here, Conan cursed. He had come to know too well the belling of hunting hounds—and this hound sought his scent, and his companions'. "We made a mistake," he said. "We should have left someone behind to deal with the dog. An arrow out of the night, and we wouldn't have had to worry about it any more."

"They would only have brought up another one." Talorc spoke with a certain grim fatalism.

"We would kill that one, too," said Conan. Some of the others seemed to think their chances poor. That calculation had never entered Conan's mind. He was still alive. He still had weapons ready to hand. As long as he could, he would go on struggling to survive.

Another howl resounded, this one closer and louder and more excited: the dog had found the Cimmerians' trail. The calls of men floated on the breeze, too. They also sounded excited. They hoped they were going to run this band of barbarians to earth and be rid of it for good.

Conan had a different idea. "They think they will come on us unawares and scatter us," he said; he had already seen the Aquilonians do that once, and had barely come out of the trap alive. "Let's give them a surprise. How will they like it if they find an ambush waiting for them?"

He had to browbeat the rest of the Cimmerians into moving. Some of them would not, and sprawled by the side of the fire, careless of what might happen to them. Conan let them stay where they were. If anything, catching sight of them would help spur on the enemy, help make him careless.

And that was exactly what happened. Spying the Cimmerians slumped there, the Aquilonians stormed forward, certain they would have easy pickings. The barrage of spears and arrows that greeted them from both flanks sent them running away even faster than they had advanced. Now they cried out in terror, not triumph. Conan made sure the dog did not live.

Afterwards, he found only a couple of his countrymen hurt, while half a dozen Aquilonians sprawled in death along the track. Now Conan plundered the corpses. He did not know what he would do with the lunas he took from a dead man's belt pouch. The man's sword, though, was another story. He knew just what to do with that, and hung it on his belt in case something happened to his father's axe.

The Cimmerians pressed ever deeper into Aquilonia. Part of that was Conan's urge to drive the knife home as best he could, the rest a half-formed hope that the Aquilonians would not trouble them so much once they moved farther from the border. That hope proved forlorn. The Aquilonians cared no more for banditry than Conan's folk would have with a gang of Gundermen loose in their land.

One by one, the other raiders fell. The band fissured: now one man, now two or three, would give up, break off, and try to go back to Cimmeria. Conan never learned what happened to those warriors. He would not have bet it was anything good. As for himself, he had no thought of tomorrow past stealing a sheep or a pig and keeping his belly full. The brigand's life, the thief's life, turned out to suit him better than any he had known in Duthil.

After a while, only eight or ten Cimmerians were left with him. He did not think they were in Gunderland any more by then. They had penetrated into Aquilonia proper. The folk who dwelt here looked different and spoke differently from the Gundermen Conan had come to know so well. Many of them did not seem to recognize the raiders for what they were, either.

Conan gulped wine in a farmhouse the men from the north had just plundered. The farmer lay dead on the floor at his feet. "It's been a long time since Cimmerians pushed this deep into Aquilonia," he exulted.

Talorc had drunk more than Conan had—had drunk himself sad, in fact. He began to weep now, saying, "We'll never go home again, either."

"Well, so what?" said Conan. "I've got nothing to go home to, anyhow. Numedides' men made damned sure of that. Best thing I can do now is pay them back in their own coin."

Talorc wept harder. "They'll kill us." He was hardly older than Conan.

"They haven't done it yet," said Conan. "They can keep on trying." He stirred the dead Aquilonian farmer with his boot. "Until they manage, I'm not going to worry about it." Some of the other Cimmerians laughed. The rest, more inclined to Talorc's mood than to Conan's, drank until the farmhouse held nothing more to drink.

They left the place before sunup the next morning. As day brightened, Conan could see a few clouds of smoke rising well to the north: the sign other Cimmerian bands still roamed their enemies' land. His companions did not fire the farmhouse. That would have brought Aquilonian notice to them, and they had already had more notice from King Numedides' soldiers than they wanted.

Later that day, a squadron of Aquilonian knights rode north past them without slowing down, without recognizing them for what they were. Conan laughed at that, but not for long. The knights might not trouble him, but they would help harry his countrymen out of Aquilonia. He wished he could do them a bad turn. The worst turn he could think of was simply surviving.

Somewhere to the south and east lay Tarantia, Numedides' glittering capital. Had any Cimmerian ever reached it? The blacksmith's son had no idea. He did want to see it before the Aquilonians hunted him down, though. That would be a triumph of sorts.

Two days later, he discovered that not all the Aquilonians failed to see Cimmerians for what they were. A raucous cry rang out: "There they are, the murdering bastards!" About a dozen men from the south, farmers and townsfolk kitted out with the same odd mix of weapons and armor as the brigands bore, came loping toward them across a field. One of the Aquilonians shouted something else: "Kill them! Kill them all!"

Another field, even broader, lay on the far side of the road. Conan did not think flight would serve the Cimmerians. A savage grin on his face, he turned to the others who had come so far from their northern homes. "If we kill a few of them, the rest will flee," he said. "We can do it!"

There, however, he miscalculated. Talorc was a good bowman despite his tears, and knocked down two Aquilonians before the rest could close. But that did not discourage the ones who still lived. On they came, shouting King Numedides' name. The battle that followed would be forever nameless, but it was as fierce as many bigger fights of which the chroniclers sang for centuries.

Talorc fell almost at once, fulfilling his own dark prophecy. He wounded one of the two Aquilonians who had assailed him. Another Cimmerian soon slew the man. The fight went on without them. Neither side showed even the slightest interest in flight. It soon became clear things would end only when either Cimmerians or Aquilonians had no one left who could stand on his feet or wield a weapon.

Up until then, Conan had dealt out wounds in plenty, but

had received hardly more than scratches. In that fight he learned edged steel could bite his flesh, too, and that it was no more pleasant when it did than he would have guessed. But not a cry of pain escaped him when he was hurt; he would not yield to wounds any more than he had yielded to his father's hard hands. And, since none of the gashes he received was enough to cripple him, he went on fighting, too.

One of the Aquilonians was a great bear of a man: not quite so tall as Conan, perhaps, but even wider through the shoulders, with enormous arms, a thick chest, and an even thicker belly that hung down over the top of his breeches. He was a farmer, not a soldier; his only weapon was a spade. But he swung it with a wild man's lunatic savagery. It split flesh, broke bones, shattered skulls. One Cimmerian after another went down before him.

Conan, likewise, was the champion for the men of the north. After half an hour, those two were the only fighters not weltering in their gore. Conan hefted his father's axe. The hulking Aquilonian advanced on him, still clutching that blood-dripping spade. A half-crazed grin stretched across his face. "One of us dies," he said.

"Aye." Conan nodded. Here was a foe he could respect. "One of us does." He threw the axe, a trick he had taught himself between bouts of brigandage. Its head should have torn out the Aquilonian's heart.

Clang! Fast as a striking serpent, the big man knocked the flying axe aside with the spade. His grin got wider. "Looks like that one's going to be you."

Conan made no reply. He did the last thing the Aquilonian could have expected: he rushed straight for him. The foe hesitated for a fatal heartbeat, wondering which blow to use to strike down the apparent madman he faced. But Conan's madness had method to it; the Aquilonian had just started to swing back the spade when Conan seized the handle just below the blade.

He heaved and twisted. So did the enormous Aquilonian. Whichever of them could wrest the spade from the other would live. His enemy would die. It was as simple as that. The Aquilonian's first couple of jerks on the handle were almost contemptuous. He had never yet met a man who could match his strength.

But then he grunted in surprise. He set his feet. He took a better grip. The youth who opposed him might have been made of iron and leather and powered by a lion's heart, or a dragon's. Strain as the Aquilonian would, he could make no progress against him. Indeed, he felt himself beginning to fail. A few more twists, and he would be without the weapon that had worked such slaughter.

"No!" he cried hoarsely, and tried to stamp on Conan's foot. But that foot was not there when the Aquilonian's boot crashed down. And, distracted from the struggle over the spade, the Aquilonian felt it rip from his fingers. "No!" he shouted once more, this time in despair and disbelief. That was the last word that ever passed his lips.

Breathing hard, Conan stood over his corpse for a moment. Then he threw aside the murderous spade. It had served him well enough, but he knew there were better weapons. He had his choice of any on the field now, and of the loot his comrades and their foes had carried.

His father's axe on his shoulder, a fine sword on his hip, his belt pouch heavy with silver lunas and golden rings, he strode down the road toward Tarantia.

A curious thing happened then. As long as Conan was part of a band of Cimmerians, all the Aquilonians in the countryside had done their best to hunt him down. When he walked along by himself, they forgot all about him. One lone youth, they seemed to say to themselves, could never threaten their grip on this kingdom. Knights who might well have slain him on sight had they found him in company with others of his kind rode past him without a second glance—sometimes even without a first.

And the deeper into Aquilonia he got, the more he began to see that the people who lived on the land did not know him for a Cimmerian at all. They should have; he resembled them no more than a wolf takes after a lap dog. But he heard one peasant woman murmur, "How big and strong they grow them in Gunderland!" to another as he walked by. He did not catch what the second woman said in reply, but it sent both of them into a fit of giggles.

Obscurely annoyed without knowing why, Conan kept on toward the capital without giving the slightest indication he had heard the peasant women or noticed them in any way. For some unfathomable reason, that only set them giggling again.

Sometimes he would stop and chop wood or pitch hay for a meal and a place to sleep. Even his bad Aquilonian got taken for a frontier accent, not a barbarous one. He began to wonder about the ignorant folk who lived near the heart of this kingdom. The Bossonians and Gundermen he'd known had been enemies, aye, but worthy enemies. A lot of the people near Tarantia, shielded for generations by the rougher men who dwelt closer to the border, would not have lasted long had they had to defend their holdings against raiders from the north.

They did not even seem to know how lucky they were to be so shielded. Conan was drinking wine in a tavern when an Aquilonian at the next table spoke to his friend: "They say the barbarians have run us out of that Cimmeria place."

The friend's jowls wobbled as he swigged from his mug of wine. They wobbled again when he shrugged. "Well, so what?" he said. "Mitra, I don't know what we wanted with such a miserable country to begin with."

"Oh, it wasn't us—not folk like you and me," said the first man wisely. "It was those miserable frontiersmen. All they do is make babies, and they were looking for somewhere to put more of them."

"Well, they didn't find it there." His friend laughed. "Not my worry any which way."

"Nor mine," said the first man. "Here, drink up, Crecelius, and I'll buy you another round."

They too were enemies. Even so, Conan wanted to pound their heads together. He doubted whether it would do any good, though. They were so sunk in sottish stupidity, nothing was likely to knock sense into their thick skulls.

Another thought crossed his mind later that day, after he had left the tavern behind. If the ordinary folk of Aquilonia had this view of the Cimmerian expedition, what did King Numedides think about it? Up until now, Conan had always assumed the King of Aquilonia would be gnashing his teeth in fury over his failure in the north. Now, suddenly, the black-smith's son wondered. Could it be that Numedides was as indifferent to the disaster as so many of his subjects seemed to be?

What sort of a sovereign was Numedides if in fact he did not care? Conan laughed gustily and shrugged. As if the do-ings and thoughts of the King of Aquilonia could possibly matter to him!

Villages grew thicker on the land. Some of them were more than villages: some were towns. Conan eyed them with a hunter's unrelenting hunger. How long had it been since any-one plundered these places? The pickings would be rich in-deed if anyone could.

Conan was walking along a hedgerow taller than a man when he heard argument from beyond it. Exasperation in his voice, a man was saying, "Everything will be fine, Selinda."

"Oh, it will, will it?" exclaimed Selinda shrilly. "I think those barbarians will cut your throat as soon as you go out on the road."

"They aren't anywhere close to here," said the man. "And

the soldiers are driving them back. Everybody says so. And my onions need to go to Tarantia. We won't get any money if they don't."

His wife—it could be none other—let out another squawk. "I don't like it, Renorio. I don't like it at all."

When Conan emerged from beyond the hedgerow, they both suddenly fell silent. They stood beside a ramshackle wagon that was, sure enough, piled high with onions. A bored horse dozed in harness. A shrewd smirk crossed Renorio's face and then, as quickly, vanished. He pointed to Conan. "You there, fellow! Can you drive a wagon?"

"Aye." Conan had never tried in his life, but had too much pride to admit there was anything he could not do.

Neither Renorio nor Selinda, plainly, had the slightest notion he was one of the fearsome barbarians who alarmed them. The farmer said, "How would you like to make two lunas—one now, the other when you bring back the wagon?"

"What you want me to do?" asked Conan.

His accent did not faze the Aquilonian, either. "Take these onions to my brother-in-law in the great market square in Tarantia. Help Polsipher unload them, then bring the wagon back here," answered Renorio. "Two lunas."

By his greasy smile, Conan suspected he would not readily part with the second silver coin. Nevertheless, the blacksmith's son nodded. "I do this."

"Good. Good! Climb on up, then," said Renorio. Conan did, as if he had done so a thousand times before. He waited. Reluctantly, Renorio gave him the first half of the promised payment. With a fine show of authority, he flicked the reins. The horse snorted in surprise—and perhaps derision—and began to walk. Behind Conan, the farmer spoke triumphantly to his wife: "There. Now you don't have to worry any more. Are you happy? You don't look happy. You're never happy, seems to me."

Selinda screeched at him. They went back to arguing.

Conan began experimenting. Well before he got to Tarantia, he learned how to use the reins to make the horse start and stop and turn to the left and right. It all seemed easy enough. When the Cimmerian came to the capital of Aquilonia, he had no trouble finding the great market square, for a stream of wagons of all sizes flooded into it. He bawled Polsipher's name until someone answered. Renorio's brother-in-law did not seem unduly surprised at finding a stranger on the wagon; maybe the farmer had hired others before.

They unloaded the wagon. Like Renorio, Polsipher had no idea Conan was a Cimmerian. Conan climbed back up on the wagon and drove away. Polsipher called after him: "Turn around! The farm's back that way!"

As if he could not hear, Conan cupped a hand behind his ear and kept on in the direction he had chosen. Now that he had seen Tarantia, he wanted to learn what lay beyond it—and riding had proved easier than walking. He would not get his second silver luna, if Renorio ever would have given it to him. But the farmer would not get his wagon or his sleepy horse. Conan liked that bargain fine. If Renorio did not, too bad for him. Conan rode out of the city and off to the south and east. He had already begun to learn the trade of thief.

The Conan Novels
in chronological order

Conan of Venarium
Conan
Conan of Cimmeria
Conan the Freebooter
Conan the Wanderer
Conan the Adventurer
Conan the Buccaneer
Conan the Warrior
Conan the Usurper
Conan the Conqueror
Conan the Avenger
Conan of Aquilonia
Conan of the Isles
Conan the Swordsman
Conan the Liberator
Conan: The Sword of Skelos
Conan: The Road of Kings
Conan the Rebel
Conan and the Spider God

Illustrated Conan novels:

Conan and the Sorcerer
Conan: The Flame Knife
Conan the Mercenary
The Treasure of Tranicos

Other Conan novels:

The Blade of Conan
The Spell of Conan